A Prelude to Nothing

Book One:
The Tom Rollins Series

Kevin Gross

Wandering in the Words Press

Requests for permission should be sent to Wandering in the Words Press: 2131 Burns St, Nashville, Tennessee, 37216

www.wanderinginthewordspress.com

All characters in this book are fictitious, and any resemblance to real persons, living or dead, is coincidental.

Cover design by Elaina Unger

PUBLISHED BY WANDERING IN THE WORDS PRESS

ISBN-10: 0990919323
ISBN-13: 978-0-9909193-2-2

First Edition

For my mother, though it may give her nightmares.

~

You're not going to find the bodies. Not intact, anyway. They're hidden, and I'm not going to tell you where, either, but I will tell you everything else. Who they were, for instance, and why they're dead.

I'm going to tell you how I got mixed up in all of this. I'm only writing this so that someone somewhere will finally know the whole story, from beginning to end. Save it as evidence, or as a warning, or for whatever reason you choose, but save it, and know that every word of this is true.

It all started about eight months ago on a hot night in mid-July. But I guess it really began a lot earlier than that. I had a mother until my father chased her off seven years ago. I was nine at the time, and I didn't fully understand, but I do now. I don't know if he beat her, but they had some bitter shouting matches and he harassed her enough. It wouldn't really surprise me if he had hit her. He hit me. He did it more than once—not hard enough to leave a very visible bruise or cut or anything, but he made his point. He was a violent man. And angry. He drank too much, smoked too much, yelled at everything and everyone and didn't give a damn about anyone.

After what I've seen in movies, read in books or witnessed in public, I wonder how families like mine come about. All those perfect moms, dads and kids smile and go camping or head to the beach. They have their bad days, too, I suppose, but they manage.

Whatever possesses a man to settle down with a woman and have a child with her, only to run her out of the house? Whatever possesses a man to hit his son? Whatever possesses a man to turn his back to the world with middle fingers raised high, stinking of alcohol? Well whatever that is that consumes a man and turns him into a vulgar, hateful piece of scum, I hope I never find it sitting in my own recliner when I'm older, waiting for me to wrap it up in my arms and embrace its obscenity with an apathetic excuse for totality. This is not the American Dream. This is not how you envision your future.

He would sink into his seat, hidden in the shadows of the living room—a sick sort of irony—staring into the blinding glare of the television through crusty, glassy eyes. Just staring drunkenly. I couldn't tell if he was actually watching it, or just fixated on the flashing lights battering his ugly face with stark shadows and unforgiving detail. When he wasn't drowning in the stale haze of tobacco and week-old canned beer, his eyes rolled around in those pits of sockets, seeking out something to turn his hatred onto. I loathed and feared him, and I stayed in my room most of the time, alone, an only child to burden all the guilt, blame and responsibility.

***

That hot day in mid-July was the straw that broke the camel's back, as crazy Aunt Josephine used to say. I spent most of the day holed up in my room because my best friend Vinny was at a birthday party and I was still too shy to hang out with Leslie alone. My room was only a few degrees cooler than outside, which is to say it was boiling. My whole body itched from the heat and several bug bites, and the summer sun coated my dusty, shadow-filled room with a nauseating yellow hue. A mix CD of my favorite bands blasted from the stereo on top of my bookshelf, but the music did little to soothe me. So I was stuck with the choice of lying around staring at the same old dead scenery, sweating until I died of heat stroke and dehydration, or hanging out in the air-conditioned living room with my father.

Maybe the heat had already gone to my head, because I chose the latter. It was possible that he would just ignore me, and more than likely he would be asleep. On the days he didn't work he usually took two or three naps, snoring louder than a bulldozer and sometimes talking in his slumber. I think if I hadn't hated him so much, I would have been in awe of his ability to crash so quickly and effortlessly. Even in the most cramped and uncomfortable places, he could manage to catch a few z's. He was a dream machine.

I rose from my spot on the floor, shut off the stereo and tiptoed out into the hall. The familiar chatter of the television buzzed from the living room and mixed with the low hum of the AC unit. I passed the laundry room on my right. It shared a paper-thin wall with my bedroom, and for the first few years of my mother's absence before I started doing the laundry, I was stuck listening to the forgotten change in my father's jeans pockets clanking around in the dryer every other night. It wasn't always just change, either. Once in a while it was his keys, and on more than one occasion I found a whole pack of cigarettes that had fallen apart in his shirt pocket.

When I took up the chore, I started removing everything from his pockets. I kept most of his spare change for myself, and never ran the washer or dryer at night.

I stopped at the end of the hall and listened. None of his sleep sounds emanated from the living room, but I poked my head in anyway. He made a garbled sound I took to be sleep-talk. I froze and then crept into the room as quietly as I could and plopped down on the couch across from him.

"What did you *take*?" he grumbled.

I shot him an amused glance and turned to see what he had been watching before falling asleep. Some poorly filmed kung-fu flick with dramatized sound effects.

"I said, 'what did you take?' Dammit!" he shouted, and I realized he had not been sleeping at all. "I heard you walking around in my bedroom, so what did you steal?"

He sat there glaring and then stood and came stomping toward me when I didn't respond.

"I thought you were asleep," I said. It was meant as an excuse for why I was there in his presence at all, but as always, he misunderstood.

"So you thought you'd go snooping around in my room while I was asleep!" He grabbed me by the neck of my shirt and pulled me up toward him until my face was inches from his. His breath stank of stale beer and cigarettes. "I raise you and feed you myself, with my hard-earned money, I put a roof over your head and clothes on your back, and there you go trying to take more for yourself! You're an ungrateful little rat!"

He lifted me off the ground and slammed me against the wall so that I was partially seated on the backrest of the couch with my legs sprawled over the cushions. I stared fearfully back into his face, which was all haggard and creased with rage. His eyes bored into mine until I looked away. Then, seemingly out of words to express his eternal hatred toward me, he pummeled me in the chest twice and threw me to the floor. I rolled over and gasped for air.

"That'll teach you to appreciate what you've got and stop biting the hand that feeds you."

I never had the chance to explain. There was no defending myself. He always assumed the worst of me and punished me ruthlessly, like a dictator fueled by his own self-serving lust for power. And there I was, a peasant, too weak and defeated to spark the revolution.

I returned to my room and stayed there the rest of the night. Even when dinnertime came around, I just lay there in my bed, staring through the single window looking out over our overgrown backyard, starving. The sheets stuck to my back and legs with sweat from the unbearable humidity. I watched night fall and slowly darken the yard. Fireflies danced around in the black-blue sky, flickering in and out of sight like aircraft warning lights. Here, then gone. Here, then gone.

I wanted to be gone.

For the past two years I had come to imagine that home as a prison. He kept me locked up in my room, my cell, to restlessly pace and ponder what I'd done to wind up there. I could feel the years of my sentence wearing on me. Dispiriting me. And my father, the jailor, turned a cold, blind eye to the truth—that I was an innocent man—and delivered my punishment with sadistic pride. But there were no bars on my window. There were no shackles binding me there. Those cement walls topped with razor wire were all in my head, and I could tear them down and walk out freely if I chose to. I could slip out into the night before my captor was any the wiser. Here, then gone.

I stood up on my bed and hooked my fingers under the window screen, then pushed. It popped out of place and tumbled quietly into the backyard before I could get a grip on it. I stuck my head through the opened window. The screen was faintly visible in the moonlight. I hoisted myself up on the window frame, placing my hands under me so the wood wouldn't dig into my stomach. Then I pulled one leg up and tucked it through the hole. I swung my other leg up and through so I was sitting on the edge of the sill, and dropped down.

A wild carpet of dead grass tickled my heels and poked up between my toes. I imagined dozens of tiny insects crawling through it, swarming over my feet, climbing up my bare legs. My whole body prickled with sweat and invisible ants. Mosquitoes buzzed in my ears, and I swatted them away. In my mind, a colony of ticks were hurrying toward me, eager to burrow into my flesh and eat me alive from the inside. I kicked the screen out of the way and ran around to the side of the house with both hands clamped over my ears.

I made it almost to the front of the house and stopped. Where was I going to go? And how was I planning to get there with no shoes? I had no money on me, no change of clothes, no food or tools or supplies of any kind. Only a vague idea that I was running away from home through a lawn of bugs. I was being too hasty. It was the heat, and my father, and all the years of mental torment finally growing to be too much for me.

And there was something else.

Freedom. I stood still, hidden from the light of the sky by the huge shadow of the house, soaking up the excitement of my escape. While the neighborhood slept, I could slink away to some other town or county. Some other state, even. I was no longer stuck living in a pit until I was old enough to be thrown out on my own. I could get a head start and vanish before the world awoke and discovered my disappearance. Free. I grinned at the idea and was once again tempted to wander off. But I couldn't leave just yet. Under the buzz of adrenaline and endless possibilities, my rational side reminded me that it would be better to wait for morning. I could rest in my bed one last time and plan out a proper getaway.

I saw myself walking aimlessly for hours, roaming through seedy streets and sleeping under overpasses like a homeless man in tattered clothes. As much as I wanted to be away from my home in Oak Ridge, that vision was equally unappealing. If I waited for morning when my father left for work, I could get into the garage and ride off on my bike. Stalking the streets at night might attract attention from the police, but passersby would be less apt to be suspicious of a lone boy riding from town to town in the daylight. Besides, it would put more miles between my home and myself if I took my bike.

I turned around and strode back to the window of my bedroom with new purpose. I smacked a few flies or mosquitoes off my arms and legs and picked up the screen. I slowly slipped it through the open window and let it fall into my room, cringing as it clattered to the floor. I pulled myself up and in after it, wiped sweat and blades of grass from my legs, and replaced the screen in the window. Then I climbed back into bed and mulled over what the next day would bring, aside from the beginning of a brand new life.

My father left for work without a word while I sat at the kitchen table eating breakfast. That meant he hadn't discovered that, while he was showering, I had taken $36 from his Rainy Day cash from the cigar box on his dresser, along with an unused Bic lighter that was laying on the floor. He probably had checked the cigar box after our incident the day before and had realized nothing was missing, but instead of feeling guilty or apologizing like a normal person, he'd gone about his day and ignored the world that refused to cough up whatever it supposedly owed him. I smiled to myself as the door swung shut. It would be the last time I ever saw him.

I finished my breakfast and left my plate and juice glass on the table. He could clean it up when he got home. I went to my room and pulled my backpack out of the closet to gather up some things for my departure. I tossed in one change of clothes, which took up about a third of the space in there even when I packed it down; rummaged through the medicine cabinet and pulled out a bottle of Advil, a travel-sized tube of sunscreen and an open box of Band-Aids; and then raided the fridge. I made three turkey-and-cheese sandwiches, wrapped them in tinfoil and then added them and a few juice pouches to the nearly stuffed backpack. I tossed in a few apples from the bowl on the kitchen counter. Golden Delicious. In a small, zipped pocket in the front of the bag, I slipped in a single steak knife.

It felt like packing for a short trip instead of the rest of my life. Granted, I was packing light with every intention of eventually finding my own place and starting from scratch there. It was more than what immigrants start off with, right? They would cross into the country with just the clothes on their backs, and no identification or papers or anything. I had everything I would need on the way, and then I would find a job and a place to settle in.

I had a tall, white plastic bottle that attached to the bar near the seat of my bike. I filled it to the top with water, slung my backpack over my shoulders, and strapped the bottle back in its harness. Then I pedaled away, leaving the front door unlocked and wide open. What would be the point of shutting it? I didn't live there anymore. It didn't matter if someone walked right in and stole everything. Let them burn it down: I didn't care.

Across the street a few houses down, Mr. Hansen sat on a lawn chair in the open doorway of his oil-stained garage, soaking up the sunlight—a glass of lemonade in one hand, a paperback novel in the other. I couldn't tell if he saw me ride off because his eyes were hidden behind a pair of oversized sunglasses, but he didn't wave or holler over to me. He and I never really spoke. As I put my back to him and weaved around parked cars and basketball hoops on that quiet street, I realized we never would.

I passed Vinny's street without slowing down. He couldn't know that I was leaving, and despite him being my best friend, I knew it was better that way. If it was any other season, all my classmates might have thought I was staying home sick. A few days later they would start to sense that something was wrong. Vinny would know right away. All his texts and calls would go unanswered by a phone left on my unmade bed, and my prolonged silence would be unlike me. He would know I was not just ignoring him for some reason, or spending time with someone else. He would think I was in trouble. But during the summer days it could be anything, and only he would notice. He and my father. The questions would last only until my father started knocking on the neighbors' doors and calling the families of my friends, wondering if I was there.

The straps of my backpack tugged at my shoulders, but I paid them no mind. The taste of freedom was even sweeter than the night before. I sped up, and a light breeze whisked the sweat from my brow. I smiled as I imagined the stupefied look on my father's face when he came home to discover I wasn't there and wouldn't be coming back. It wouldn't be for another seven hours, and by that time I'd be miles away. Maybe a squirrel would run in through the open door and make a nest for itself on his pillow, or knock a lamp off a table, or get into the pantry.

Another block down, and then I rounded a corner. The firehouse sailed by on my left. Harry's Comic Books passed on the right. The pungent odor of motor oil hit me, and I heard men shouting over the cacophony of the auto shop. Soon Oak Ridge was at my back, and I was crossing the bridge into Mapleton, with its storefronts and corner cafés. I swear, even the girls are prettier in Mapleton. I steered clear of Main Street and rode into the neighborhoods and passed a sign welcoming me to Brighton Township. That was where Leslie lived. I would have to stay away from her, too—all of the general public really, but especially anyone who'd recognize me.

The streets were more shaded here, lined with tall white oaks, but with more shade came more mosquitoes. A few other kids rode around on bikes nearby like a preteen biker gang. They popped up and off the curb, amusing themselves more than each other with their wheelies and amateur tricks. I felt bad for them. Their days were anchored there on that block. They had no idea about the world beyond, and everything they could be if they just walked away from the mundane routine of their cookie-cutter lives.

I took a swig from my water bottle and reminded myself to preserve it as much as possible. I had only limited supplies and no way of knowing how long I would go before being able to replenish them. I'd only spend the cash in my pocket when I had to, and not at all if I could get along without it. I placed the bottle back in its harness and rode down street after street, wondering where I was headed. One town melted into the next. After a couple hours, I began to consider just pedaling until I died. Where could I go? Anywhere I wanted. Where would I sleep? Wherever I passed out from exhaustion. It's the overlooked glory of being an orphan or homeless man: I had nothing to hold me down or hold me back from chasing a whim.

***

I didn't have a watch because I always just checked my cell phone, but I left that when I rode out of my old life. Since that moment, time became irrelevant.

Now I have no need to count the hours or days. Months and seasons melt into each other with only the changing weather to show that any time has passed. I have a watch now, and I wear it, but mostly as a reminder of what's happened, so that once the scars and bruises fade, I'll at least have something to hold onto.

***

With no watch to remind me how long I'd been pedaling, I was taken by surprise when my stomach began to cramp with hunger. I'd been gone for several hours before I hit the brakes and found myself in the ancient parking lot of a mostly deserted shopping plaza. I got off my bike and walked it up to a closed-up pizza place. The concrete was cracked and crumbling so bad that large chunks of it wobbled underfoot, like I was walking on uneven cobblestones. It felt weird walking after so many hours of riding, but I held my balance and propped my bike against the side wall of the building. A large sculpture of an Italian man with a thick black mustache and a tall white hat and white cook's uniform stood on the roof of the restaurant brandishing a pizza on a tray. Under him, a sign declared the name of the restaurant in thin red letters: Papa Tony's. I wondered if it was the original owner's name or the name of the stereotypical character that stood watch from the roof.

I peered in through the front windows, holding my hands to the sides of my face to block out the sunlight reflecting off the glass. I don't know what I expected to find. There were neither pizzas on display under the bare counters nor an abandoned soda fountain. No signs of life. No ghost of Papa Tony haunting the shadowy kitchen. The emptiness seemed to say, "Go away, there's nobody here. Nothing to take. Find someplace else, why don't ya?"

I went back around to the side of the building and shrugged off the straps of my backpack, glad to be free of the weight. I sat against the wall in the shade, eating one of the sandwiches I'd made earlier that morning and sipping a Capri Sun.

There, marooned on the island of my independence and forbidden to socialize again for fear of being caught and dragged back to the prison of my old life, I decided I had made the best choice. Friends, family, school, a home—what are they but societal ties? So many ropes binding you to what the idiots so generally label "The System." The more you network, the more you wrap yourself up in the net. But I had come unraveled. I looked out over suburbia—sun glinting off the windows of storefronts and passing cars, air shimmering over the baking streets—and saw a Hollywood backdrop to the road leading to my future, ripe with possibilities.

I let a light breeze snatch up the Ziploc baggie that held a few crumbs from my sandwich and send it sailing while I stood and urinated on the restaurant wall. Then I zipped my backpack, slung it over my shoulders and resumed my bike ride to an unknown destination.

The first twelve hours on my own were pleasantly uneventful, and I began to ease up on the occasional thoughts that a police cruiser might pull up alongside me and ask me what I was doing riding across highways and through towns all alone. I got a few glances but otherwise went unnoticed. No one would give me a second thought. The world had not yet discovered I was a runaway. In the minds of any passersby who took the briefest moment to wonder, I was just a kid on his bike, probably headed to a friend's house or a campsite.

And on considering this, I aimed for the woods. There I could bike into the night without having to worry about attracting attention from the authorities, find a place to sleep out of sight, and grow a bit more accustomed to the wild outdoors I was bound to find myself living in now that I was a nomad.

I followed road and campground signs until I came upon a dirt road covered in footprints and tire tracks leading into Olsten Pines. The sun was just beginning to set, which, in the peak of summer, meant that it was already pretty late. The road stretched on in a mostly straight line for a mile or so before branching out into three separate trails. I took the one on the left, thinking that Robert Frost would be proud. Clumps of foot-tall grass and weeds stood in the center of the trail where truck tires hadn't worn them down. Discarded tires and broken bottles littered the edges of the path among the trees. I ducked under low-hanging branches when I could and plowed through them when I couldn't, hoping no spiders or ticks came tumbling out to land in my hair.

When the road became too sandy to keep riding and the ground seemed to give way under me, I quickly hopped off and walked the bike across the sand patch. The sun was behind me, spilling a few last rays down to earth before clocking out for the night. My shadow stretched ahead of me and was gradually swallowed up in the shadows of the woods until I was in complete darkness. Moonlight peeked through cracks in the canopy overhead. I squinted, barely making out the trail.

The ground was once again hard, compacted dirt, but I was too tired to climb back onto the seat and resume my ride. I pushed the bike for maybe a quarter mile, then brought it to the edge of the path and laid it down in the brush. I stepped around it and into the trees. Sticks snapped under my feet. Limbs and branches clawed my face and clothes.

Someone grabbed hold of me and pulled me back.

"Hey!" I grunted. "Let go!"

I stumbled and pulled against the assailant, who said nothing, and only held me tighter. I thrashed out, kicking backwards. A moment later I tugged free and spun around. Nobody was there. I realized the branches had tangled in the straps and zipper-pulls of my backpack. I shook my head, glad I was alone, and continued my search for a place to rest.

The night in the woods was cooler than the night before outside my bedroom window, but my skin still crawled and itched. I found a space hidden away from the path, yet still close enough to my bike so I could find it the next morning, and sat down on a carpet of pine needles. I leaned against the base of the nearest tree and closed my eyes.

I've never really gone camping. I've been in the vicinity of campgrounds hundreds of times, swum in lakes and fished, taken a couple leisurely strolls through the woods in parks. But I've never slept in a sleeping bag in a tent in the middle of the woods, and especially not alone. Even if I'd had more experience, I'm pretty certain that first night on my own would still have been far from comfortable. There was the feeling of being lost, but I pushed that aside, reminding myself that maps and geography meant little to me. I had my whole life ahead of me to explore, so why not start now? No, what kept me awake—and woke me when I happened to doze off, though I'm not positive I managed to sleep at all— was the strangeness of the place.

I kept my knees bent and huddled close to my chest, not wanting to lay them down in the dirt and risk a bug crawling up my pant leg. The rough bark of the tree dug into my back. The woods were mostly quiet, though very clearly awake and alive. It was like I could sense the silence of the rest of the world, but was stuck listening to the buzzing and scampering and ticking of a million tiny creatures going about their nights the same way I would go about my day. Wandering, searching for food. Seeing and smelling things I couldn't. Seeing and smelling me.

I wasn't afraid. I was lost and alone deep in the woods at night, but I was more concerned than anything. What comforted me was that my father would never find me there. He was undoubtedly awake and pulling out his hair wondering where I was, and he wouldn't suspect I was balled up somewhere in Olsten Pines, unzipping my backpack and pulling out one of his golden delicious apples and nibbling it more out of boredom than real hunger. I pictured him enraged, storming out the front door and pounding on Vinny's door. Vinny or his parents would answer and say I wasn't there, and he might start getting worried. Or grow more furious. And had one of the neighbors gone rooting through the place after I'd disappeared? Snooping in his house—in his room. Had someone swiped the stash of cash hidden away in a cigar box on his dresser?

News would travel fast through the neighborhood. Oak Ridge is that kind of place where everybody knows everybody, and even if most of the town was asleep when my father raised the alarm, they'd be on high alert by morning. They would set up search parties and set out to the places I'd most likely run away to. And that's where they would fail. I was five steps and several hours ahead of them, and I'm not dumb. Foolish, yes, but I'd argue I'm one of the brightest kids from the Ridge. Too intelligent to live there. Then again, I've always thought of myself and my few friends as too good to live in a dead-end town like that.

A shrill scream broke the silence. I dropped the partially eaten apple, unsure if I had fallen asleep in the middle of eating it. The scream had come from somewhere in the distance, though definitely somewhere in the woods. I held my breath and listened. The world was still, silent. I sat there, frozen for what might've been only a minute or two but what felt like hours. No breeze rustled the leaves. No screams echoed through the trees. No footsteps charged down the path.

Then a stick snapped somewhere, much closer than the scream but still far enough away so that it could be anything from a restless squirrel to a psycho killer stalking through the Pines. Far more likely to be a squirrel, but I was already too awake to try to sleep again, and I might as well put more distance between myself and the Ridgeans, so I stood and shouldered my backpack. I wished I had packed a flashlight. Then the thought of that woman's shriek killed that idea. If someone was sneaking around and attacking random campers, a flashlight would attract his attention and send him my way.

What if he has night-vision goggles, or a sniper rifle with an ultraviolet scope?

No, those were just paranoid thoughts. It was just a squirrel back there. The night makes everything more ominous, that's all.

The scream?

I could've dreamt that. I wasn't sure I'd fallen asleep, but I had to have, because if someone had really been calling out for help, a ranger or campground attendant would have gone to check it out. Right?

I tripped over my bike in the darkness and fell hard. A pedal pounded me in the crotch. I rolled off it in pain and scrambled to my feet. Still hunched over, I grabbed the handlebars. My shins throbbed. My nether regions ached. I lugged the bike onto its wheels and hobbled out of the trees and into the path. I stopped again.

Which way?

My tired, skittered mind tried to trace its way back to the moment I had turned off. I decided to head left. I eased myself onto the seat and pedaled off. If someone was out there, they would be close. Too close. I pushed harder, all the while working on convincing myself I was overreacting.

I had a knife in my backpack. I just had to get to the front pocket in time and it would be in my hand, and then I could strike out at anyone who came at me. Kill them before they killed me. There was no one there anyway, so I wouldn't need it. But just in case.

That was ridiculous. How could I expect to kill someone bigger than me? He'd probably killed someone in the middle of a campsite, probably illuminated by a bonfire, his face clear as day. Here in the darkness he would seem even larger, more vicious. And the victim had only screamed once. Didn't have a chance to scream again. Probably strangled the breath right out of her.

There isn't a killer.

I was just speeding away because of all the bugs crawling around me, carrying all kinds of diseases. And to stay a few steps ahead when the inevitable search party started scouting the area. Would they come this far?

I was thinking through a dozen different methods of distracting a serial killer from my path when I crashed into some unseen obstacle and went sailing over my handlebars. I fell hard for the second time that night. My body struck the ground and I found myself in a large sandy patch in the middle of the trail. It wasn't soft enough to make for a graceful landing.

"Wrong way," I groaned.

I couldn't tell if I was bleeding, but I was definitely bruised. If I kept beating myself up like this, I would be dead before anyone could come bursting out of the trees wielding a machete or a chainsaw or a glove covered with bladed fingers. I shook the horror villains from my mind for a whole four seconds and got to my feet. I blindly brushed the sand from my arms and legs as best as I could, then found my bike—a dull black shape amidst a hundred gray shadows.

There was a chance I'd gone the right way, and that running into more sand patches was just something I'd have to deal with, so I ran with the handlebars in hand and pressed on in the same direction. When I felt hard, sturdy ground under my feet once again, I got back on my bike and rode it as fast as I could go. Branches full of leaves whipped my cheeks until I ducked down and rode with my face nearly buried in my chest. They snagged and snapped on my backpack. There was nothing to do about that.

After a while I realized the road had widened, and the branches were no longer smacking me from both sides. The canopy split apart, revealing a starlit sky and crescent moon. I returned my gaze to the trail ahead of me.

What I saw made me hit the brakes hard enough to almost send me flying over the handlebars again. The bike dipped forward and I jumped off it and hit the ground running before it toppled over.

There, a few yards away, a dead body lay crumpled at the edge of the trail. Looking back now, it could have been the perfect trap to catch another victim. I could have used similar tactics to lure in some unsuspecting girl and slit her throat, though I'd have to consider a proper location and means of disposing the body. But thoughts like those didn't come until five months later, and there in the darkened woods my heart was more set on saving lives rather than taking them.

There was no saving that life. The stench of rotting meat and decay hit me from a few feet away. I gagged, paused, covered my nose and mouth and stepped closer. I saw what looked like a dozen sticks protruding from its skull. I stared at it for a moment, confused and revolted. The corpse just looked...wrong. Like it was twisted around the wrong way, and far too big. I was reminded that bodies sometimes bloat and swell after death, but I couldn't imagine how a human could become so monstrous.

After a minute, I realized I was looking at a dead buck. I quit gaping at it and turned around, took a deep breath and gagged again on the stench. I managed to not vomit and got back on my bike. The smell stuck in my nose for a short while. The grotesque silhouette of the deer carcass never left my mind. The night was taking on the air of a strange, morbid dream that was not quite yet a nightmare.

I stopped at a fork much farther along down the trail, which confirmed my thoughts that I was headed in the same direction I'd been going rather than back the way I had come. There were two paths this time instead of three. I turned right and found myself looking out over a lake. Instead of a sandy beach leading up to it, there were rocks and broken glass. Not the kind you'd want to walk down to barefoot. I could only imagine what waited under the lake itself.

A car was parked to the left between the trees and the lake, but as I rode toward it I saw it had been there for some time. It was rusted and very likely broken down. Even if it had a working engine, it wouldn't be going anywhere soon, because three of its tires had been replaced with cinder blocks. The windows were all either broken out or cracked, and grass was poking up through the floor in various places.

I scanned the black lake but saw no camps on the other side, or docks or lights or anything. A small island near the center of the lake caught my eye, and I contemplated swimming to it and sitting it out for the rest of the night, but I decided to press on and keep dry.

Another shriek emanated from somewhere in the woods. This one was more clear and distinct, and only sort of sounded human. Probably a screech owl or some other bird. I must have heard it and got myself worked up. The nighttime can fog your mind like that. Pull at your deepest fears, no matter how irrational. Drives you a little crazy, or builds to your madness, or just points out that there's still a fear in you that's alive and waiting to come out and stretch its legs when the sun goes down.

***

If you've ever seen the things I've seen, or have been through half of what I have, you know that after a while it doesn't matter if the sun is down. That horror creeps in the moment you wake—if it lets you sleep at all. It flicks on the reels of your memory and replays the worst parts like a montage from hell. And you're stuck there, forced to watch it *Clockwork Orange* style. It gnaws away at your being until you're left to choose between suicide from guilt or a life of sadomasochism. You can run, run, run, but there's no place to hide from yourself.

***

By morning I was out of the woods. The last thing I saw as I exited the trail was a lone white sneaker lying in the middle of the path. It struck me as out of place, but I didn't hang around to investigate. I was making better progress keeping my eyes to the horizon. I kept in mind that my father and our neighbors would likely be traveling by car to find me. I doubted they would follow the same roads I took, but you never know.

The paranoia of the previous night had dispersed. All I felt was tired. I'd hardly stopped moving since leaving home, and while pulling all-nighters wasn't uncommon, traveling a hundred miles during that time was taking its toll. I rode down a mile-long paved road that cut through the edge of the woods. Gradually, the wall of trees thinned out and was replaced with billboards and township signs.

The road led to another toilet of a neighborhood. Every house appeared to have a chain-link fence with an angry dog behind it. The beasts ran around the front yards and yapped their heads off as I passed by. A few kids darted around in swim trunks and shorts, tossing a beach ball over a sprinkler and screaming excitedly. Several houses down, someone was getting a head start on their lunchtime barbecue, and the smoke of the grill wafted up from the backyard. A light breeze caught the mouthwatering smell of burgers and hotdogs and blew it my way. My stomach gurgled and growled. I put the street behind me and kept going, promising myself that as soon as I found a place to sit and eat, I would.

No more than five minutes later, I decided to quit starving myself and eat wherever I damn well pleased. It's what exhaustion, hunger and freedom will do to you. I rolled up to an open basketball court, laid my bike on the ground, pulled a sandwich from my backpack and sat down to eat it. The court was across the street from some dilapidated houses, which I suspected were built after the court itself. The paint on the pavement was faded at best and rubbed off in some spots. The hoops all had missing nets except one, which had a net of chains hanging from the rim. A crushed beer can stuck out of the crack that served as midcourt. Other trash blew around in the wind like tumbleweeds.

I ate slowly, trying to make the sandwich last. I only had so much food, and I wasn't eager to spend the stolen money I kept stashed in my pocket. Despite the hurry I'd been in to distance myself from Oak Ridge, I enjoyed eating at my own pace. It was a luxury I hadn't been able to afford before. Dining with my father was always uncomfortably tense. Most nights I would excuse myself from the table early, or quickly eat whatever was on my plate and not bother hanging around for seconds. I had breakfast by myself, but I was rarely awake enough to care about such things at six in the morning.

My thoughts turned to lunches with Vinny and Leslie. Vinny had moved to town the summer before seventh grade, was in most of my classes, and lived close to my house, so we naturally became best friends. We sat together at lunch. Funny how a thing like matching schedules can bring kids closer together. So middle school came and went, and we moved on to Brighton Township High School, where all the students of the three local middle schools come together.

We claimed one side of one of those long, gray, fold-up tables in the cafeteria. A few guys from the Brighton Middle School crew joined us and so did two particularly cute Brighton girls. One of those girls sat next to Vinny, but over time, our seating arrangements shuffled around. She was pretty cool—good-looking but not stuck up about it. She hung out with us guys, but she was neither overly flirty, nor was she a tomboy.

I don't think I've ever met anyone as easy to get along with as Leslie, and I may never again. By the end of that first day, we were all friends, and the three of us—Vinny, Leslie and I—hung out every week since. Always the three of us, unless the one missing was her. I guess Vinny had this crazy idea that I was into her, and didn't want to leave me out any time I couldn't hang out. I didn't hang out with her alone, either, but that's because Vinny's crazy idea wasn't far off the mark. I sort of relied on him to keep things from heading into relationship territory. As much as I liked her, I didn't want our friendship to become awkward, as I feared it would.

A group of teens, three blacks and one white dressed in various sports jerseys and basketball shorts, came up to the court and started shooting hoops a few feet away from where I sat. I looked away and finished my sandwich, feeling their eyes on me. The last thing I needed was people familiarizing themselves with my face. I caught a bit of their conversation and could tell they were talking about me.

"…little white boy…" one of them said, apparently unconcerned by the fact that one of his friends was also white.

They laughed and joked, clearly at my expense. My scalp prickled. I told myself it wasn't nervousness—that I probably had bugs in my hair from the ride through woods, all those branches slapping against my head. That didn't help. As if they could read my thoughts, they laughed again. I zipped my backpack to close it, and it caught on a bit of the material. I struggled with it, and felt the pressure of those four sets of eyes boring into me. Sizing me up. No, mine wasn't a face they would forget if a policeman happened to come through town with a photograph of the missing boy from Oak Ridge.

I left the backpack partially unzipped and threw it over one shoulder, then picked up my bike shakily, got on the seat and pushed off.

"Where you goin'?" one of them called over to me.

I rode off the court without a word or glance at them. I sensed one of them walking my way, and then something hard struck my head and threw me off balance. My bike slid out from under me and I fell over on my side, bewildered and angry. The basketball bounced a couple times and rolled across the street. I cringed, half from the pain and half from the looming confrontation I had been unable to avoid.

A cloud of dust and dirt sprayed up around me from my bike's jerky fall. A shadow fell over me, then another. I pushed myself up from under my bike and winced. My right hand was scraped and bleeding, caked with dirt. Another hand reached down to help me up, but I didn't take it.

"Yo, my bad. My hand slipped," the white guy said. The others laughed. I kept my head down and picked up my bike.

"We got a problem?" one of the guys asked, slapping the bike out of my grasp and pushing it back to the ground. "My boy just apologized. You gonna stand there or you gonna say something back?"

I continued to ignore them and bent over to pick my bike back up. The second guy shoved me to the ground. More laughs.

"You gonna need to learn some manners, little boy," the white guy said. "When someone talks, you talk back. Feel me?"

My silence didn't break. Once again I reached for my bike. That time, he grabbed a hold of me by the collar and pulled me over to face him. The fabric around the neck of my shirt stretched and tore.

"You disrespectin' me?" he said, making a show of it now. Looking tough for his friends. If they hadn't been there, it might've been different; he might not have approached me at all. But around these guys, he felt the need to prove himself. He glared at me through eyes that said, *You may be better off than me, but I'm still a hell of a lot stronger.* "You wanna see what happens to people who disrespect me?"

Before I could answer, his fist slammed into my jaw. And again. I fell back. A pair of hands caught me and held me up. I knew they weren't helpful hands. They were holding me in place so I could receive my punishment. I pulled against their grip. Someone was tugging at my backpack. I might've noticed they were unzipping the pockets and trying to pull out whatever they could find there if I wasn't busy getting the crap kicked out of me.

All at once, the four of them were on top of me. Two holding me, the other two punching and jabbing and pummeling me around. A fist socked me in the eye. Another rammed me in the nose. I was lost in a swarm of thrashing limbs. I kicked at them helplessly.

I tasted blood. I spat, and immediately regretted doing so. One of them yelled out in revulsion and punched me hard in the side. Pain rocked me from every inch of my being. The two guys holding me let me go and joined in on the beating. I fell to the ground, screaming for them to stop. Screaming for them to get off me. Screaming. Bruises, cuts and scrapes covered my body. Everything hurt. And I was all alone, getting kicked to death. Where the hell was everyone? Far away, enjoying their summer. Running through sprinklers. And there I was, screaming my head off in vain.

My hand hooked onto the closest foot and I pulled. A body came down on me, feeling like a pillowcase filled with meat as it fell on my face. My nose throbbed, and I couldn't breathe. I writhed and struggled to pull my hands free so that

I could push the guy off. His friends kicked at my shins and crotch and head.

I turned my head and sucked in air from the side. A small, silver sliver of something caught my eye. With fists and feet flying all around me, I took a deep breath coughed up blood, took another breath, and tugged my right arm as hard as I could up and out from under the guy. I grabbed for the steak knife that had fallen out from the front pocket of my backpack. It was just out of reach. I bent my arm back at an awkward angle and fished for it desperately.

My fingers caressed the handle. I curled my fingers, trying to get a grip on it, but it eluded me. The pounding in my head, arms, legs and chest made it almost impossible to focus. Sharp little needles of pain all over. My body was one big, swollen bruise. I formed my hand into a claw and dragged my fingers closed around the edge of the handle, scraping my fingertips against the rough ground. Slowly, I brought my index and middle fingers together.

I had it. Barely, but I had it.

Then one of the guys stopped wailing on me, and swore.

"He's got a knife!" he shouted.

I slid it closer and plucked it from the ground, turning it in my palm in one swift move so the blade was aimed down. I stabbed the guy on top of me and felt the blade sink into his flesh with surprising ease. He jolted and flopped off me like he was having a seizure.

"Ugh! I'm bleeding! Son of a bitch stabbed me! Gah!" he shouted, holding his arm away from the place in his side where the blade protruded. There was about four inches of stainless steel in him. The others backed off and gathered around the guy I had stabbed. They looked from him to me, stunned for a few seconds before one of the black guys came charging at me.

"Stay back!" I yelled, and reached into my pocket, unsure of what I was even reaching for until my fingers locked around my father's lighter. I yanked it out despite my aching muscles and flicked it. "I've got mace too! You know what that'll do? Turn this lighter into a goddamn flamethrower! You'll be disfigured forever!"

I stared at him, doing my best to look like a maniac. My voice was hoarse, and I could hardly see out of my swollen right eye. One of the guys was helping pull the knife out of his friend, and the white guy stood in the middle of it all, trying to assess the situation and make sense of what was happening. I approached my bike, taking one cautious step at a time. I held the lighter out in front of me, threatening to turn his face into a fireball at the slightest hint of attack.

"We gotta get him to a hospital," said the guy helping the knife-wounded one. Then he turned to me. "Fuckin' *freak*!"

A large, crimson gash leaked freely from the one's side as his friend pulled the knife out. He let out a quivering moan and shook violently. The white guy took the knife from him and ran up to my bike. He stooped down and sliced the back tire before I could stop him, then dropped the knife and called to the others, "C'mon, let's get him some help!"

They took off running, shooting me fearful, disgusted glances every few seconds as if to make sure I wasn't going to start chasing after them. I watched them go and then grabbed the knife, my backpack, and my bike, and started walking. More like limping, really. The shredded tire flapped with each revolution. My legs throbbed with every step.

I pushed my bike for a mile or two, passing rows of houses where families and neighbors chose to enjoy the warm summer day in their backyards. I passed a closed-up Laundromat, a pawnshop and cash-for-gold combo and a car wash on the Main Street of Wasteland. Then I shut out everything and focused on puttering along the road without collapsing or fainting. My strength was failing me, but I pushed myself on one laboring step at a time.

I finally stopped at a run-down shop with a rusted sign that read: ANTIQ ES. I needed rest, and by that point anything would do. It was all boarded up and looked to have been abandoned for at least ten years. I made my way around the back of the place and, banged up hands and all, worked at prying the rotting boards off the back door. I won't even try to remember how long it took, but for a while it was seeming to be damn near impossible, until one warped and splintered board shifted outward a little. I started pulling harder and kicking at it to knock it the rest of the way off. My knees protested, but I carried on. Occasionally I would look around to make sure nobody was around to catch me breaking in. Nobody was.

There were a lot of boards, but not enough to completely hinder a homeless kid's desperate attempts to find shelter. Once each one was pulled loose, I broke in without too much trouble. I propped the bike against a wall and unhooked my water bottle. Then I sat in the doorway and unscrewed the cap. I took a big gulp, indifferent to its warmth, and used the rest of the water to rinse my hands and wash the dirt away from my cuts. After that I went in and shut the door behind me and felt around blindly. I found the nearest corner and dragged my foot across the area to sweep away any litter. Once I was satisfied it was relatively clean, I set my backpack down and lay on my back, using the bag as a pillow, and tried to sleep. The floor was hard, cold and dirty. None of that mattered. I was alone and in a place where I could think and plan out the next step of my life in peace.

I drifted in and out of sleep on the floor of the old antique shop while I let my mind wander. Thoughts came and went, most of them useless. Memories of Vinny and Leslie. Of school and responsibilities. Of dreams and expectations. I wondered about my mother and where she'd run off to. Had she found another man to replace my father? Did she have another child? It never occurred to me until then that I might have a half-sibling. She very well might have lit a match and set fire to the photo album of her past, erasing everything and starting over. Would she be relieved if I found her—greeting me with open arms and an, "Oh, thank heavens, you made it out all right!"—or distraught by the return of a small piece of her previous life? I'd always sort of had a sense that I'd see her again someday, but now that I was as much a refugee as she was, I understood that it was impossible. It was necessary to completely cut ties with the people and places we knew.

It seems like a universal law that all realizations are sudden. Maybe the idea that sparks the realization is hovering overhead for a while, but then one day it rains down on you. Some days the storm hits you so hard you fall over, blindsided by the blow. When that happens, as cliché or simple as it may sound, you know you've reached a moment that is changing your life. From some unseen place, on an otherwise ordinary and uneventful day, a truth is revealed. You take note of it because there is no question of its importance. The epiphany is not something you can ignore. It's an earthquake. A tidal wave. An answer to the question you never knew you'd been asking yourself all this time.

With the quickness of a whim, I suddenly realized that this was not the next chapter of my life; this was an entirely new book. This was the opportunity I'd been wishing for and had finally granted myself: the chance to start over. The time to close the door to my old life and begin anew. I was reborn. No regrets could bother me; no memories would plague me. I had no past. Only a future. I was overwhelmed and overjoyed by the possibilities that greeted me. Like a dog no longer tethered to a pole in a yard, I saw the great big world around me and ran into it with a newfound wonder.

An idea formed from nowhere. I snatched it from the air. I would get to Boston, one way or another, and work as a trapper catching crabs or lobsters. Both, even. Why not? I'd make enough money to live comfortably, far from the world I once knew. It was a job I was sure anyone could do, yet most ignored in favor of more prestigious professions—lawyers, bankers, doctors. A life for the nobody who skated under the radar.

With the destination in place, I began working out my means of getting there. My bike was useless unless I could find a new tire and air tube. That would cost money I didn't want to spend. Or I could steal. It would be faster to travel by car, bus or train, and more cost effective still to go by boat.

I woke up some time later, surprised to find I'd fallen asleep in the midst of my planning. A few incoherent threads of memory from a dream I couldn't fully recall dangled at the forefront of my mind. My one good eye scanned the four bare walls of the empty room. Boards covered the windows, making it hard to figure out what time of the day it was, but I doubted it was far beyond noon. My stomach rumbled, but I was too stiff and aching to pull any food out of the backpack. I lay there for the rest of the day and into the night, mulling over my next few days.

My third day of independence was really just a continuation of the second. My back hurt worse than before. Probably from lying on the hard ground, though it could have just as easily been from the soreness settling in. My limbs were dead weights and my mind was too groggy for me to think properly. I tried to get up and pace around the shop for a while. When that got to be too painful, I tried resting. It was all right in small doses, but if I lay there too long, my muscles started to stiffen, which made getting up later feel worse.

I struggled against the aches and pulled an apple from my backpack. My jaw refused to open wide enough for me to take a bite. I pressed it against my lips and worked my teeth up and down, but the action amounted to little more than the equivalent of a cheese grater. I put it back and took out my last sandwich instead. I tore small pieces from the sandwich and squeezed them between my teeth, wincing while I chewed. I ate and thought about the guys who'd attacked me. What would the hospital attendants think happened to the guy I'd stabbed? Would the police get involved somehow? How much would the teens say? I hoped they were as afraid of the authorities as I was. It could be my only hope in escaping detection and remaining hidden.

Countless hours passed with nothing to do but go over my plan again and again. When I was strong enough to leave, I'd travel up the coast through New York and Connecticut, walking when I could and swimming when I had to. If I could steal a boat, I'd get there that much quicker and with fewer chances of running into roadblocks—namely police or concerned citizens who might wonder what a teenager is doing walking around all alone, beaten and bruised and likely skinny as a rail.

I grew restless. I flexed my leg muscles and cringed against the pain. My jaw popped loudly, and for a second I thought I'd done worse damage to it. I slowly opened my mouth and realized I'd set it right again. My face still hurt—a line that would set up every damn comedian in my school for the lamest of punch lines. I pulled my backpack over to the door and sat up against it.

An idea I hadn't given much thought to the previous day occupied my mind. I'd plunged a knife into a kid's side in order to defend myself. I never thought in a million years I'd stab somebody. And of course it was only permissible because of the self-defense factor, but still, I did it. I could have killed him. Maybe that wasn't enough of a wake-up call for him to stop with the gang-like violence and think twice before he did something rash, but it was more than plenty for me to realize what I was capable of.

I wasn't used to this kind of life. I had to do better to avoid people at all costs. Especially the trashy delinquent types. Another fight like that could get me dragged right back to my father, or worse. Would it be worse to be caught or dead? I wasn't ready to make that decision. I sure as hell wasn't looking to get others hurt, either. But if I had to kill someone to save my own life…

I saw something yellow on the far side of the room. Window-level. A small crack or spacing between the boards covering the window where a little light was pouring through. I steadied myself, stood slowly and crept toward it. Once there, I put my left eye up to the crevice and peered out into the street. A soda can rolled by, but I saw no people or cars. I stayed there for a moment, watching the nothingness in front of the shop and then went back to my spot on the floor and drank some juice.

I rubbed my eyes and then winced.

"Four days," I croaked. My voice felt a little rough, and I figured I was getting a cold. It wasn't that surprising. I had gotten by on hardly anything. I hadn't even showered or changed my clothes in that long.

I heard a car drive by and wondered if I could just walk out the back and continue in whichever direction I was headed. I sat on the floor and contemplated this, and what my next move would be, until I decided there was only a single train of thought running through my head and I might as well get off my ass and follow it. I took a minute to stand up, peed in the corner, grabbed my bag and left. I didn't bother taking my bike with me; if I ever returned, I could take it someplace and get new tires. As it was, it was useless.

I kept out of sight behind the rows of buildings, thankful for the shade. Even the dim back alleys seemed oppressively bright after almost two full days spent in total darkness. I eventually came to a blockade of twisted, rusty fence that I didn't dare climb over. That was a bad case of tetanus waiting to happen. I left the alley and went around the front of what turned out to be a tobacco store that was still operating.

I hurried along before the geezer in the window could frown at me disapprovingly, though he probably did anyway. That's how old folks are, always frowning or giving those nervous little teary-eyed chuckles. And they're miserable, which is understandable, considering they've probably lived through losing a lot of their old friends and family members. But, Jesus, they could lighten up a little. So critical and cynical and suspicious of anyone under thirty-five. Is it that they think kids are really all as screwed up as everyone says? Like we're too naïve or immature, and we're going to ruin everything and let it all go to hell? Maybe they haven't noticed, but not every teen is like how they are in the movies.

I headed into town, following eastbound signs. My scalp itched, and once again I wondered whether I had spiders, or maybe fleas, crawling through my hair. My arms were too sore and heavy to lift them over my head, but I promised myself I'd wash up the first chance I got. My shoulders burned under the weight of the backpack's shoulder straps. A bus route pamphlet skittered around the sidewalk at my feet. Not a bad idea. Buses were cheaper than taxis, and I could hide in the crowd that way. Fifty cents, maybe a dollar at most, and I could be on the fast track out of there. Miles further from my old life, and that much closer to my new one.

"Excuse me," a girl about my age said. And though it was said in an abrupt sort of *you're-about-to-walk-into-me* way—which was exactly what I was about to do in my oblivious state—it still managed to sound sweet, like this girl was incapable of being rude. I blushed, but didn't bother looking up.

"Sorry," I said, though my apology sounded more like a mutter, and a little more blood colored my face. Enough so that I almost wished someone would cut me so the blood had somewhere else to go, because I hate blushing. I feel my embarrassment seeping through, and that makes me even more embarrassed until I'm a damn beet on a body wondering if I might pass out from the overload of blood in my head.

"Hey, don't I know you?" she said as I started to walk around her, and this finally made me look up. I hadn't expected to run into anyone I knew this far from home. It may only be a few hours by car, but even then, who would I know out here? And it turned out I didn't know her after all. She was mistaken. I saw her surprise at my appearance—a swollen, busted and bruised face and hair that was probably matted to my skull from dirt and grease. Her jaw dropped. It was hard to say whether she was expressing concern, or just shock.

If I had ever met her previously, there wouldn't have been a moment of hesitation of whether I'd known her. That was a face you wouldn't forget. And even as beautiful as she was, and how red I would've been on any other occasion to come face to face with this gorgeous girl talking to me, the surprise of it had given me enough pause to let the blood drain out of my face in a split second. I stood there staring back at her in confusion. I could only guess that maybe I looked like someone she knew.

"I don't think so," I said.

"My God, are you okay?" she asked, looking torn between wanting to help me and wanting to run. "Your face…"

"I'm fine," I lied, and turned away.

I felt her staring me down as I walked, but I couldn't hang around. I was surprised enough that she'd want to waste any more time talking to a stranger, even if he was a vaguely familiar-looking stranger. This stranger was dirty, smelled awful, and hadn't been using the most kosher environments as a bathroom lately. But when I went a dozen paces and shot a glance back, she was leaving.

I walked on and came to an NJ Transit bus stop across the street from a tiny outdoor ice cream stand. I sat on the bench and watched customers come and go while I waited for the bus. I wondered if Leslie would've recognized me if she'd been the one passing me by on the sidewalk.

I contemplated getting up and leaving every few minutes until the bus finally rolled up and took it's sweet old time shooing passengers out the slow-opening mechanical door. A half-dozen brainless kooks moseyed out into the street. Some wore heavy-looking jackets. I wondered how they could bear the heat. Maybe that's all they had to wear, and they probably didn't have homes and closets to hang their jackets up in. One guy was mumbling to himself. I noticed he never closed his mouth all the way, as if he'd caught himself mid-sentence and realized he had nothing to say. I gave the kooks a wide berth and then climbed onto the bus, reluctantly paid my $2 and found a seat near the back.

It was the first time I had ridden a bus since the previous school year had ended. All I could think of were the early-morning and after-school talks with Vinny each day. We'd sit together, always in or near the back seat, joking and listening to music on his Walkman—and then his iPod, when he got one. I don't remember any of our bus ride conversations clearly, but that's the thing about bus ride conversations: They're almost always small talk. Class projects and forgotten homework assignments and why a band's newer music will almost never be as good as their older work. I'd mention how much I hate my dad, he'd listen attentively and at some point change the topic to whatever happened to be on his mind or troubling him at the time.

We never argued about anything serious. I think that's what made us such good friends. We'd debate about music, girls or school politics, and rarely actual politics, but we tended to agree on most subjects. Our debates were never meant to prove any point besides the fact that we were able to think for ourselves and stray from the like-minded social conformers that made up most of the school populous. Not that he and I ever discussed that point, but it was sort of implied. Sometimes I'd even sit and listen to him rant without adding in my two cents. I'd just nod and agree and wonder how much time he spent consuming all these facts or ideas, churning them over in his mind. He was a smart kid—pessimistic to the point of cynicism, but intelligent, and funny as hell despite his brief spells of moodiness.

I stared out the window for a while, thankful for the cushioned seats and smooth ride. Trees and buildings whipped by—a whole world full of people who didn't know me. I was just another kid on the bus. I closed my good eye and relaxed. Things were going to get better. I listened to the static of distortion blaring from someone's headphones a couple seats in front of me and let my present dilemmas roll off my shoulders. My right hand rested on the backpack in the seat next to me. I thoughtlessly fiddled with the small thread knotted through the zipper hole.

Something—not exactly a voice, but just an unsettling feeling—from my subconscious told me I was in trouble, but I ignored it. It's just something I feel once in a while, usually when I take some time to sit back after hours or days of heavy stress. I get that itching in the corner of my mind, like I'm not doing something I should. Like I'm ignoring my priorities.

My left eye opened and settled on something fastened to the back of the seat in front of me. Then I realized what my mind was trying to tell me. The something I hadn't taken the time to notice, or at least not consciously. The something that told me that sitting there on that bus was endangering myself, and wasn't worth all the travel time I was saving.

The sign read:

FOR YOUR SAFETY, THIS BUS IS
CLOSELY MONITORED VIA SECURITY
CAMERAS AND AUDIO RECORDING.

The police had to be out looking for me by then, posting missing person fliers around Oak Ridge and the surrounding towns and assisting my father in the search by any means possible. I wasn't sure to what extent they would go to find me, but video surveillance on public transportation wasn't out of the question. It was too risky to ride the bus, especially as beaten up as I was, without a disguise. My cuts and bruises made me stick out like a sore thumb, and I was already getting recognized on the street. I had to find some cover.

I got off at the next stop and looked around. It was more of the same. Pizza, supermarket, office supplies. I scratched my head—more from the itching than wondering what to do—and happened to spot an electronics store between a Chinese buffet and a greeting card store. I couldn't count on them having more than adapters, music players and cords, but with any luck I would get my hands on an electric razor. Then I'd find a public restroom and shave my head, solving two problems: the itch and my recognizable identity. I'd work on the rest of my disguise later, if and when I found the right places. A wig shop, maybe. Or a different style of clothes. I'd figure it out when the time came.

The inside of the store was surprisingly bigger than I expected. A variety of headphones hung from one wall behind and next to the front counter. Pre-paid phones, chargers and battery packs filled bins below the headphones. A television sat on a raised platform facing the counter, and the news was on with the volume turned down. Speakers of all sizes lined the far wall near racks of neatly displayed microphones and microphone stands, audio recorders and extension cords. Printers and cartridges filled the next tiny aisle over. Miniature televisions lined a small shelf across from the front counter, on the off chance there was still someone left in the world who would buy one.

I didn't get far enough into the store to learn whether they sold electric razors. I stood fixated on the television for a moment. The news anchor was quietly describing a story I couldn't hear, but understood anyway. Next to the talking head was a photo I'd seen only a few times and had completely forgotten. I gaped at the screen. The image stared back.

It was me with my father, the both of us smiling cheerfully. His arm was around my shoulders. The ocean was visible on either side of us in the background. The sun peeked over my father's head like an ironic, off-kilter halo. His belly had been in all right shape; it hadn't yet spilled over his waistband as a full beer-belly. My legs were covered in sand up to my shins.

A more recent high school photo then replaced the one from my youth. My freshman yearbook picture showed a noticeably older boy, but anyone could tell it was the same kid from the beach. The photos did not reveal any of my life story other than a typical boy from a typical family, though the truth was far from this implication. It was impossible for viewers to know that my mother was missing from my life, and that my father was anything but Saint Dad. He'd chosen the pictures that would put him in the most favorable light.

No doubt he'd given the cops and reporters some great quotes on how much he missed me and wanted me to come home. And if I was returned home? He'd say something about wrapping me up in his arms and thanking the Lord I'd come back. Because that's what the media wanted, and that's what the people—both neighbors and strangers alike—expected to hear. He'd leave out mention of the ass kicking he'd serve me, and whatever other punishment he deemed fit.

The anchor finished up the story, probably advising anyone who saw me to report my sighting to the local authorities and spread the word so I'd have no chance of escaping. A video appeared on the screen, showing volunteers at a soup kitchen. I kept my back to the clerk and left the store.

I was screwed.

My face was plastered around Oak Ridge for sure, but that wasn't even half the problem. Now the Philly news station was reporting on me. Anyone in the tri-state area would hear of my story, see my face. Nobody would hesitate to call the police. There could be a reward for anyone directly responsible for reuniting me with my father. The bastard who turned me in would think he was the damn Citizen of the Year, and I'd be locked up and kept under watch for the rest of my sentence in that prison of a home.

I'd have to stick to the back roads and stay out of sight, disguised or not. It wasn't safe to travel among other people.

I left the shopping plaza and walked toward the neighborhood with my head down. It was easier to get caught by someone who noticed that I didn't live in the area—especially if they happened to see me on television reported as missing—but I preferred to cut through areas with fewer people out and about. That way I could cut through increasingly quieter and less-populated parts until I made it to the long stretches of empty roads that cut through the farms and wheat fields I thought of as New Jersey countryside.

After a few uncertain turns, hours of walking and occasional jogging through pocket communities, and hesitant trudging along streets lined with sprawling homes, I found myself plodding down one such country road. Night was on its way by the time I got there. I was numb from walking so long with tired legs and sore muscles.

My stomach grumbled. All I had left in the bag was a partially eaten apple, and I knew that if I stopped to rest and eat it, my body would refuse to budge until it got a few more hours of rest. I wasn't ready to call it a day, so I unzipped my bag and pulled out the apple, shouldered the bag again and ate while I walked. The spot where I'd started in on the apple the day before was browning, so I avoided it. My jaw clicked while I chewed.

With a couple bites of apple in my stomach, I suddenly became ravenously hungry. I finished it quickly and tossed the core into the trees, aware of the dull weight in my stomach. It had shrunk from my lack of eating. I was nearly dehydrated, too. I'd have to spend some of the thirty-seven dollars and some change on some food. I had found a little over a dollar in change since leaving the electronics store and walking around with my head down, reminding me that the streets were a goldmine if I took the time to search them.

I followed the same road for miles. It led me on a straight path through large expanses of open fields. The road was mostly uninterrupted, but it occasionally intersected with other back roads with four-way stops. No cars in sight. The only people around for miles were indoors. So far, I had been successful in eluding the police and anyone else who might be looking for me. My next problem to tackle was getting a haircut and finding some new clothes for a disguise. Until that was out of the way, I would put off my plans of getting to Boston for the time being.

A large structure stood out in the dimming light. It was set back about a half mile down a dirt driveway at the center of a fenceless multi-acre plot of land. A smaller building stood about ten yards from it. I guessed that the larger building was a barn and the smaller one was the farmer's home. I was already deciding that sneaking along the fields would be safer than walking the roads when it hit me that there would be plenty of sharp objects to cut my hair with in the barn. There would be no mirror or light by which to give myself a proper haircut, but whatever was inside would have to do. I'd just fix it the next morning if I had to.

My heart raced a bit as I approached the barn. This was big. I was going to deliberately break into private property while the owners were home and close by. What awaited me inside was a mystery. Tools? Shears? A knife? I hunkered down close to the freshly cut grass in case anyone happened to look out the window and see a strange kid snooping around their property. My calves, thighs and back argued with my plan. I bit through the pain and inched closer.

It was strange. In broad daylight, I'd look like a maniac crawling across such a wide-open area, my backpack poking out like a tortoise shell. As it was, the darkness was my closest friend. I felt like I should've had someone there to sneak into the barn with.

Once at the large double doors, I hesitated. There would be no alarm to set off, but what about horses or sheep? They could be asleep inside, and my entry would startle them. I pressed my ear to the rough wood and listened. Silence. It occurred to me that farm animals probably were not noisy sleepers, and then I found myself scanning the rows of corn behind the house, noting the lack of fences. It was not an animal farm. Inside, I would find mowers and equipment.

Nothing that would make noise and wake the farmer. A car, maybe, but I was not going to steal that; it was too easy a way to get caught.

I reached for the latch, praying the doors' hinges would not squeak. Then I saw the lock.

Of course it was locked.

Breaking in would be riskier. Whoever was in that house would be up before I even stepped foot inside the barn. The whole thing would amount to a waste of time and the possibility of having the cops called on me. I didn't need that. I could move on to some other place, maybe settle down for the night and come up with a better plan in the morning.

I stared at the lock, unsure of what to do. The cons seemed to outweigh the pros, but I couldn't shake the desire to force my way in. I had come all that way. I was already there. I did not want to walk another few miles and try again.

For the second time, I wished someone else were there with me, to encourage me to make the decision I'd already made upon crossing the field. Someone like Vinny.

What would Vinny do?

He'd find another way.

I walked around to the side of the barn...then to the back...the other side...and finally back to the front again. There was nothing but the double front doors and a mountain of hay bales piled on the right side—not a single hole in the wall by which to pry apart the wall paneling and climb inside. If I was going to do this, I'd have to find the key or break the latch off the door. Finding the key meant breaking into the house first, and that was nonsensical.

Thus, I made my decision. I'd have to make it the quickest search of my life, by only the light of my lighter, but I would break in. I pushed one hand against the doors to test the wood. It didn't budge. Pretty sturdy. It would be tough to kick them in and force the latch to snap off. I didn't think I'd have the strength to do so, anyway. Additionally, the hinges were on the inside, so I couldn't unscrew them even if I had the right tools.

I looked over at the house, then to the barn doors, and back to the house. By the moonlight I could make out a porch that wrapped around to the side of the house, with steps leading down at the front and backside. All the lights were out inside. I couldn't make out whether the shades were drawn.

"Screw this," I whispered to myself.

There was no way to break in. Not in the condition I was in, and not alone. Maybe a character in a movie would find a way, but in real life you come to understand that things don't always work out. I just had to accept that and give up, find a place to sleep and—

Oh, the way the mind works.

Nothing inside that barn would be of more use to me than whatever I could find in the house. And getting in there would be a piece of cake.

I went around to the right side of the barn, rooting through my pocket as I did so. I produced my father's lighter and flicked it. The little flame leapt from the head. It looked so beautiful and harmless. I let it blow out, glanced back at the house, and stepped closer to the stacked bales of hay. I extended my hand to the second layer of hay, flicked the lighter again and held it there until the hay caught fire.

The stalks smoldered quietly for a minute, burning a deep red. It reminded me of the inside of a pomegranate. Then the flames spread outward, feeding off the dry, compacted fuel. Once it got going, I turned and ran to the side of the house. I watched the fire grow from a distance, waiting for the farmer to wake up and come rushing out the door at the sight. It was a small fire for the time being and would not catch his attention immediately. Not until it was a raging hell storm of destruction.

The flames began to spread more rapidly, climbing the mountain of hay and eventually licking the wall of the barn. I could hear it crackle from where I squatted at the foot of the porch. It was amazing. The blinding light hypnotized me as it ate away at the darkness. It kept mostly to the hay, rather than burning the building next to it, but I was too fascinated to care. Some of the blaze might have stripped the paint from the barn—I couldn't tell. If so, that was about as much damage as the barn incurred.

The stacks, on the other hand, looked like a rose garden of light. Thick smoke blurred and dimmed the light, leaving patches of crimson peeking through clumps of black—a bouquet of destruction, sending ghostly puffs into the night. I thought I felt the heat even from yards away, but it might've just been my excitement. Or my searing leg muscles crying out from crouching.

Something off to my right squeaked loudly. I fell backward and landed hard on my ass. Two loud stomps, and then the slamming of a door. The silhouette of a man ran from the front steps of the porch and halfway to the barn. Another figure followed him.

"Goddamn rotten punks!" the man shouted at the conflagration. Then, after a moment of silence only broken by the roaring fire, he yelled, "Don't just stand there! Call the fire department! Christ!"

I'd become so hypnotized by the incinerating haystacks that I'd forgotten I'd set them aflame as a distraction. I crept backwards like a crab on my hands and feet and came around to the back steps of the porch. The figure who'd followed the farmer out ran back inside to call 911. I stayed where I was, peering over the edge of the porch and waiting for the farmer's son—as I assumed it was—to return. I checked on the farmer twice, looking through the bars of the railing to do so.

The second time I looked for him, he wasn't there. My heart pounded in my chest. I glanced behind me, dreading my capture or the unlikely race for my escape, but he wasn't behind me, either.

Must be around the other side of the barn.

I heard the faint voice from inside stop talking, marking the end of the quick phone conversation. The farmer's son came storming out the front door to inform his father that the police and fire departments were on their way. He stopped between the house and the barn, looked around and then ran around the side after his father.

The wall of the barn was burning, but the fire didn't appear to be spreading beyond the haystack. I tiptoed to the front of the porch and froze when a third figure came through the front door. An older woman held her untied robe around her thin frame. She let out a gasp at the sight, totally oblivious to my presence a few feet from her. She lifted a hand to her face and scrambled down the front steps.

"Steven!" she called. "Steven, where are you? Where's Richard? Richard! Steven!"

I hesitated for a second, unsure whether someone else would come out of the house, then decided everyone was out front gaping at the fire. I snuck through the open door, my backpack slapping me with each hurried step. I found myself in the entranceway that opened to the kitchen on the left and a hallway leading straight to the dining room and living room. Beyond that, glass doors looked out over the garden in the backyard.

I came in through the hallway and turned right to where the bathroom and bedrooms were. Photos lined the walls. One showed a smiling family standing in front of the farmhouse. A second showed a black and white of the same house some unknown number of years earlier, with whom I guessed was the farmer at a much younger age standing next to his own father. The boy held a hoe and looked seriously at the camera. His father looked a tad grim himself, as if he knew what I'd done. Both were covered from head to toe in dirt.

I passed the rest of the photos without checking them out. The door to the first bedroom on the left was shut, and when I opened it, everything was dark. I found a neatly made bed and a few pieces of dusted furniture in an otherwise empty room. The guest room. I closed the door and moved quickly to the end of the hall.

The second room was a little larger than the guest room, but I knew by the twin bed that it was the son's. The blankets had been thrown off in the excitement, and there was an indent in the pillow where he'd been sleeping maybe ten minutes earlier. I went straight to the bureau and rummaged through the top drawer. Under a tangle of socks and boxers, I found a ring of keys, a wallet and a note scrawled on a folded piece of paper. I snatched the wallet and opened it. Three dollars and change. I took the cash and stuffed it in my pocket. There was no time for much else, so I stuck the wallet back in the drawer and shut it. One quick look around the room, and then I was off to the next.

The master bedroom was just as plain and modest as the other two, yet noticeably larger. Two shaded windows faced the garden. The double dresser displayed a small clock and a watch with a broken face. Next to the dresser, a doorway opened to a private bathroom. The walls were pale blue. A ceiling fan rattled above, looking and sounding like it would fall at any minute and break into a hundred wooden pieces. It was a wonder they could sleep with it on, but I suppose the noise was more tolerable than the heat.

Lit lamps sat on both bedside tables. I went to these first, but found little more than personal effects—tweezers, nail clippers, a paperback novel. Next, the dresser drawers. They were filled with nothing but clothes. Frustrated, I went to the bed and lifted the mattress. Nothing hidden underneath.

Sirens whined nearby. I told myself I had four or five minutes at most, though I knew there was no way to really tell until flashing lights came pouring in through the front windows.

I ran to the closet and felt around in the pockets of the jackets. The first two were empty. I stuck my hand in the right pocket of the third and excitedly pulled out a bit of paper, but put it back when I discovered it was a receipt.

Forget the money. It's not what you're here for.

I turned and went to the private bathroom, tugging my backpack off as I did so. I flicked on the light switch and then realized what I'd done and quickly turned it off. By the light from the bedroom, I scanned the sink area and medicine cabinet. There was a razor on the bottom shelf of the cabinet, along with a can of shaving cream and extra blades in a tiny plastic container on the next shelf up. I unzipped my bag, tossed them in and then checked the rest of the cabinet. Content with what I'd stolen, I swung the mirror back into place and ran out through the bedroom and into the hallway.

A chorus of police and fire alarms clamored out front. I sprinted for the kitchen. I passed the guest room just as the sound of running footsteps raced across the front end of the porch toward the door. I doubled back and ducked into the guest room. The front door opened and someone entered the house mere seconds after I'd shut the door behind me.

I was draped in darkness. Steps echoed from the kitchen area. I held a hand over my mouth and nose to stifle the sound of my panicked breathing. I moved slowly to the back of the room and ran my hand carefully along the wall. I bumped into a chair and stopped, sure that I'd hear the steps come down the hall. I didn't. There was an opening and closing of cabinets or doors somewhere near the front of the house. I couldn't figure out what was going on out there, but I wasn't concerned as long as nobody discovered me.

My fingers brushed against a curtain. I retracted my hand in surprise and then reached out and found closed shades blocking the room's one window. I felt around until I found the drawstring for the shades and pulled it slowly. From where I stood I couldn't see the fire, but a large, shapeless glow reflected off the lawn.

I hooked my fingers under the windowpane and felt an odd sense of *déjà vu*. I lifted the window open, making sure to make as little sound as possible. Men around the side of the house were surprisingly silent as they worked on extinguishing the fire. The sirens had been cut and now it was just the sounds of the trucks and hoses battling the flames. I dropped the backpack out ahead of me and then began the excruciating process of trying to climb out after it.

My leg seized and trembled as I lifted it to the sill. It refused to stretch. I tried again with the same result. The other leg was just as stubborn. I winced and forced my right leg as far as it would go. My whole body had not stopped aching from my run-in with the thuggish kids at the basketball court, and now my muscles were heavier than lead. I was trapped in the farmhouse, surrounded by police, unless I could pull myself out through the window.

I cursed under my breath, remembering how easy it had been a few nights earlier. I looked back at the door to the room, wondering if I could be sneaky enough to run out and through the sliding glass door leading to the garden. It wasn't a bad idea, but I decided against it. No way to tell whether someone was still in the kitchen, or if I'd be spotted running out the back door. It was going to be tough enough getting clear of them once I was out the window.

My arms shook as I heaved myself over the sill. I pushed off and tumbled out, turning myself as I did so I wouldn't land on my head. There was a thump as I hit the ground next to my backpack, but the noise wasn't enough to alert the family or firefighters. I shouldered the bag, bent as low to the ground as I could get, and snuck through rows of cabbage, carrots and cucumbers. My empty stomach mimicked the roar of the fire behind me. My body begged me to stop. Up ahead, I saw a cornfield that would provide the food and cover I would need to get through the rest of the night. I went down on my hands and knees, crawling to it.

I neared the six-foot wall of stalks, shooting glances back every few paces at the silhouettes of the dozen or so firefighters—and maybe police. I was sure they'd rule out the possibility of an accident. Despite the initial heat of the night, it was beginning to cool down. When the family discovered the missing razors and the son's empty wallet, they could put the facts together. And there was the open window in the guest room, a clue that was undeniable, even if they overlooked what I'd stolen.

I crawled faster, straining against my exhaustion. Luckily, everyone's attention was on the barn and the burned haystacks. My bag stuck up awkwardly, and the speed at which I was moving made it jostle on my back so that it was practically waving at them.

Crickets chirped. The distance I'd placed between the farmyard and myself muffled the discussion between the family and the first responders. I felt myself slipping out of consciousness, my senses dulling from lack of sleep. I'd spent all day and night in overdrive. The scent of corn and the muted sounds of the farmland closed in. I crawled faster, hardly able to focus on the vegetables I was racing toward. Pushing on and on and on, as slow as a dream. Behind me, black smoke drifted up into a blacker sky. It already seemed miles away.

I stood up straight as I reached the edge of the cornfield and shoved my way through the cramped space between stalks. Leaves everywhere. No room to stretch out and sleep. Too dark to see where I was going. I just had to trust that I was moving in a straight line forward. I was swimming through a sea of dead limbs. They reached up from the earth, barring my path and creaking as I forced them aside. I stumbled deeper, swatting at the tassels and husks.

Finally I gave up and lowered myself to the ground, where I curled up around a stalk. It was dirty and uncomfortable, but I didn't care. I let go of my thoughts and worries, and slept.

***

It's strange how long ago that feels. To be honest, I had forgotten all about it until I started writing. Being alone in the world like that. Like this. Sleeping in strange places and just barely escaping all the trouble I'd set up for myself. It was fun back then, I think. I was banged up and worn out, running on fumes, but the thrill of it was still there. As close to death as I sometimes felt, I always thought I'd land on my feet. Like I was too young to die. It was Tom Rollins against the world, and I was thus far the undefeated champion.

***

I woke up surprised that it took me no time at all to remember where I was and why. I could tell it was still early in the morning, even though the sun was hidden behind a gray sky. Using the surrounding stalks for assistance, I pulled myself up and stood in the cornfield, looking around to find some trace of which way I'd come from and where I was going.

I thought I remembered keeping my feet pointed in the direction I'd arrived when I'd lain down, so I put that spot directly behind me and pushed forward. After a while, the rows became less crowded and more even, and I followed a single open column the rest of the way out, bagging five ears of corn on the way. Just as I'd hoped, I came through on the other side of the field and found myself a quarter mile from a simple, hand-carved wooden fence that marked the boundary between that farm and the next one over.

The unpainted fence was composed of two long horizontal logs with ends carved to a point to fit in the cut-out slots of two vertical planks sticking out of the ground. The slots were cut tall enough so the carved ends of the next section over could fit in, too, and so on. The fence wrapped around the entirety of the adjacent farm. I walked along it and eventually came to the east corner.

Across the flat plain of grass, I found another dirt road leading away from the neighboring farmer's driveway. This barn was larger and longer and more likely housed animals, which would explain the fence. The walls were the color of dried blood, and the paint was chipped and worn off in some places, exposing the blanched wood underneath. A weather vane in the shape of a rooster perched on the roof, facing off to my right and gently turning to either side in the light breeze.

The bright mass of cloud that shaded the sky gradually darkened to a deeper gray. The first of the raindrops fell one by one like a hint of what was to come. I blinked and noticed the swelling in my right eye was down to a puffy circle. My vision was only a little fuzzy. My muscles were still stiff and sore, but the aches were lessening. I guess if I'd stayed in the antique shop for a few more days I'd have been well-rested enough to loosen up and start feeling better, but I couldn't stay stuck in one place for too long. It wasn't just that I was afraid of being caught, either. I was free to roam, and that freedom kindled a desire to explore.

Sure, five days on the road brought on the kind of strangeness similar to culture shock you get when you're alone in a new place, but I wouldn't call it homesickness. You just start craving those feelings and emotions you associate with home: routine, familiarity, safety. This was uncharted territory for me, so I would take to hiding a lot. But there was also the pull. An unseen force had cast its line and hooked me. It was beginning to reel me in. The danger excited me. It was magnetic. And at times, it offset the scales to the point where I sought it out more than the safety of the ordinary life I should have been building for myself.

I followed the dirt road out of the Jersey countryside and into an industrial worksite just as the wind picked up and the clouds broke into a steady drizzle. I ran to it in hopes it would be deserted. From the outside it appeared to be, but I thought the workers might all be there.

Under the cover of a large metal tower constructed of five wall-less floors encased in a tangle of pipes and beams, I shrugged off my backpack and scoped out the place. Across the gravel driveway, the face of what I presumed was a power plant had a series of arches carved into it, though they looked to be more stylistic than functional. Three thin, column-like smoke stacks protruded from the wide cement and brick building. A filthy pond was situated beyond that, with smaller structures scattered about. The whole area, from the plant to the surrounding field of rock and glass and sand, was a boring rusty red and gray made more boring and gray by the lazy rainfall.

When I was positive nobody was around, I stuck my head out under the rain, letting it soak my hair. Then I took the razor from my backpack, removed the used blade and stuck a fresh one in. I ran my fingers through my slick hair like I was spiking it. I held the strands by the ends and, unaided by a mirror, sawed away at it with another unused blade. I was careful to avoid slicing my scalp or hand in the process, but I cringed anyway, expecting any minute to make one wrong move and slash my wrist open. And what a fittingly anticlimactic end that would be: an accidental suicide. As much as I'd previously hated my life, and as much as I'd want to die months—hell, even weeks—later, I was not intent on going just yet.

The work was tedious, but by the end of it a small pile of hair lay at my feet, and I knew it would make the next part of shaving my head easier. I dropped the blade and grabbed the razor and can of shaving cream from my backpack, sprayed the cream on until it covered at least most of the top of my head, and began pulling the razor over my scalp in slow, straight lines. I tensed my whole body and held my breath. A couple times I snagged a tuft of hair that was a little longer than the rest due to my uneven slicing, at which point the blade would stop cutting or slide over the hair. I was deathly cautious of peeling away a strip of skin.

I sawed away the excess hair even more carefully than the first time, holding the little tufts with pinched fingers, and eventually finished shaving. When I ran my hand over my newly bald head, I felt a few places where I'd missed, but it was good enough. I put everything back in my bag and left the hair on the ground where it was.

I walked around the plant for a while. I didn't want to break in for fear of running into someone, so I continued on with the rain pelting my bare head.

Across the weedy plain I came to a stream that was just barely too big to jump across. I could've waded through it, as drenched as I was, but I walked around it and came to a bend in the first paved road since leaving the neighborhoods behind. The blacktop stretched on like an endless ribbon of film. Farms sprouted up on my left, nothing but trees on my right.

Miles and hours later, while I walked along the shoulder after a handful of cars and trucks had sped by, a sputtering pick-up truck rolled to a stop beside me. I ignored it and kept walking. The walk and the rain didn't bother me, and while I was dying to find a market or food stand or someplace to get a bite to eat, I wasn't ready to start showing my face around to strangers. I needed more of a disguise—a wig, a costume, something—before that happened or else I risked being recognized again. Still, the guy in the truck didn't let up. He rolled down his window and called over to me, driving slowly to keep up but not get ahead of me.

"'ey, boy!" he said. "I ain't gon' letcha jus' wander 'round in da rain. Come on 'n hop in! I'll take ya where ya headed. You gon' catch a cold!"

He repeatedly insisted, and after a moment of weak refusal I gave in and slid into the passenger seat with my backpack in my lap. The man had a round face made rounder by a full red beard that wrapped his entire jaw line. A flimsy, weathered hat crowned his curly red mop. He wore overalls over a mold-green T-shirt. When he spoke, I noticed his teeth were yellow and unevenly spaced, with a large gap between his front two. Despite his hillbilly demeanor—or possibly because I was a stranger—he was exceptionally kind and pleasant.

"Wha' were ya doin' walkin' down dis highway all by yerself, anyhow? Where ya goin'?"

I shrugged. Could I trust him? I figured I probably could, at least to get me as far down my path as he was willing to go. But then once I was off on my own again, he'd likely tell his wife or friends, if he had any, and if any of them caught word of a boy who'd recently run away from home, they could piece the facts together.

"Just walking," I said. A lame response, but he accepted it.

"Just walkin'" he repeated, nodding. "I guess I'll never understand kids 'ese days. Gon' catch a cold out 'ere you know. Get ammonia! Ricky's boy was out near damn e'ry day las' winter, got ammonia. Ricky's my neighbor. Been friends since we were tots. Kids, you know. Tha' was somethin' people'd call kids when we were kids, *tots*. Pro'ly before yer time."

I didn't correct him in saying ammonia rather than pneumonia, and I don't know why I remember a detail like that. I've got a habit for retaining useless information. I listened, trying to figure out a way to get myself back on the road and away from him.

"Ricky and I grew up 'ere, stayed right 'ere all our lives. We'll be 'ere 'til the day we die, I s'pose. Friends always. It's a good way to be. Kids 'ese days get all in a hurry to leave 'n go livin' someplace else, scatterin' 'round the world like someplace else'll be any different'n where they is. Ain't no place any different 'n the next. So where you headed? You goin' home, or what?"

I opened my mouth to answer, and in a flash I imagined unbuckling his seat belt, pulling the steering wheel to the side and running the truck straight into a telephone pole. I imagined his body ejecting from his seat, through the windshield and onto the pavement. He'd shatter several bones and ribs and die on impact. I'd sprint away from the scene if the truck was too damaged to drive away.

It was becoming a problem; I was consistently choosing destruction over more humane and friendly means of getting my way. This man had decided to do me a favor out of the kindness of his heart, and I wanted to eliminate him and any chance of a normal life because I could no longer bear social contact. Anyone and everyone I met could potentially lead to my ruin.

"Ah! I bet I can guess," he said before I could answer him. "That there carnival."

He nodded towards a park filled with rides and refreshment stands set up between the last of the cornfields and the neighboring town. A large yellow banner with pink lettering read: BILLSTOWN SUMMER CARNIVAL! The whole arrangement looked out of place in the dreary weather, but during a hot summer day it would've been hopping with activity.

"Looks like it's closed, due ta the weather, though, so maybe not," he said without slowing down.

"Actually, that's it," I said, hardly thinking it through. "Could you stop here?"

"Stop here, for the rained-out carn'val? You sure?" He shot me a look, as if trying to figure out if I was joking, but he slowed down and pulled over to the shoulder.

"I just want to check something," I said. "I'll be right back." I unbuckled my seatbelt and hopped out of the truck. I ran through the entranceway under the colorful banner and passed the "Closed" sign taped to a podium where carnival employees probably sold tickets.

No locked gate or chain-link fence blocked my way, so I went in and walked briskly between empty concession stands, collapsible booths and portable rides that made up the three-day event, as noted by several posters stapled everywhere. That day was supposed to be Day Two, but for obvious reasons it was either canceled or postponed. Everything was still set up and left as it would've been so they wouldn't have to work extra hours taking things down and setting them up again the following day, and as I toured the vacant park an eerie sensation engulfed me. It was like passing through a ghost town.

The rain was tapering off, but it wouldn't have made sense for the carnival runners to open shop until the next day. The rides were all too slick, and the grounds were specked with muddy puddles. I looked down into one, but the cloudy sky provided little daylight for a reflection. I went from booth to booth, searching for anything I could use as a tool, or a disguise. Those things appeared to be packed up. All that was left was a child's wonderland, rained on like a parade. Here, a miniature carousel with various breeds of horses; there, a mallet game to test strength; and a few yards away, a bounce castle partially covered with a large blue tarp.

Straight ahead, a short building donned with shiny silver lettering across the top of its doorway caught my eye: "The House of Mirrors." Interested in witnessing my handiwork with the razor, I shuffled over to it, favoring my still-aching right leg. Two life-sized, plastic clowns stood on either side of the attraction, beckoning me inside. Unlike most people, I was indifferent to their massive, hyperbolized grins and button noses, abnormally large feet and colorful apparel. Clowns neither scared me, nor made me laugh. I followed their outstretched arms and entered through the unlocked door.

As I should have expected, there was no visible light switch in the entranceway. The daylight that poured in behind me was a dismal gray, and while it filled the maze-like room somewhat effectively via the mirrored walls, it didn't help much when I stood directly in front of the glass. I shut the door behind me, casting myself in a darkness I'd learn to call home months later. The room was curiously void of smells. Even the scents of popcorn and cotton candy that filled the air outside were blocked out, and I found that I'd hardly noticed them until they were gone. I pulled out my lighter and flicked it. It didn't light. I tried a second time, and was suddenly encircled by tiny, floating ghost flames dancing in the million reflections.

With the light held out before me, I saw that my head was more spotted with random scraps of hair than I had thought. But there were no ticks. I'd done an all right job for shaving blind, and I was content with how different I appeared. I hardly recognized myself. That was, of course, partially due to the ghastly shadows draping my cheeks and exaggerating my bruised face in the multiplied images of me scattered about the room. My darkening tan looked yellow in the flickering flame of the lighter. I had dark circles under my eyes—a purple ring around the half-closed one—and an unusually pronounced jaw line and cheekbones. I was possibly thinner. That could have just been a trick of the light.

With no brown hair to identify me by, I could move on to changing the rest of my looks until I believed no one would pick me out of the crowd. I would also clean up the shaving job I'd done once I was settled.

That reminded me that, in my haste to get out of Farmer Joe's pickup truck, I'd left my backpack on his passenger seat. Naturally I hadn't planned on cutting through the carnival and walking east, abandoning my chauffeur to sit idle for hours before realizing I wasn't coming back, but I remained undecided as to my next move.

Kill him and take the truck.

A fine idea theoretically, but I was incapable of murder. I couldn't even fathom hurting someone, despite the stabbing incident. That just wasn't me. And besides, the police would find his body, or his family would declare him missing and somebody would match his license plate to the stolen vehicle report. Something would go wrong.

Just to the coast.

But they could track my path based on where he disappeared and where his body and truck turned up. Forensics would pull my fingerprints from the steering wheel. I'd go to prison. How would I kill him, anyway? As weak as he might be, he was a full-grown man.

Pull a razor blade across his throat.

I shook off my sinister thoughts and let the flame go out. My hunger and fear of being found were making me paranoid and moody. I'd go back to the bucktoothed hick and put on a show of charming him into driving me as far east as he'd go, bid him a farewell and hope he'd write it off as a good deed that warranted no mention to his wife or friends. I could be persuasive. Or pay him not to talk. One way or another, everything would work out. It always did.

I felt around for the knob and exited the House of Mirrors. I wasn't ready to leave yet, but I had no reason to stay. I didn't want to keep Farmer Joe waiting. Back into the world of postponed splendor. Being there in the middle of the empty carnival felt like walking across a stage that was all set up and ready for a show no one would ever see. There were all the props and none of the action, none of the magic. I think that's what the husk of our childhood would look like once we've lost our innocence. Just a bunch of lifeless cartoon characters left to gather dust and mold under overcast skies, or old toys in an attic with missing screws and exposed springs. When the music stops and the sweet smells grow stale, there's no more denying it was just a well-disguised charade designed to distract us from the tragedy of reality.

Resolved to hitchhiking, I returned to the pickup and got in.

"I thought maybe ya ran off wit da circus," the driver said with a crooked smile. "Didja find what you were lookin' for?"

"I don't know," I said, propping my bag on my lap and shutting the passenger door.

He gave me a curious look, but apparently thought better than to pry.

"A'right, then," he said. "Where to?"

"Well...how far are you willing to drive?" I bit my tongue and shifted my gaze around, finding it hard to meet his eyes for longer than a few seconds at a time.

"Anywhere yer goin' can't be so far, is it? Aren't cha goin' home?"

"I...the thing is..." I fumbled over my words. It was one of those moments where you know that either immediate outcome—getting a ride, or being kicked out and forced to walk—didn't matter so much as the long-term consequences. Depending on how I answered, I could wind up as just another mystery of this man's life that gets lost and forgotten in the folds of his mind, or an instant problem that only the police could solve. And what the hell could I say, anyway? Some guy I never knew and would never meet again was being polite and offering a ride, unknowingly putting himself in a potentially dangerous situation. Some kid whose life story he'd never know and could hardly relate to happened to stroll by on a rainy day while he'd been driving to who-knows-where.

***

The way people stumble upon each other's paths and affect each other's lives is unimaginable and undeniably happenstance, directed entirely by personal needs and goals and moods. It's just crazy. I think about that a lot these days. I wonder about how my life would be changed had I made a single decision differently, or had a certain class at a different period of the day, or walked down a different road at some point during my travels. All these consequences are absolutely nuts. How are we able to ever take on all this responsibility, knowing that if we totally screw up, we could ruin, or even kill someone? Things like being at the wrong place at the wrong time never concerned me before, but now my mind reels with the possibilities. Now, I can waste all the time I want playing out all the scenarios in my head, believing hindsight is clearer than all the crystal balls in the world—and sometimes convincing myself that hindsight is a load of crap, and there's no way to ever know how things will unfold.

***

"I don't have a home, or family… but I…I was hoping maybe you'd drive me up to New York. Unless that's too far for you, and I'd understand if it is, it's just that's where I'm going."

Before I knew it, one lie spawned another and another, finally spilling out into one tall tale. My words came out rapid-fire, spewing out so he had no time to interrupt me.

"My parents are dead, but they were from New York, or at least I think my mom was, and that's where I was born and raised for a while. They died when I was young, from a car accident. I was in the backseat, but the car seat saved my life, and ever since I've just been on my own, and I never knew where to go, but I think if I can get to New York, there might be someone, like a neighbor or a relative, or a family friend or someone who can help me… I don't know, find other relatives I can live with, or something. If you can't, that's okay, but I was hoping, since you offered to drive me…"

"Well, son, dat's a sure long drive and I 'ouldn't be back 'til late, but I tell ya what. Why don' I drop ya off at th' police station, and they can set you up wit some food and a place to sleep?"

"No, that's all right. I can get there myself. It's really nothing I want to bother the police with," I said.

"I'm sure it's no trouble at all. Dat's what they're 'ere for, t' keep everythin' in order. The police are your friends, 'spite what some people tell ya."

"Forget it, I'll just walk—"

"Now, hold on, then," he said, raising a hand to signal me to stay. "If yer insistin' on not lettin' the p'lice help, even though I know that'd be th' best course of action, if you wanna ride along fer…say, another half hour, I'd be happy to take you. An' if I can't convince ya to go to the p'lice by then, I'll let you out and turn 'round and come back home w'thout another word about it. How's that?"

He flashed that crooked smile at me again, which must have been his way of trying to prove he was an all right guy after all.

"Okay," I said. "But please don't tell anybody, and especially not the news or anything like that. I don't want that kind of attention. It's embarrassing and…uncomfortable to talk about."

"Don't worry 'bout it," he said, waving his hand. "I won't tell a soul."

We drove off, keeping as much of a northeast path as the roads would allow. During that half hour, he grilled me about my past, and I lied through my teeth, staring out the passenger window at times so I could avoid looking at him. The less contact I made, the easier it was to weave a story with what little information I'd provided him. I don't remember everything I said, but I made a point of making myself sound like the unluckiest kid in the world. Death, sorrow and misfortune were merely nicknames for my shadow. I made him feel sorry for me, and pitied him in return for eating up all the bullshit I fed him. He clung to my story of woes, totally in awe of the hardships I'd supposedly endured. The first half hour came and went, and we were still driving. I kept us off the topic of what time it was and how far he'd driven, but after an additional fifteen minutes passed and he finally pulled over to the shoulder by Jax Burgers, I was more than ready to end our conversation and stuff my face. He wished me well and left. I went into Jax and ate my first full meal in days.

I was too hungry to be bothered by the number of diners inside. I made my way to the service counter and blocked everything else out. It's a reckless way to be when you're hiding. Any one of them could've seen me and called the cops or pointed me out to their friends. But by the time I ordered my food, took a seat in the corner by two windowless walls and began eating, I noticed that my surroundings weren't all too menacing. The kids were glued to their cell phones. The grandparents were too out of touch with the news to know a boy was missing, and that the boy looked suspiciously like me. The parents had their hands full with crying and misbehaving kids, or the dramatic gossip of the day. I was just another nobody.

The restaurant was just like a McDonalds or Burger King. It just wasn't a chain. The whole place smelled like french fries and grease. My table, and seemingly every other one I could see, was covered in salt and smears of ketchup or grease or half-wiped-up soda. A tiny metal napkin dispenser and a plastic tray holding packets of salt, ketchup, mayo, mustard and sugar sat at the wall side of my tiny couple's booth.

I wolfed down my burger, stealing occasional glances at the other patrons while mostly keeping my head down. They were preoccupied with their own lives. I wished I could be, too. This was supposed to be a new beginning for me, and I couldn't even focus on what I wanted. I was so busy worrying about being found out. I was sure people would stare at my bald head or my beat-up face. But as nosy as humans can get, they also don't care that much for strangers. At least not when they've got other things on their minds. Family, friends, work.

I missed Vinny and Leslie. Had they tried texting or calling me? God, it's been forever since I called or texted anyone. Texts had just started replacing note-passing in class last year. For one, it was easier than writing out a message, folding it up and getting the person's attention so you could hand it off to them; notes were even worse when you had to pass it down the length of an aisle or row and hope nobody else would intercept it. And notes were mostly harmless, unless the teacher actually got a hold of it and found something written about him or her. But if they took your phone? Then you'd have to hear about it from them, the principal and your parents, and you'd lose your phone.

Somehow, Vinny had mastered the art of texting without looking at his phone. He'd tuck it behind his textbook or under his notebook while the teachers lectured. He mostly only texted when the recipient wasn't in that class, but sometimes he'd shoot me one even when I was sitting next to or in front of him. He never got caught. I rarely checked my phone, though, until class was over. That way I wouldn't lose my phone or wind up cracking up at whatever he said. He did that enough with the ridiculous faces he'd make at me while the teacher was talking.

Leslie was the real troublemaker, though. Tyler Pitt had given her his number early on in the school year—an act I wasn't too thrilled about, but shrugged it off later just the same. He was the biggest tool in our grade and had the most annoying, smug grin. He thought of himself as the king of comedy, but his jokes were always vulgar and raunchy. I was amazed he even had friends. And though he never talked to me much, it got to the point that his presence was all it took for me to want to bash in his face.

Leslie neither gave him her number in return, nor did she call him to go out or anything. But when she found out that Tyler always left his ringtone on loud during school, she started calling him in the middle of class. His cheesy hip-hop tone would blast from his jeans pocket, and then he'd make a show of not being embarrassed. He'd get his phone taken away each time, and it didn't matter that her number wound up forever in his phone's history, because she didn't have an identifying voicemail; just a generic this-phone-owner-missed-your-call one. He might've suspected Leslie, but never let on if he did. So the joke continued until later in the year when he got suspended for three days. He never learned to just silence the phone.

Her goofiness drew me to her even more. She liked the same things we liked, hated the same people we hated, and knew how to make school more interesting. She didn't take life too seriously. I liked that. I still do. And now I'm out of her life. I up and disappeared. What did she think of that? Does she miss me as much as I miss her? For all I know, a new guy might've moved to town. Or worse, she could be dating Vinny. I shouldn't do this to myself, thinking this way. I was the one who left them behind, and if they want to be together, who am I to complain? It kills me to think I might never meet friends like them again.

***

One time I had excused myself from class and went to the bathroom, and either on the way there or on the way back—I don't remember which—I overheard a conversation going on in one of the other classrooms. I stopped by the lockers near the open doorway and listened in for a few minutes. It was a sociology class, I think. They were discussing why people are the way they are, based on two areas of study: nurture and nature. The former claims that how we were raised either fucks us up for life or sets us on the right path to becoming a healthy, intelligent adult. The latter claims that it's based on our genetic makeup. Supposedly, the student consensus was that it's a combination of the two.

I remember getting ready to head back to class, because I didn't want to get yelled at by my teacher or a passing security guard for hanging out in the hallway, but I stuck around for another moment when a girl's voice chimed in. At first I thought it was Leslie, but when I peeked around the lockers I saw it was a pale, twiggy girl with curly red hair and glasses. I'd never met her before, but after hearing her argument I almost felt like she and I should've been friends. She was so in tune with my view on things, and was able to word it better than I ever could have.

"I think it's a combination of three things," she blurted. This captured everyone's attention, including mine, and the teacher waited silently while she elaborated. "There's nature, which explains how some of our behavioral aspects are genetic, and that makes sense with what we've talked about in regard to addiction and twins who are separated at birth, yet maintain identical or near-identical personalities. Then there's nurture, which explains how, given a certain setting or culture, we may act accordingly. But I think there's a third factor, too: experiences. The things that happen to us over the course of our lives can change or mold our personalities. For example, accidents, or near-death experiences, or getting married, or conversely, a lack of any traumatizing experiences or milestones in a person's life, can affect how they act."

The girl may have sounded like the biggest nerd in the class, but I thought she made a pretty damn good argument. It was cool hearing a kid close to my age pointing out things an adult had overlooked. I was impressed, but the teacher apparently wasn't. He thanked her for her input and then right away turned her argument around and tried to file experiences under the category of nurture. I looked in again and saw her jaw go rigid like she was clenching her teeth. She nodded along to his assessment, but I sensed her frustration. He was wrong. The curriculum was wrong. I was on her side, but of course I couldn't walk right in and say so. It was bullshit how he just shot down her well-thought-out point and said that experiences were the same as how you're raised. But that's how teachers in that school are. The answers to the questions of the universe can only be found in the teacher's edition of a textbook, and everything else is wrong.

I never ran into that girl, and even if I had, I wouldn't have any good reason to bring up what I'd overheard her say that day in class, but her words stuck with me.

I've explained a little bit of the nurture factor of my life and its affect on my decision to leave home. I'll get to the nature part later. Now, I think I need to indulge myself and use the redhead's argument to defend how I've behaved these past nine months. Because I'm not the same boy I was when I left, and the things I've done can't be explained away by a hereditary diagram.

***

A day and a half passed uneventfully, and for that I was thankful. The forty-five minute drive in Farmer Joe's truck had brought me significantly closer to the coast than I could've hoped to get on my own, and by the end of that thirty-six hour trek (broken up by infrequent breaks to eat, sleep under the bleachers of a baseball field, change my clothes and move my bowels) I arrived at the shore. It was the first time I'd been to a beach since my mother had left, other than a two-day visit with Vinny and his family one summer earlier. I was excited to beeline up the coast and settle down in Boston, but a short break filled with sand, sun and saltwater sounded too good to resist.

I half-jogged the rest of the way through the sunny street of ugly pale pink and blue beach shacks, by little kids smeared with splotches of sunscreen, old convertible cars and giggling girls in bikinis. I probably looked like a maniac, and on top of that, a homeless maniac, but I was so close to the sand, and I couldn't wait any longer. I ran as hard as my body would allow up the salt-worn boards of the walkway and then fell over when I reached the sand. I'd gotten my only other pair of clothes dirty.

I can just wash off in the ocean. And steal another outfit once the sun sets.

A smile cracked my face, thinking that I'd actually made it that far. Gone, finally, from my old life and the stress of looking over my shoulder. That paradise that stretched out in both directions for as far as I could see, it was all mine, and the waves ahead of me were reaching out and pulling back in as if beckoning me to float away and let all my problems disappear.

I sat up, took my shoes off, pulled each sock off, balled them up and stuck them into my sneakers. When I got up, the soft sand was a relief. I went down to the water and stood there looking out to the horizon, watching the whitecaps form and pit themselves against the smooth, muddy sand. I breathed it all in—kids' laughter, the screams of seagulls, the smell of the ocean, the ease with which my feet sank into the ground. I stepped on a seashell and cracked it, but it didn't hurt, and I didn't even avert my gaze from the water as I picked bits of it from the pad of my foot.

I stared at the deep, distant blue melting into the sky, which was beginning to darken from an oncoming storm. Let it come. I wouldn't mind. Wash away the last few remnants of my bitter past and shower me from the heavens. I was more than content; I was at peace. I stood like that as the minutes passed and the sky deepened to purple and almost black. Sunbathers packed up their things and left, and if they looked at me questioningly, I didn't notice. I was only vaguely aware of them while I let my thoughts wander out into the vast depths of the Atlantic. It was both calming and intimidating. I regretted tearing my focus away from it.

"Hey champ, you might want to head on home!" a man called over to me, and I turned to face him. He pointed to the sky, which was now completely blotted out by one enormous, purple-gray cloud. "It's about to rain!"

As if on cue, a crackle of lightning sounded somewhere over the horizon. I nodded to him, turned most of the way away, then took one last look out over the ocean before giving him a small wave and heading off up the beach, as if returning to a family beach house. I had no further plan regarding a place to stay or even what I would do with my life once I reached the coast, so I roamed around, passing buoy after buoy.

The storm broke suddenly and came down hard, but I stuck around for a while, unperturbed. I let the wind-wall of rain pound me for about fifteen minutes. Shivering uncontrollably, I turned back towards the street in search of cover. I contemplated waiting it out under the slope of a dock that protruded from the sands and out over the ocean, but it provided little shelter and would just make me more uncomfortable in the cramped space. The sheets of rain became blinding and I could no longer make out the paths that led off the beach and into the streets. It was as if I was walking along the ocean floor, fighting my way through the rip tide.

Finally I gave up looking for an exit and stepped carefully over the thin spikes of wood that fenced in the dunes, climbed over the clumps of sand and grass, and made my way over the fence on the other end. It was difficult to maneuver through the dune area in the storm, and even more so with my shirt and shorts clinging tightly to my freezing skin, but eventually I made it back to the street. It was rough and slippery, so I pulled the socks out of my shoes and stuck my feet into the sneakers. Struggling to pull my socks back on would have been useless. I peered through the rain in every direction, looking for somewhere to dry off and rest.

After walking a block and a half, I came to a beach house with a "For Sale" sign flapping in the heavy winds. I took my chances and ran around the back side of the house, and then checked in all directions to make sure nobody was looking before fitting both wadded socks over my fist, winding back, and smashing through the window of the back door. I reached in cautiously, avoiding the shards of glass jutting from the edges of the window frame. I unlocked the door and yanked it open, jumped in and swung it shut hard behind me.

Once I was safe inside, I sank to the floor and sat dripping and panting. I didn't feel bad about it. I was happy just having a dry place to crash. I wiped the water from my face with my wet hands and smiled. Anyone who was looking for me wouldn't find me there. As far as I was concerned, it was my new house, and it would be all mine unless someone came around and realized the vacant home was not exactly vacant. I wasn't planning for how I would deal with that either, or at least not at the moment. I got up, acquainted myself with my new pad, and found the bathroom, where I stripped down and dried off with a towel from the closet.

I stepped out of the bathroom with the towel wrapped around my waist and took a tour of the house. I was mostly interested in the layout, but if there was anything valuable hidden in the rooms or attic, I would be more than happy to claim it. Whoever owned the property was looking to sell it, and so I didn't expect to find money or jewelry lying around, but it wouldn't hurt to search every drawer and cabinet just in case. I was feeling lucky. What I found, though, was nothing more than a good place to hide out until something better came along.

The place was spotless. There was a kitchen, a living room that was a little bigger than the one I'd known growing up, a small dining area between those rooms, three bedrooms upstairs, two bathrooms total, a couple of hallway closets, and an open garage area with a shower-and-changing-room section. A sliding glass door at the rear of the master bedroom opened to a balcony with one staircase leading down to the back entrance and another leading up to a sitting area on the roof.

The refrigerator was empty, as were the bureaus and the pantry, but a few things were left behind, either to be picked up at a later date or to be saved for the future owners. There was an umbrella in a hallway closet, a few towels in the bathroom and some books—mostly about nature, but a few novels, too—on the bookshelf in the second bedroom upstairs. A bulky television sat on a small wooden table, though I guessed it was originally arranged on an entertainment stand that had already been moved. Most of the decorations were gone save for a couple paintings on the walls and a wooden plaque with a flock of sandpipers in flight etched into it.

I picked up *The Call of the Wild* by Jack London from the bookshelf and lay on the couch in the living room, flipping through the first few pages before growing bored and falling asleep.

Three flies buzzed around the living room when I awoke, reminding me that I'd need some way of patching up the window I'd broken in the back door, but I told myself I'd figure that out later. I stretched and sat up, relaxed and grateful for the comfortable sleep I'd gotten—and indoors, at that. It was a little breezy because I'd slept in nothing but a towel, but it was still the best sleep I'd had that week. I didn't want to get up from the couch, but I had to go to the bathroom, and I knew that I was lucky to actually have a bathroom available exclusively to me at the moment, so I went. Then I tested the shower and was happy to find it was still working. I stood there with hot water cascading over me for longer than I had to. Long enough for my fingertips to prune. There wasn't any shampoo or soap, so I did without.

I stepped out of the shower and dried off with the towel I'd slept in earlier. Then I gathered my wet clothes off the floor and brought them out to the balcony to dry on the rail. The sun was setting, but it was still in the mid-seventies and the temperature wasn't dropping much. Still, I didn't think they'd be dry by morning. That was all right. I wasn't in a rush to go anywhere, and I could wear my other clothes as long as the rain hadn't soaked through my backpack. I stood with my hands resting on the rail, looking out over the backyard and nearby beach houses like a king observing his kingdom from the tower of his castle. I imagined I could still hear the waves crashing against the shore from that distance. The sun dipped lower and disappeared. I didn't budge.

The promise of a happy life never felt so close. The last time I remembered really looking forward to anything was years ago. Back when things were okay. After a year—or maybe a year and a half—of fighting for it, my father had finally gotten the raise at his electrician job. A pretty significant raise, too—one he'd deserved for a while and had been waiting for without much fuss until a coworker had been awarded a similar one. He and this coworker, Barry, did the same job running full-office maintenance and electrical, but Barry had been hired a year after him. They'd each been cheated of raises for too long, and when it came time, Barry got one and my father was left out.

When Dad got his raise, along with a bonus for being so patient and understanding, he announced that he was taking us—my mother and me—on a family vacation to the Caribbean. I was ecstatic. It'd be the first time I was anywhere outside the states. I pictured us swimming in clear blue water, lounging by tropical beaches filled with palm trees, cracking open coconuts. My mother made it sound like we were going to be rich.

Every day, I woke with a beach scene floating through my mind. Each night I stared up at my ceiling, wondering what sorts of cool stuff I'd find. Sometimes I dreamt about it. And then, ten days before we planned to hop on a boat and set sail for the Caribbean, my mother announced that we weren't going. The night before, my father had gone out with some friends and coworkers to celebrate in Atlantic City without telling Mom. It had been a long time since there had even been mention of my father's gambling problem, and my mother was sure those days were long gone. Even when he came home very obviously drunk and incoherent at two o'clock in the morning, she had no idea what had happened. Only after he sobered up that afternoon did he confess to having lost his entire bonus check, and $3,000 of savings on top of that, over a course of just a few hours playing black jack and poker. Our vacation was canceled and my hopes were wrung out.

Then, to make bad times worse, my father's boss caught wind of something else that had occurred that drunken night in AC. Whether one of his coworkers snitched on him will forever remain a mystery, as will what happened. My best guess is that they brought some hookers up to a hotel room after they'd wrapped up at the casinos, and maybe some of that money my father lost wasn't lost to a bad hand. In any case, he was fired. That was the beginning of when things got worse. My mother disappeared shortly after.

Since then, I'd get most excited about just getting out of the house and spending time with my friends, or going on a class trip. But that flame sparked up again on the balcony. As dark as the night was, there was a glow in the night sky, as if God had forgotten to turn out heaven's light. I've seen that night glow a few times since that, too. I think it's all the light from the stars, dimmed a bit by the polluted air. By the glow, I lost myself in my thoughts and hopes for the future. I was happier than I'd been in so long. Like the sky, I was glowing even through the thick veil of pollution that encased me, caused by a thousand careless assholes.

A car pulled up and parked out front of the house next door, and while I didn't really notice it right away, I subconsciously assumed that it wasn't as late as it felt. I started to notice, however, when someone got out of the car, said goodnight to the driver, and wandered around to the back of her house. By her unsteady zigzagging I could tell she was drunk, though I couldn't tell if that was why she'd chosen the back route as opposed to coming in through the front door.

So you snuck out tonight, eh?

If so, it was only for some social excitement rather than an escape from her family. That would also explain the reason for coming in the back way, avoiding the front entrance and all the sounds of turning locks, which would wake up her parents. She'd snuck out and had gone drinking with some friends—or new acquaintances—at a bonfire on the beach, like in all of those teen summer movies. The weather had likely put a damper on things, and the party probably had to be moved inside where there was even better access to liquor.

She wobbled a little as she came to the back patio and leaned heavily on whatever was in her range. She grabbed hold of a garbage bin, threw too much weight into it and fell over, knocking the trashcan down with her and spilling its contents. I laughed. She heard me and looked up. I stepped back from the rail, not wanting her to catch sight of me, but I was too slow.

"Hey!" she yelled up at me. "You spying on me?"

I said nothing, hoping she'd go inside. Instead, she waited for a response.

"Hellooo-ooo?" she called.

"No," I said, trying a little harder than she was to not wake up all the neighbors. I came back to the rail and leaned over it so she could hear me clearly. I couldn't quite make out her features, but I guessed she was about my age. "No, sorry." I laughed again, watching her drunkenly climb to her feet. "I just happened to be standing here when you tripped."

"Riiight," she said, and put a hand on the trashcan. She tried using it to prop herself up, but it rolled away under her weight and she fell to the ground again. She cursed the trashcan, and I laughed again.

"You're going to wake everyone up," I whispered.

"Then help me up," she said, lying on her back. She held her arms out, closing and opening her hands. I couldn't help thinking she was cute, even as pathetic as she looked. And despite my every instinct to go inside and avoid people, this girl was too drunk to recognize me in the dark even if she did see my photo on a missing person flier the next day. Besides, the sooner I got her inside, the less likely it'd be that one of the neighbors would come out and find me living next door. Then they'd ask if I was the owners' kid, and it wouldn't be long before my web of lies caught up to me and they called the police.

Or, you know, maybe I was just making up excuses to get close to her.

I descended the wooden steps leading down from the balcony, adjusting my towel so it didn't slip off as I walked. When I got to her backyard, she was still lying on her back, and beaming up at me like we knew each other.

Of course she's smiling. She's drunk, and you're naked.

She clapped her hands at me, and I took them and lifted her to her feet. She leaned against me and held on tight. I had to throw a foot backward to hold my balance so she wouldn't knock us both over. I smelled the beer on her breath, but her perfume was stronger. Not a fruity smell, or any sort of smell I could identify, but it was sweet and overpowering. I realized I didn't know what to do next. Her chest was pressed against mine, and her hands were clasped against my bare back. Her hair fell to my shoulders. She was hugging me so close, and I knew it was just so she didn't fall over again, but in that instant I wanted to kiss her.

I told myself to escort her to her back door and let her find her own way to her bedroom—she didn't need my help beyond getting safely inside—but I couldn't move. She was holding me in place, leaving me to hug her back and breath in the mixture of light beer and strong perfume. I didn't mind one bit.

She shifted her chin off my shoulder and looked into my eyes, keeping her face a centimeter or two from mine and then flashed an unmistakably mischievous grin. Her eyes shined with the glow of the sky. Then she contorted her face into an expression of faux surprise.

"Oops," she whispered, and pulled my towel loose. She cackled as it fell away from my waist, revealing everything.

Without thinking about it, I chose to hide my genitals from her view by holding her closer against me.

She laughed. "Oo-oh! You think you're smooth, Mister Spy-Man?"

"You tell me," I said.

She smacked my butt with both hands and howled with laughter.

"Very smooth!" she blurted.

"All right, time to get you inside," I said. I tucked my foot under the towel, which was laying on the ground, and kicked it up into my hand, so I could wrap it back around my waist before attempting to walk her to her door.

"Hmm-hmm-hmm, nooo…" she said, shaking her head teasingly as she placed a hand on my shoulder.

I stood frozen, as if her hand held all the weight in the world. Of course I didn't want to be rid of her just yet, but what else could I do? I wasn't witty enough to sweet-talk her, drunk or not. I'd never been the best at talking to girls. But she was flirty enough for the both of us, and playing along was fun. Once I took her inside, I'd just be stuck alone in my beach house, kicking myself for blowing yet another chance at even kissing a girl that cute.

"Aren't your parents home?" I asked. "Aren't they going to hear us out here?"

"My *brother's* home, but he's asleep upstairs. My parents are out with my aunt and uncle. I'm stuck babysitting tonight." She rolled her eyes. She was standing on her own, hands on her hips, eyelids occasionally drifting shut. "Aren't *your* parents home?"

"I'm…kind of by myself here, too," I said. "And you probably wouldn't wanna wake up your brother this late…"

"Mmmaybe we should go back to your place, then?" she asked, raising an eyebrow at the suggestion I'd clearly made yet failed to put to words. Then she suddenly hitched forward, and I swooped to catch her.

In the process of dropping down, grabbing her by her hips and scooping her up before she could topple to the ground for the third time that night, I pulled her in close and kissed her awkwardly on the lips. It was an instinctual act. The kiss was too rushed and desperate, so that even a drunk girl could tell I didn't know what I was doing. I practically crushed her soft lips.

She pulled back slowly, giggled, and put her hands on her hips over mine.

"Guess you're not so smooth after all," she said.

"Even James Bond slips up now and then," I whispered, taking her wrist. I took a step toward her door, but she stopped me.

"I never fucked a spy before."

And just like that, I was redeemed. I guided her in the other direction, around the spilled trash and toward the house I'd broken into hours earlier. I laid my towel down over the small pile of broken glass in the doorway, ushered her inside, then shut the door behind us and led her upstairs to the master bedroom. All the way to the bed, she couldn't keep her hands off me.

Things were really turning around. I had a house of my own, a hot neighbor who wasn't going to let me sleep alone, and all the time in the world. Life was good. Why would I want to get up and leave so soon for Boston? It wasn't going anywhere. Losing what I already had, on the other hand, was a mistake I was tired of making.

I was vaguely aware of someone moving from the bed the next morning. The previous night was a bit of a blur, though the more I let reality seep in, the more parts came back to me. I rubbed my eyes and checked the clock. There wasn't one. For a moment, I thought about the odd dream I'd had. Then I heard the storm door shut downstairs and realized the girl from next door hadn't just gotten up to go to the bathroom;

she was sneaking back home. I was reminded of how drunk she was when I'd met her, and how I'd led her to that room and had sex with her. Both of us were too tired and relaxed to go anywhere or do anything afterwards, so we'd just lain there and fallen asleep.

She's sober now. Shit.

I took my time getting out of the queen-size bed. It was hard to get up, and even more difficult to not let my eyes roam around the room. A television faced the bed, taking up about half of the space on top of the dresser. Pastel paintings of sailboats hung from the walls to my left and right. The walls were painted eggshell white. They reflected the sunlight that poured in from the glass door of the balcony and through a small, round window that reminded me of ships and submarines.

Finally, I sat up and swung my legs over the edge of the bed. My foot fell on something other than the hardwood floor, causing me to nearly trip. It was her bra.

Double shit.

Despite her looks and the fun we'd had, I wasn't ready to track her down right away. I was sure she'd be pissed at me for technically taking advantage of her. But I had to return her bra. I swear, before my days were filled with blood and guts and dead bodies, you'd have thought I was living in a bad teenage comedy.

I padded down the hall with it clenched in my fist, went down to the living room, and pulled my clothes out from my backpack. They were a little damp from the rain, but not bad. I got dressed, slipped my shoes on, and stood around for a few minutes wondering what I'd eat for breakfast. Then I quit stalling and went out the back door. Glass crunched underfoot beneath the towel I'd left out the night before. With so much running through my head, I paid little mind to it.

I knocked on the back door, because I'm an idiot and didn't think about going around front. After knocking three or four more times, the door opened. A young boy answered, looking up at me in confusion and curiosity. He wore a *Batman And Robin* T-shirt and khaki shorts that ended a little higher than his knees. I quickly hid the bra behind my back.

"Yeah?" he asked, appearing troubled.

"Is…" I started, and remembered I'd never asked about her name. "…your sister home?"

"Yeah." He made no move to get her. Instead he asked, "Did you get blown up or something?"

"What?"

"You're all banged up, and your hair's missing. Did you get blown up? I saw it on TV before."

"No, I just shaved my head. Can you get your sister for me?"

"Just a minute." He shut the door.

I waited, rubbing my hand over my bald head.

I *really need to do something about this.*

When he came back, he was unaccompanied.

"She's in the shower."

"All right," I said, sighing. I couldn't decide whether I was relieved or frustrated. "Can you just let her know when she gets out that Tom from next door needs to talk to her?"

"Yeah."

"Thanks." I adjusted the position of my bra-holding hand so he wouldn't see it as I walked away.

I found a broom in one of the hall closets and swept up the broken glass from the back door. While I swept, I watched my neighbor's house for any movement. The day was hot and humid. I scooped the glass into the outside trashcan, smiling at the thought of her clumsiness the night before, then ran up the wooden steps and took my dry clothes off the railing. I brought them inside, laid them out on the bed, and then a terrible thought struck me. Fishing through my pockets, I pulled out a crackling wad of bills nearly glued together from the rain. I carefully pulled the bills apart, tearing one of the fives in the process. Then I tested the lighter. It still worked.

A knock at the door downstairs shook me from my daydreams and drifting thoughts.

"Coming!" I called.

I went the wrong way and ended up in the kitchen. I had momentarily confused the house I was in for Vinny's. When I backtracked and came to the door, she was peering in through the broken window, looking a little amused and very unsure—of me, I guess.

"Tom?" she asked. God, I liked hearing her say my name.

"Hey," I said, opening the door to let her in.

"Hi... I can't stay long. My parents are going to be home any minute. My brother said you came over looking for me?"

"Yeah, I have something of yours. Hold on," I said. My cheeks grew warm. I took the bra off the coat hanger in the broom closet and handed it to her.

"Thanks. I figured that's what it was. What did you say to Drew?"

"Is Drew your little brother?"

"Yeah. You didn't...tell him...?"

"No, no, of course not. I just said I was looking for you. I didn't know your name."

"That's fine," she said, implying that she didn't feel like giving it out. "Listen, about last night. I was really drunk. I had just come back from a party with some friends, and I made Drew promise not to tell my parents I went out. I let him stay up all night and eat ice cream and watch TV, and told him I wouldn't tell if he didn't. But I can't have you coming over or talking to him, and my parents cannot know we ever met. Okay?"

"Yeah—"

"Because if they find out I've been drinking and fucking guys while they're not around, they'd fucking kill me."

The way she came right out and said it left me a little stunned. The fact that she said guys, plural, was also a little surprising, though I shouldn't have assumed anything one way or another.

"I totally understand. But we can still hang out and stuff, right? I mean, I don't mean like last night, necessarily, I just—you seem cool, and while we're living next door to each other I'd like to get to know you."

She smiled and tucked a lock of chestnut hair behind her ear.

"Sure. I did have fun last night. And I can't really blame you for what happened."

"Cool," I said. "Besides, now that we've been through that, there's really nothing to be shy about, right?"

"I'm not very shy at all, but yeah," she laughed. "All right, well I'm gonna get going. I'll see you around, Tom."

"Bye..." I said, hoping she'd fill in the pause with her name. But she just smiled and waved as she walked back to her house, leaving me to stand there awkwardly watching through the broken window. *Whoever you are.*

With that over with and a full day ahead of me, I slathered on some sunscreen and took a leisurely stroll out on the town. I remember the oppressive heat and tons of families and couples swarming the sidewalks, shopping or making their way down to the beach, but it was hard to take in my surroundings with Ms. No Name distracting my thoughts. I told myself I wasn't going to socialize, but she made it so easy. Plus, she obviously had no idea who I was, even if she now knew my name. Her easy-going nature and effortless charm put me at ease, and I began to wonder if I could get away with showing my face to hundreds of strangers with the same result. Neither she nor her little brother appeared threatened by my appearance, but I personally thought I looked like a delinquent and a half with my shaved head and unwashed clothes.

Things always had a way of working out for me. And most people meant well, even if they had a hard time showing it. I certainly did. I had to stop worrying that things would take a turn for the worse, and just live life the way I intended: free, and without fear. Independence is scary at first, but it was only my path changing, after all. Not me. Not the world around me. Just the decisions I made and the people I met. And of course I wanted to meet people; trying to isolate myself from the outside world was absurd. I didn't have to be alone to start over.

What I had to do was get some food. I'd been starving myself for fear of spending all my money, and as of yet I hadn't thought of a way to make more money. That was a problem that could wait. I stopped in at a brick steakhouse with a green awning, momentarily surprising myself with the sudden decision. The place was crowded with early birds catching a quick lunch before a day on the beach and night owls grabbing a late breakfast. A nineties rock station played quietly under the clamor of conversations. The lights were dim, but the windows let in enough sunlight. The atmosphere was not that of a beach-area restaurant, but a typical steakhouse. I felt a little out of place smelling of sunscreen, but that was nothing new.

I approached the hostess at her podium by the door. She briefly looked over at me and then went back to her conversation with a coworker. Discussing some guy, no doubt. She was pretty, though not as pretty as her friend. I looked beyond them to the tables in the dining area, cloaked in white tablecloths and topped with linen napkins folded neatly around bundles of silverware. Almost all of the tables were taken, though I noticed a few empty ones scattered about the middle of the room.

"Can I help you?" the waitress talking to the hostess finally asked. She smiled the way girls do when a boy is about to say or do something foolish; that face that says, *you're not joking, but I'm sure as hell laughing.*

"Yeah," I said hesitantly. "I need a table? But I didn't make reservations. I'm here for lunch."

She waited, not saying anything for a moment. She was intentionally making me feel more awkward. Just holding eye contact and deepening that smirk. The bitch wanted to watch me sweat. She probably did it to every guy in her class, making a game out of it.

"Are you eating alone or waiting for someone?" she asked, and I got the hint that she was assuming the former.

"My friend is meeting me here, but he told me to grab a table for us," I said, averting my gaze as I lied.

"Oookay," she said. "Do you want to sit on the bench until he gets here?" She gestured to a rigid, wooden bench by the door.

"Would it be okay if I sat in there?" I asked, nodding to the dining room. "You could send him over when he gets here. His name is Andrew."

"Uh, sure. Do you want to get started on a salad in the meantime?"

"Yeah, that works," I said, relieved that I was finally going to get some food.

She led me directly to a table in the center of the room, facing straight to the entrance so that Andrew would see me as soon as he came in. She didn't have to know that there was no Andrew, though she probably assumed as much. I ordered a Sprite and a Caesar salad, then watched her disappear to the other side of the room.

I was making too much of an impression on her. I didn't want to believe it, but I was. She wouldn't see me on the news, because there were bound to be other newsworthy things going on closer to the coast—shark sightings, or boats crashing, husbands lost at sea—but making any sort of impression could be a bad thing. I was better off blending into the crowd, as hard as that was to do while I looked the way I did.

No, I was overreacting. As much as I told myself to relax, every little thing was still setting off my paranoia. It was the hunger. Once I got some food in my stomach and headed back outside, to the ocean or wherever, I'd start thinking rationally again.

As much as I hated to spend more money, I settled on the idea that I'd go shopping after lunch. There were surf shops and gift shops every block or two. There I could buy a hat and some new clothes, maybe even a bathing suit. Blend in. Strip away the Tom Rollins look in favor of something new. Then I wouldn't worry so much.

The waitress brought me my soda and salad and then left me to peruse the menu. I ate greedily, eyeing what meals I could afford. Then an image rose up in my mind, causing me to nearly choke on a mouthful of lettuce. I'd laid out all my money on the bed back at the house. I'd forgotten to grab it before heading out, and now I was about to order lunch. The waitress probably suspected I had no money right from the start; that's why she was so weird with me. She expected me to come in with family, or a group of friends at the very least. Not alone.

But I told her I wasn't going to be alone. I was just waiting for a friend. And when the check came? Well, then I'd just tell another lie. What did I care? It's not like I'd ever have to see her again. She could smirk and make me uncomfortable all she wanted, and I'd screw her over by skipping out on paying.

When she came back, I ordered their most expensive cut of steak with a side of tortellini, mashed potatoes and gravy. If I was going to eat for free, I might as well make the most of it. She asked if I wanted to wait longer before having the food sent over, so that Andrew could show up and have some salad or soup, too. I told her not to bother.

"He won't mind," I said. "Maybe I'll even save room for dessert, too, just in case. So when he gets here I'll still be eating."

She clearly thought I was the worst friend in existence. Not that I cared. Once I'd confirmed for the third time that I was too hungry to wait to eat, she went back to the kitchen to put in my order.

***

It's hard not to think about how easily it came to me. Lying. It's funny. I used to lie all the time, and especially in those days. The thing about lies, though, is that they lead to more lies. You tell one, and if you're sloppy enough to slip up or get called out on a hole in your story, you find yourself weaving more and more. Your fabrication isn't just a veil you use to cover someone's eyes; you've woven a web, and eventually you'll become ensnared in it. And it doesn't matter how many people you convince yourself will benefit from your lie, because, honestly, you're only doing it to cover your own ass. To believe otherwise would be to lie to yourself. At that point, there's no hope at all.

I haven't had to lie in quite some time now. It's something I'm thankful for. Not that it makes up for the terrible things I've done. Nothing I ever do for the rest of my life can make up for that. But at least I haven't had to lie to myself or others. I've learned from my mistakes, and what I've learned is that lies rarely do me good. Despite that, I know there have been times—not many, but some—when a lie has paid off. Usually that only happens when it's a small lie, one that is of little consequence because ten minutes later it doesn't matter. Consequences are what I fear most lately, so I tread as gently as I can to avoid them. I believed I was a pretty careful guy back then, too. Not hardly as careful as I am now, but you know what they say about hindsight.

***

The longer I played out my act, the more suspicious I could feel my waitress and her coworkers becoming. Sometimes people can tell you're up to something, and they keep their eyes on you, just waiting for that moment when you slip up so they can catch you in the lie. They know it's coming, and the only question is when. Did they think I was only making up a story about meeting with a friend, or did they know I planned to leave without paying? I'll never know, and I don't care. What matters is that when the time came for them to collect the check, I was already out the door, with my boxed leftovers in one hand and the taste of red velvet cake fresh on my tongue.

I wanted to see the girl next door, but I didn't know how to get her alone with me. If her parents went to the beach, so did she and Drew. If they were home, she was, too. I couldn't show up to her place, and she wouldn't invite me over, because I'm a teenage boy, which means a dick on a stick in the minds of parents. I'd simply gotten lucky that first night, and beyond that, I had to make my own luck.

I spent that second night alone lost in thought, picking at my leftovers. I couldn't find any silverware in the kitchen, or napkins or paper towels, so I ate the steak with my hands. I wondered how many more times I could skip out on the check before restaurants started posting warnings about me, and whether that was even something restaurants did. I wondered if the police were still investigating the fire at the farm. I wondered if the kid who I'd stabbed was recovering well and if he thought about that day every time he undressed and saw the wound. Above all, I tried to push away thoughts of everyone in Oak Ridge.

***

Right now all I can think about is the pile of corpses. Does anybody know what happened? Has anybody figured out what I've done? I'm still holed up in here, so at least I don't have to run. For now, anyway. I try to drink to forget these things now and then, but I know I've got to keep writing. Some days are hard. What can I say? How the hell do I even say what needs to be said? No sixteen-year-old should have to live like this. Wondering if he's going to be caught and strapped to an electric chair, or whatever they'd do to me. I guess it's lethal injection, right? I imagine that would be better. If I have to go, I don't want to feel it. I know I don't deserve to get off that easy, but life is painful enough without adding the unimaginable torment to ending it.

I went shopping that week and got a beanie to hide the fact that I didn't have hair, plus another set of clothes and some bread and lunch meat to tide me over when I wasn't out hitting restaurants. But what am I talking about? You don't care about all that shit. This isn't a diary. You're here for the answers, and I guess I've just been dancing around them. To tell you the truth, I've been anxious about telling it. Not that I'd lie, but it's not something I'm proud of. Not something I'm eager for you to read. Just something I need to say or it'll eat me alive from the inside. Ha. That's a joke. It's already started to.

Experiences. The third thing, along with nature and nurture, which helps shape our lives. They make us do things we never thought we'd do in a million years. Terrible things. Unbelievably stupid things. Things like putting your life on hold for a girl, because you think she's the answer you've been looking for all this time. Things you may never recover from, if you manage to live through them.

***

I broke into her beach house six days after meeting her. It was driving me crazy—not being able to see her. I'd steal glances out the window from time to time when she and her family were heading out to the beach, but that wasn't enough. I kept wanting to call out to her, run up to her, kiss her. Bring her back to my house, into my bedroom. Finally, the idea occurred to me. I was surprised with myself for not having thought of it sooner.

I waited until they were far down the road and out of sight and then ran out onto the deck and down the steps, bee-lining for their house. I'll admit it was more than a little exciting, thinking that, while she strode along the hot concrete in her tiny bikini and flip-flops, carrying a boogie-board and a white-and-pink striped towel, she had no idea what I was planning. Hours would pass before she'd discover the note, and I hoped at least some of that time she was thinking about me. Hell, I could hardly go five minutes without thinking of her.

Their house was a structural twin to mine. I was grateful for whatever architect was lazy or thoughtful enough to mass-produce those identical vacation homes; it meant less time I'd have to waste figuring out which room was hers. I'd paced around my own house for an hour the night before and had concluded that her parents would most likely have given her the second-largest bedroom. I'd stood in the room, mostly bare and empty due to being up for sale, and tried to imagine it as she would have it decorated. Her perfume bottles scattered across the dresser, her clothes folded neatly in the drawers. Her bed…

Standing on their deck and looking in through the sliding glass door, I saw the lock was set. That was all right. I'd foreseen the possibility of it, and had practiced using the steak knife to slide through the cracks and pry the lock open. It wasn't easy, but I got it on the third try. I stepped into her parents' room and quickly shut the door behind me. It was unlikely that anybody would see me breaking in, but I wanted to get in and out as fast as I could. No point in hanging around longer than I needed to.

Her room was exactly where I'd expected. The door was ajar, and as soon as I peeked inside, I knew. No pink walls or posters of boy bands, though that only suggested that it was a rental home rather than their permanent address. Still, the thick, fruity aroma and short shorts and tank tops crumpled by the closet door told me what I needed to know. I was in the bedroom of the hottest girl I'd met in a long time, and with whom I'd slept. A place I'd dreamt of going. It was almost surreal, so filled with her personal touches and yet so devoid of life. Unfortunately, I was all by myself. I saw her letting me in and sitting me down on that bed, shoving her rumpled clothes aside and climbing on top of me. I saw her leaning in close. Wanting me again.

I took the note from my pocket and tucked it under her pants, then hesitated for a moment. It didn't make sense for anybody else to come into her room before her, so it was doubtful that anybody would find the note before her, but it wasn't impossible. I read over the note again, imagining how it would sound to someone without the proper context:

> *I want to see you. Sneak out of the house tonight and come on over. I'll leave the doors unlocked.*

She'd know it was me, and where to find me. Her little brother might even make an educated guess. Her parents, on the other hand, would be hard-pressed to figure it out. I placed it on her bed and threw her clothes over it, then darted out of the room as silent as a thief in the night.

You're acting like a stalker.

I slid the door open a foot and squeezed myself through.

Go back and get it. Tear it up. Throw it out. Never talk to her again.

But it was done. I'd thought it over, carried through with it, and went sprinting back to my house to wait for her to return. All that while, I worked myself up playing out the possible scenarios of that night. Of course, my teenage mind focused on the two extremes that seemed most inevitable: her absolute adoration, or fear and loathing. The latter is all I ever expected to find from the girls who occupied my mind, though, in reality, girls generally overlooked me and rarely addressed me about my affection. Every teen has a crush. Every teen is a boiling pot of emotions and hormones.

***

And then there's this teen, who's mostly a boiling pot of rage, paranoia and a distant remembrance of feelings I used to identify with. Regret seeps in fairly often, quickly followed by a defeated sort of cynical apathy. A shrug and a, "what's passed is past, and can't be undone." Some days I really truly believe things will work themselves out as they always have, and I'll be able to soak up the sunlight in peace again. But depression and despair aren't ever far behind, and then the voice in my head tells me it's only a matter of time, and that this will only end one of two ways. Death, or prison. Though those aren't really any different from each other, are they? It's death either way.

Some days, I think it'd be a relief.

***

I moved all my personal belongings up to the roof, where I liked to hang out and look out over the town at night. If she came around, I didn't want her to ask why I kept all my stuff in a backpack. It made me look like a drifter, and while I had been one at one time, I'd found a home for the time being. She would be more likely to stick around if she didn't think I had any plans to leave, and I honestly had none. No plans whatsoever. I was a fly-by-the-seat-of-my-pants kind of guy, and that lifestyle was suiting me just fine.

She didn't show up that night. I sat on the porch for at least three hours as soon as the sun dipped below the horizon, all for nothing. I took it as a bad sign, but still the possibilities were there. Maybe her family stayed up late. Maybe they were light sleepers, and would've heard her sneaking out. I wasn't stupid—I knew she was avoiding me, Needy Tom—but sooner or later we were bound to bump into each other, and then I'd do my best to convince her I wasn't crazy. And I don't mean to brag, but I am a pretty damn good liar.

Two days later I did it again. Ms. No Name hadn't shown up at all, and I was beginning to worry that I'd driven her off. Naturally, that would mean that breaking in for a second time would drive the nail deeper into the coffin, but I did it anyway. I had no other way to contact her. And as unlucky as I often am, I was surprised she accepted my offer.

I asked her to visit me at the boardwalk amusement park. I didn't even request her to come alone; I added that she could bring her brother along. It was probably what made her comfortable enough to come, and that was the plan. Also, it gave her an excuse to come unsupervised. She just had to pretend we were friends who hadn't seen each other for a while and suddenly bumped into each other unexpectedly. Not so totally farfetched, even if Drew had already met me.

We met at the Ferris wheel, a bad pop song in the making. My skin prickled as my pores opened up to the heat. The sun fried my brains, scattering my thoughts and filling my world with pus-yellow light, an over-exposed photograph. She was neither late nor was I early, though I'd waited too long for her. We hadn't agreed on a time, just a place. The Ferris Wheel. A pointless ride, though only one of many. It takes you up, just to bring you back down. At least roller coasters have the added excitement of speed and corkscrews, so you feel like you're about to be decapitated at any moment. But it ends the same: you get off and walk away.

Her eyes told a story I wasn't expecting. More than simple recognition, she seemed glad to see me. At least, that's what I read from them behind the light tint of her shades, under a bouquet of hair. She smelled like her bedroom. The thought squeezed the words from my throat, so she spoke first.

"Hey," she said. Then, to Drew, "Here's $5. Go get some cotton candy. I'll be right here watching you."

"But the line's so long!" Drew's face contorted in the most tragic of frowns, as if he'd been asked to carry out some miserable task. He thought he was going to ride in a shaded seat of the Ferris wheel, and instead he had to wait in a long line in the simmering sun.

"I'm paying for your cotton candy, Drew," she said, so maternally. "Don't be a brat, okay? Afterwards, we can go on any ride you want. I promise."

"Can we go on the Matilda-whirl?" he begged.

"Yes, we can go on the *tilt-a*-whirl, right after you get some cotton candy. Now go! I've gotta talk to my friend for a minute."

"Okayyy," the boy said. His tone was that of unmistakable annoyance, and I began to wonder. Was it because he was doing something he was told to do, or because he didn't have his sister all to himself? He seemed put-off at joining the line on his own and leaving her with me, if even for a few minutes. But he trudged along just the same, and when he was out of earshot, I turned my attention back to her.

"Something you wanted to talk about?" she asked.

"Yeah. Hey. We haven't talked in a while." I bit my lip, immediately regretting the clichéd preamble. "I've been kinda bored, stuck in the house by myself, and I wanted to spend more time hanging out with you. If that's cool with you."

"Of course," she said, flashing her big, perfectly white teeth. They blindingly reflected the sun so that I had to squint. She wasn't making this easy. "I was hoping we'd get together again, but I've been so busy with family stuff and watching after Drew."

"He doesn't like me, does he?" I asked.

"He's just shy. You know how kids are around anyone older than them."

"Right."

"But *I* like you," she said. "And that's all you're concerned with, right?"

"Are you flirting with me?" I asked.

"Maybe," she said, masking the inflection on the word so it was difficult to gauge.

"Do you think you could get some time away from your family? Away from Drew, too, I mean? Alone?"

It was the question I'd been trying to pose to her a thousand times over, thus far with absolutely no luck. In the oppressive heat, I was starting to not care what her answer might be. I knew how strange I'd been acting those past few days. Breaking into her house, watching her from my window, leaving private letters on her bed. I couldn't blame her if she wanted me to keep my distance, at least for a little while. But every word that rolled off her tongue was encouraging me to press on, push my luck. Her lips parted, an open invitation. She reached out to me with one hand and pressed lightly on my shoulder.

"I'll see what I can do, and I'll let you know," she said, and I knew she meant it. "Maybe I can get a little time away from them on the beach—like, walk a few beaches down from where we usually hang, and meet up with you. How's that?"

"That sounds good. Yeah. Just let me know where to be."

Drew came running up to her with the five-dollar bill still squeezed tightly in his little fist.

"It costs five-fifteen, Katie!"

"Oh, jeez, I thought five was more than enough," she said, and I smiled at her young brother's use of her name. "Here, there's a quarter. Hurry up and get back in line before it gets any longer."

"Well, *Katie*, you're an awfully nice sister," I said, smirking.

"Why thank you, Tom. And it was fun talking to you, but I should get back to him before he starts calling you my boyfriend."

"That wouldn't be so bad, would it?"

"Not at all," she said. "But I thought this was gonna be our little secret."

"Right. The beach then."

"The beach." She gave me a sly smile. "If I can, maybe I'll sneak out tonight and give you all the details in person."

"Okay. See you."

"See you," she said and briefly held my hand in hers.

"Bye Katie." I brought her in for a little one-armed hug before heading off back to my house. Then, as drunk on success as I am now on vodka and beer, I walked merrily on through the crowds of cheery beachgoers, down the boardwalk, and stopped off at a pizza place to eat alone. It didn't bother me, though—being sent off after only a short conversation, even when I'd chosen the meeting place. My singularity was no longer a thing to dwell on. Soon I'd have her all to myself. Another bad pop song in the making.

She climbed into bed with me that night, as promised. I didn't ask her about how she'd snuck out, thinking it best not to bring up her family. She wasn't there to discuss that; she was there for me. I remained silent and she lay on top of me, slipped my beanie off and ran her warm fingers over my bald head. Then we kissed, and everything that followed is a bit of a blur. Bodies and blankets tangled together. She lay cuddled against me afterward, naked, and explained where to meet her the next morning. I listened, filing away the directions in my mind, but *tomorrow* had never felt so distant. I already had her with me, right where I wanted her, and I couldn't remember a single time I'd seen another person so content. She was so peaceful with her head on my chest and her arms around my waist. Quiet and happy. I didn't care if the morning never came.

I was swimming when she walked down my section of the beach. We had identified the sections by the strips of sand between jetties. I've gotta say, swimming in the ocean first thing in the morning is nice and peaceful, but it's also chilly as hell until you get used to it. Then it gets nice. Katie asked me to come out and go for a walk with her, but I talked her into taking a dip with me first, so I could prolong my swim for a few more minutes before letting the ocean breeze freeze me on our walk. She swam close, and we kissed. Then she wrapped her legs around my waist under water and floated there.

Then we walked and talked, discussing a little about our pasts and what we hoped for our futures. I learned that she was a year and a half older than me, but I didn't reveal my own age; I was tall for fifteen, and looked roughly seventeen if you didn't know better. She told me her father was a salesman and her mother a teacher, though she didn't teach at any of the schools Katie had attended. Her parents were happily married and though she occasionally argued with them, they were a happy family. She had her little brother, who I already knew, and an older sister, Amanda, who was studying abroad in England for the summer semester. She told me she still wasn't sure what she wanted to do with her life, which was one thing she and her parents argued about. I couldn't blame her. With so many different choices and only one life to throw away, how do you ever decide? I'd thought I was going to run away and catch crabs in Boston, and while that was still an open possibility, I wasn't making any progress down that road.

Hand in hand, we strolled along the line of crashing waves. We shared my first real conversation in about a month. I was getting to know her, more than just what her body felt like against mine and how loud she got when she was drunk. This was the real Katie, exposed and displayed just for me. Then she led me up a small, narrow dock that acted as a jetty. We stood there looking out, and she moved a little closer, to the point where it made more sense to stop holding her hand and put my arm around her waist instead. Then we made out on the edge of the dock, while splashes of saltwater sprayed our legs.

We took our time walking back, ankle-deep in the ocean for the most part. Halfway back we paused to dig up sand crabs with our feet and poke at them with our toes, and she playfully threw a white jellyfish at me. I chased her around with the remains of a horseshoe crab. Then we kissed again and continued home, laughing and joking. I stopped three beaches away from where her parents and brother were building sandcastles, kissed her goodbye, and made my way back to the house to shower and get changed.

I was in such a good mood; I almost didn't notice the SUV in the driveway. Then I stopped in my tracks. Someone was in my house. They were walking around *in my house.* Every little thing I'd left out of place was a red flag signaling that it was not exactly uninhabited—the broken window in the back, the toiletries in the bathroom, the food in the fridge. And if they went up to the roof...

I scoured my memory for anything else I might have left out. Nothing came to mind. But then again, I hadn't really kept inventory, because I wasn't expecting company. I inched slowly toward the house, sizing up the situation. The SUV belonged to the realty company, meaning they were either preparing it for an open house or taking a possible buyer on a tour. The shades were pulled away from the windows, but I didn't see anybody inside.

Could be because they're up on the roof, rifling through your backpack.

I had to get inside and see what was going on. I had to keep my distance. A realtor was in there, trying to sell my hideout, ruining my chances of spending the summer with Katie. If it sold, I'd have to find somewhere else to live, and that somewhere else could be blocks away. Towns away. States away, if it got that bad.

If it sold.

I snuck up to the SUV and tried the handle. I didn't know what I would do inside, other than search through it and hope to find something valuable—the deed to the house, or something—but it was locked. I quickly looked around to make sure no one was watching and then went around to the back and listened in through the broken window in the door.

Nothing. I opened the door, gritted my teeth as it squeaked and tiptoed into the hall. It felt wrong. I was the one who had broken in—fine—and I wasn't paying to live there, but I couldn't shake the idea that the realtor was the imposter. I wasn't used to being so careful and guarded there. Halfway to the stairs I heard a man's voice above me. I hunkered down and searched for a place to hide in case he came downstairs. With no suitable cover in sight, I crab-walked toward the stairs, ready to dart into the kitchen at the first hint that he was coming.

Listening closely, I realized no other voices accompanied him. He was on the phone talking to the police, or his real estate company—I couldn't tell. But he was definitely discussing a serious problem. He used the word "squatter" more than once. While I personally hadn't been found out, it was about to be very public knowledge that someone was living there uninvited, and that's not the kind of thing the authorities take lightly. Regardless of whether they sold the house, they would treat it as if the place was the site of an infestation; they'd root out whatever pest was holed up inside and evict it from the premises. There was nothing I could do but gather my stuff and get out before anyone found me.

After the most perfect couple of days with Katie, I'd have to leave her without saying goodbye. I was disappointed, but I had nobody else to blame but myself. I couldn't expect to actually live comfortably and independently the way I was. I wasn't free. I was even claimed as a dependent on my father's taxes. I didn't own myself or my future. Everything's run by the big guns, the ones with the power and money to say how we live. It didn't matter if I refused to play by their rules, because they didn't just run the game, they owned the game, they owned the fucking factories that manufactured the game, every little piece of it. And I thought I'd figured a way to challenge it, make my own rules. I was lying to her, and lying to myself. The only way to make it right was to go back to my original plans and leave her behind.

"All right, I'm on my way out now," the man said as he headed toward the stairs. "I'll talk to you later."

I bolted up and into the living room. He was right there, *right there* and coming down the steps. I had to move, and quick. I ran for the couch, thinking I'd climb over it and jump behind it, then looked down at my feet. They were still a little wet, and covered in sand. Not exactly the most inconspicuous squatter, now, am I? The man was on his way down, and there I was, standing around and staring at the evidence of what was beginning to look like the last great moment of my life. I ran around to the side of the couch, lay down on my side, and snaked the rest of the way behind it, forcing myself into the tight space between it and the wall.

He left after taking one last, long look around. Probably to take inventory on how obvious it was that some punk had been living it up in an empty house for a couple weeks. I waited for a few more minutes, just to be sure that he wasn't coming back. Then I sprinted up the stairs two at a time, through the master bedroom, out onto the balcony and up to the roof. I immediately checked my backpack. If he had searched through it, he hadn't taken anything. I packed everything up and shouldered the bag, then stood there looking around for a minute.

Where was I going to go? I didn't want to leave, but I didn't have much of a choice. Pretty soon they'd have cops and lawyers and realtors and whoever else might show up. I had no idea what was going to happen, only that I had to make myself scarce.

I sat on the edge of the roof, taking it all in for the last time and wishing I could just live up there if I had to. Down below, the quiet street was so colorful and pleasant with its repurposed rope fences lining yards filled with stones and shells. Rash shirts, swim trunks and bikinis hung on clotheslines in backyards, surfboards perched atop cars or leaned against the backs of the houses. Moving on from there meant leaving my ideal home, my paradise. I'd gotten to know my way around town, and had even come to think of the beach house as my home. I knew the place so well, I'd been able to walk right into Katie's house, the twin to my own, and know where every little thing was, where her room was, probably even which cabinets they stored their glasses in versus where they stored their plates and bowls.

I jerked upright so fast I almost wobbled right off the edge and plummeted to my death. That was it. I couldn't live hidden away on the roof of my own house, naturally, because whoever investigated the squatter situation would find me up there, but they wouldn't be looking in Katie's house—or on her roof. Her family probably didn't even go up there to hang out, and why would they? It was too dangerous for a kid like Drew, and in any case, I couldn't remember ever seeing any of them go up there. Not Katie, not her parents. I'd be perfectly undisturbed, and they'd have no idea. Best of all, I wouldn't have to leave her. I'd be closer than ever.

A few minutes later, I was lying out in the sun on her roof, covered and cushioned by towels stolen from the house where I'd once resided. I watched the clouds pass by and form shapes. That's about the time I realized how little I was living my life. I told myself I was gonna do whatever I wanted.

***

I guess wasting it and spending it are just matters of perspective, but when a third of every day of your life is lost to sleep, that adds up to a third of your life, and a man who dies at sixty has dreamt away twenty years. When you get old enough, you start to wonder, *What would I have done with all that time, had it been consecutive?* But the answer, if we're being honest with ourselves, is the same as what's been done with it. We'd sleep it away, or stay up at night thinking about what we should've done differently. I mean, who gives a shit about the shapes clouds make? They're clouds. It's like tracing constellations and letting yourself get all mesmerized by the twinkling of faraway balls of fire that burned out fifty years ago in a universe that's supposedly ever-expanding, though we have no way to prove it. Why do we keep looking up for answers? Here's an answer: I'm nervous because I'm in control, and that means I've got the ability to ruin everything.

Of course I'm nervous. I was the moment I slipped out my bedroom window and felt that urge to run. I got on my bike that day so many months ago without any idea of how things would turn out. I've been nervous all my life, though I don't make a point to announce it. What the hell am I going to do if someone catches me? I'll have to face all my friends and acquaintances, teachers and peers when they drop the noose over my head and tighten it around my neck. I'll have to look them in the eyes and say, "Yes, I did. And now it doesn't matter how eternally sorry I am, because soon I'll just be eternally damned." And I was nervous that night, on the roof, trying to sleep a few feet above the girl I'd become infatuated with. Because there are so many possible ways for things to go wrong, and all I wanted was to hold onto how things were. But preventative measures are only effective because they prevent anything from happening at all, and at some point I'd have to come back down from daydreaming on her roof and live.

***

Her rhythmic breathing in my ear told me I was where I wanted to be. Every time we were together, she seemed to make it a point to be touching me, holding my hand or pressing her body against mine. We didn't have to talk to say what we were thinking, but when we did, it only confirmed what we already knew. For almost every day from the night we'd met to the end of summer, we found some way to be together.

The day after I'd moved to her house, we went for another walk. I wanted to tell her everything that had gone on since I'd last seen her, but those thoughts dissipated the moment she appeared on my section of the beach. As we started down the shoreline, she took my hand and led me up through an exit between the dunes. An ice cream vendor—some Don Cheadle-looking guy with an Orioles cap and a neck tattoo that read "Shana"—stood behind his cart at the base of the exit, playing on his phone. He put it down long enough to scoop out a cone of chocolate-vanilla swirl for me and mint chocolate chip for her, and luckily I'd started keeping my cash with me, so I paid for the two of us. It killed me a little to spend my money so lavishly, but I tried to put it out of my mind, because it was for her.

We walked a few blocks, joking and teasing each other until we came to a souvenir shop. All the shirts, sweaters, baseball caps, towels and mugs boasted the name of the shore against bright pastel colors and a few darker shades. Out front, tables displayed some sale items—mostly T-shirts and hoodies—under a white awning. All the store clerks were inside, manning the cash register or helping shoppers find something in their size. I snatched a pink tank top off the table outside and tossed it to Katie. She laughed and threw it at my face, giving me a good whiff of that new-shirt smell. I unfolded it, stripped off the price tag, whispered, "put it on," and then took off running down the sidewalk. She let out a little gasp and chased after me. When I turned around, I saw her pulling it over her bikini top. She stuck her tongue out at me and called me an ass.

That day, as I'd been coming back from the beach a little earlier than Katie, with her shirt tucked under my arm—she'd wanted me to bring it back for her so her parents didn't see her with it and question where she'd been—some guys were standing around the front yard of the home for sale. I gathered that there were probably more inside, taking a look around.

"Excuse me," one of them had called to me, beckoning with a quick wave. "Got a second?"

I walked over to him, heart pounding and palms suddenly slick with sweat. I forced my tensed face muscles into a half-smile and said, too quietly, "Yeah?" I cleared my throat and tried again. "Yeah?"

"Do you live in that house?" the man asked, pointing to Katie's house. His words were quick and snappy, no-nonsense. Cold blue eyes stabbed at mine under arched eyebrows. He made a show of looking patient and asking me calmly. I couldn't tell if he was an investigator, or real estate agent, or what. Regardless, I knew where the conversation was headed.

"Yes. I'm Drew."

"How long have you and your parents been here?" he asked, unimpressed with my introduction.

"All summer," I said.

"All summer, and do you know the folks who live here next to you?"

"Not well." I shrugged and averted my gaze, because it's impossible to focus when you're weaving a lie on the fly. "I saw a man a few days ago, I think. He went around back, long hair, like a hippie. I guess that's who you're talking about?"

"What did he look like?" the man had asked, leaning in, obviously excited behind his mask of stern determination. I'd offered a brief description of his squatter. Eyewitness evidence of the man he was after.

"Well, like I said, he had long hair, about down to here." I raised my hand halfway between my elbow and my shoulder. "Scraggly and thin, pretty pale. That's all I really remember, though. I didn't take a good look at him."

"That's all right, that's all right. Did you see anything else, or anyone with him?"

"No," I said, looking him straight in the eyes and shaking my head. I had him completely subscribed to my story. "That's it."

"When did you see him last?" he asked, jotting notes into a legal pad while another man came over to join in on the conversation.

"The only time I remember seeing him was…"*Jesus, we need to make this quick.* "Maybe two or three days ago, I'm not really sure."

"Did you ask him about a car or anything?" the second investigator muttered to the first.

"What about a car, or a bike? Did you see anything like that?" the first guy asked.

He had a backpack full of clothes and shaving supplies.

"No, nothing. But I really need to get showered and cleaned up, we're going out for lunch when my parents get back, and then we're gonna be gone for pretty much the rest of the day." My best lie to keep them out of my hair for at least twenty-four hours.

"We're looking for the man you saw in this house, Drew. He's wanted on criminal charges, and specifically breaking and entering. The man you saw doesn't live here, so he may be moving around from place to place, breaking into homes and staying for short periods of time. Possibly a day or two, maybe longer. We have very little information on him, and while we suspect he's already moved on to a new home, we're starting our search here. The homeowners are dealing with enough as it is, with the realtors and insurance agency and everything, so we'd all really appreciate your help with whatever information you can pass along to us," the first guy said.

"Yeah, okay. Well, I'm pretty sure that's it. Sorry I couldn't be more help," I said, backing toward Katie's house.

"Let me give you my card," he said, fishing through his pocket and pulling one out of his wallet. Clean, unblemished leather. A badge visible from the ID pocket. "Give me a call if you remember anything else. We'll be here."

Two nights later, I heard her sneaking out. I peeked over the edge of the roof to find her tiptoeing up the steps to the deck of the house next door. The one where I used to live—until I was sort of forced to pack up and leave.

Watching Katie peer in through the sliding glass door, I imagined investigators peering at her from another rooftop, binoculars in hand, expecting to find a long-haired hippie, or possibly the hippie's dreadlocked girlfriend.

"Oh, Katie," I whispered into the silent night sky. She tapped quietly on the glass, looking around at the dark bedroom, wondering where I was. "What are we going to do about this?"

I crept down from the roof and found her window open. I had to climb onto the railing, balance as best as I could and finagle my way in, which was even more difficult than it sounds because my flexibility isn't the greatest, but I managed. For the third time, I snuck into her room. But this time, I stuck around and waited for her to return.

Her perfume drowned out the pungency of sea salt on the air. It might have been dizzying had the window not been open to air it out a little. I lay back on her bed, grateful once again for the comfort of a mattress. For days I'd been laying on the rough surface of the roof, and before that, before even coming to the beach, I'd made my bed in more than a few unpleasant spots. By then, I was also used to finding myself in unfamiliar places, to the point the unfamiliarity was becoming commonplace. So while I probably should have been uneasy about entering a stranger's home unannounced and uninvited in the middle of the night, it didn't faze me in the slightest.

As I stretched out on her bed, I toyed with the idea of what her life must've been like. Eating breakfast with both parents and a younger sibling every morning. Getting a ride to school rather than taking the bus, no doubt. Basking in everyone's attention, because how could she not? She was hot, and flirty, and naturally outspoken. At night, she probably curled up under her covers and slept peacefully, with no thoughts or worries to bog her mind. She wouldn't have a perfect life—nobody does—but she'd hardly realize how great hers was, with only the smallest of obstacles peppered in to make things interesting. I envied her. And most of all, I wondered at how I'd come to be a part of it.

The low crackle of stones and shells alerted me to Katie's arrival. I lazily sat up and waited for her head to appear over the windowsill. In a matter of a couple minutes she was padding up the steps and climbing onto the railing, pulling herself up and standing right there a foot away from me, a thin silhouette eclipsing the moonlight.

Then she saw my own silhouette, draped in her shadow, and almost screamed.

"Hey, shh, it's just me," I whispered. "It's Tom."

"What the hell are you doing here?" she said a little too loudly.

"Calm down, you're gonna wake everybody up," I hissed.

"Well what the hell, Tom? I don't expect to come into my room and find you on my bed."

"I saw you looking for me next door, so I thought I'd pop by for a minute," I said. "But you're right, I shouldn't have scared you like that. Sorry."

"What were you doing? Watching me?" she asked, hands on her hips. I could barely see her, let alone make out her facial features, but I assumed she was glaring at me. "Why weren't you home?"

For the thousandth time in my life, I hesitated. She wanted to meet up with me a few minutes earlier, but gave up after not finding me. She'd gone out of her way to spend time with me. If I told her the truth—and nothing but the truth, so help me God—she'd never want to see me again, and hate me for making her believe I was the kind of guy worth seeing, spending some of her time with—time surely coveted by every guy she knew. Of everyone she met, at parties and in classes, or chance encounters down the shore, she was sneaking out of the house to see a homeless kid who'd spent the past couple weeks crashing in a vacant house next door. A house that, pretty soon, would very likely be the death of our relationship.

"I wasn't expecting company," I said. Truthful enough, or just skimming the surface of a lie. "And I couldn't sleep."

"So, what? You went for a nighttime stroll?" Her anger, if it had been anger, was lessened to a skeptical sarcasm.

"I was bored," I said, shrugging. "But hey, I wanted to see you, and it looked like you wanted to see me. What's up?"

It was her turn to quietly hesitate. She walked around to the pillow side of her bed and sat down next to me, staring at the shadowy bookshelf topped with an assortment of seashells and a lone starfish.

"I couldn't sleep either. It's easier when I'm in your bed," she said.

"I don't think we should keep sneaking in and out," I said, trying not to sound like I was hiding something. "We might wake up the others. What if I sleep over here tonight?"

"We can't exactly fuck here without waking everyone up, either," she said. Her and her filthy mouth. She was so charming.

"I'm not the loud one," I teased, placing my hand over hers and leaning in. She locked eyes with me, and I stopped talking. We sat like that, frozen, for a solid minute. Maybe longer. Just staring into each others' eyes. But I wouldn't say it was like those sappy chick flick kind of stares—only a prolonged silence, underlined by the faintest buzz of an invisible electric current running from her eyes to mine, some imagined pull. There was nothing to say, but neither of us made a move to break the stare.

***

It's dark here, like her bedroom. There's an unobstructed window, unlike in the warehouse where I spent so many months, and sometimes at night I look out, and I think of her. I think of that night a lot, when I'm not thinking about what came after. I don't have much of a view, but that's all right. I'm not here for the scenery. I'm here because I'm hiding from the police and everyone else who might be out there looking for me, seeking retribution. And while there's nobody left to pin the blame on besides me, I'd argue that a lot of it was done under the influence of a mind-numbing cocktail made up of love and hate and rage and apathy.

***

Fast-forward to the end of August. Love-struck Tom Rollins is perched on a rooftop high enough to make for an unquestionably effective suicide, watching as Katie's parents pack luggage into their ugly tan minivan. Little Andrew, affectionately addressed as Drew, runs out the front door, tugging a yellow duffle bag along with him. Everything's getting loaded into the van, and soon the family will be on the road and heading home, wherever that is. And Tom, stupid with joy at having worked his way, almost effortlessly, into the arms of Katie down below, is just smiling. He doesn't care where her home is, or how far away it is. Home could be on the other side of the world, for all Tom cares, because he's overheard some particularly great news. Gorgeous, funny, wild, mischief-seeking Katie isn't going home with her family. She fought for one more day of fun in the sun, and her ruthless defiance got her just that.

I watched the minivan until it rounded a corner, and then I descended the steps to the deck. I hadn't gotten to see her for two whole days, other than coming and going, and I stayed out of sight so neither she nor her family spotted me camping out on the top floor of their vacation home. The last few times we'd hung out, I took her out to lunch—and skipped out on the check—rode all the roller coasters on the boardwalk—on stolen tickets—and made out on the beach at night. It was the summer of our lives, one neither of us would ever forget. And I was preparing to end it with a proper finale.

The sliding glass door was still unlocked, as I'd left it a few days earlier. I went in and shut it behind me, elated with the sensation of free rein of the house with her for a full day. Whatever she wanted to do, that was the plan. And I had a pretty good idea of what she'd want to do.

I caught my reflection in the master bedroom's dresser mirror. My hair was more than just a prickly fuzz coating an otherwise bald dome. The bruises and scars were faded or gone. Any sign of what I'd been through was washed away, replaced with a new me. I smiled and hurried out of the room, through the hall and down the stairs.

Oddly, halfway down the steps I thought of the guy who was looking into the squatter situation. He wouldn't have uncovered anything since I'd left. I'd slipped out of his hands from right under his nose, and he'd be forced to give up after a while. As much as I didn't want to think about Katie leaving, I wondered if I could pull off living in her house during the fall. I only had a few dollars left to my name, but living for free hadn't been an issue lately. And maybe I could arrange for us to meet occasionally, wherever time and distance would allow. It wouldn't be right for things to end so soon.

"Hey, is that you?" she called from the kitchen. "My parents just left. What are you doing upstairs?"

"Yeah, it's me," I said. "Thought I'd surprise you. I saw them leave—"

"Holy shit," she said, dropping a spoon to the floor. "Tom."

"Yup!" I said, coming into the kitchen. I scooped the spoon up off the floor and handed it to her. "Surprised?" I pulled her into a one-arm hug and kissed her.

The front door opened, and in walked another guy about my age.

At first, standing in her living room on the second floor of her parents' beach house, looking back and forth between them, it didn't register. There was no fury immediately. No desire to lash out at them both, scratch and tear at their throats, stab them repeatedly and leave them together in a mangled, bloody mess of tattered flesh. It didn't hurt so deeply that I wanted to tie them to a chair and glare at her, stare into her pitiful eyes as I soaked them in gasoline and burned the place down around them. It was so abrupt and unexpected that I stood there, blinking dumbly at them, incapable of believing what was happening. All the love I'd felt for her melted and reshaped itself into something else, like a solid wall of brick and cement forming between us, an emotional barrier to signify that I, in fact, did not know her at all. This girl, with all the beauty and perfume in the world to intoxicate an unassuming boy and blind him to truth, had secrets enough to fill the ocean we swam in together and as many lies as grains of sand on the beach.

As he stomped towards me, winding back to sock me in the jaw, I saw myself helplessly being held under water. She on my left, he on my right, with the faintest hint of a smile on her face as they drowned me in her betrayal. It was too vivid, far too real, but it was gone in an instant when his fist connected with my face and sent me sprawling onto the floor. I'd come there to make her happy, to give her what she wanted, only to be given a black eye. I'd shown up unannounced, like the bad boy she wanted me to be, to take her right there on her own couch, or her own bed, hell, maybe even on the goddamn floor, I didn't care. And there I was—on the goddamn floor—while a guy I hadn't even known existed beat me senseless.

He was the reason she hadn't planned on coming over or arranging anything with me for her last day at the beach. He was the reason she was ever busy when her parents were away. The reason she got so much joy and excitement out of seeing me. And what was I? An escape from him. I'd spoiled her big secret. She'd ruined my life.

I said nothing, and once she finally screamed for him to get off of me, I scrambled to my feet and darted out of the place. Let me guess; you would have handled it differently? You would have kicked his ass, right? I knew what I was up against, and he was clearly stronger than I was. There was nothing I could or would do as a means of standing up for myself, and there was nobody in that room I felt the need to prove myself to. I understood I wasn't wanted there. Not anymore.

I hardly remember the time that had elapsed between running out the door and into mine. My old beach house, back to where it all started. Once I was inside my living room, though, the stunned emptiness wore off, and I exploded. I threw my fists at everything within reach, pounded the walls and thrashed around like a madman. The lamp on the end table became her sensuous smile, and I destroyed it. I picked it up and slammed through doors and mirrors. Any bruise or cut I incurred just infuriated me more, and in my blind rage I obliterated everything until I fell over, sore and out of breath. My throat burned, and I realized I'd been screaming—or probably roaring—while I wrecked the place. I beat my palm against the floor and cursed myself, my house, my town, my entire existence, but I knew none of those things were to blame. I'd fallen victim to a girl's urges, and I'd played along in her game without knowing I was being played. I was in the right place at the wrong time, and was available for her to take advantage of. That was all. Not all of the pieces were in place, and it took the entire next week to play it all over again in my head, rewinding my happiest moments and reviewing them with a bitter, tormenting revelation that it was all a charade. The worst part of it was that, even though I hadn't known her for all that long, I at least did feel like I knew her, and that she let me in because she wanted to have me there. It wasn't about me, though. It could have been anyone, and by chance I was there.

***

It's all right now. I screwed up, and she screwed up, but it's okay. We lied to each other, and we lied to ourselves. Maybe she learned from it. I know I did. And distancing myself from it, taking a step back and looking it all over, I know it was all just a mistake, tangled up in lust and greed and teenage idiocy. But I harbored that anger, and it lay dormant inside me even after I thought I'd expelled it. The beach house I'd broken into was trashed, and the guys investigating it would later find it much worse for wear than on their first visit, but by then I'd be long gone. Again. It was my first victim, so to speak, and while I didn't realize it, there would be more. Experiences help shape your identity, and this was a defining moment in mine—the moment I finally snapped.

***

Gulls cried out as if in warning as the last faint wafts of salty air trailed behind me. The sunburn I'd acquired from spending most of the past month or so outdoors was already darkening to a tan on my arms and legs, while my face and neck maintained a pinkish hue. I was haggard and almost lifeless as I placed one foot in front of the next.

The pit of my stomach was left charred and empty after my rage-fueled bloodlust, but I was too disgusted to eat. Cars passed dismally slow, heading home to their rules and rituals. I no longer envied them. I pitied them. We are raised to think life is a wonderful, beautiful mystery. One we can solve by growing up and becoming anything we want. Parents plant seeds of aspiration in our hearts, and ever-expanding dreams flourish from them, and each morning we awake eager to begin. It's not innocence we lose as we grow and mature. It's ignorance. It's a belief in the unwavering truths that turn out to be lies, and faith in those who broke our trust by feeding us the lies. But I guess we should take a small part of the blame, too, for not taking the time to wonder: Had they achieved their dreams? Of course not. They'd given up on themselves and put their last hope in the possibility that we wouldn't turn out like them. The irony is that we can't help it. It's all we've ever known. Maybe I could break the mold, though. And I'd keep running 'til I did.

A group of older teens laughed and called over to me mockingly, but I ignored them. A tall, skinny black man smoking a cigarette nodded to me as he walked by, and I warily nodded back. A flashy billboard boasted a nearby casino—"FROM A PAIR O' DICE, TO PARADISE!"—to drivers who were willing to lose a few hundred dollars before leaving the beach for the summer. Lawn flamingos dotted the yards like customers waiting in line. I couldn't grasp what everyone was so happy about. The sunny season was on its way out, and the cold weather was approaching. The world was filled with people whose beauty was only skin deep, and whose values were even shallower. And I was only one kid, hardly enough to even attempt to change the way things were. I puzzled over it for a couple minutes before shrugging it off and assuming my mood was affecting my thoughts. A girl had got one over on me. It wasn't the end of the world. I stepped over a deflated soccer ball and kept going.

A thin white line stretched across the sky, and I watched it grow, wishing I was on a plane. I'd never been on one, but I'd seen videos, and anyway it wasn't just that I wanted to look down and see the patchwork quilt of clouds blanketing the world below me, blotting out any view of what lay there. I was tired of walking, and frustrated with trying to find my own way without a map. I also wasn't thrilled about having to find a new place to sleep each night, and in an absurd way I was beginning to feel homesick—or more specifically, room-sick. I was dying to crash in my own bed, but I blocked it out of my thoughts and forced myself to consider where I was headed.

And you left your backpack on her roof, genius. You've really left everything behind this time.

I was still pondering what exactly I wanted to do with my life when I came to a convenience store. Before I walked all the way up to the door and inside, where I probably would have looked for something to swipe rather than purchase with a few lonely dollar bills, a lime green bicycle resting against a post caught my eye.

"Even better," I muttered, and grabbed it by the handlebars without a second thought.

I rode all day, pedaling until my legs were pumping mechanically. I didn't want to stop. Even if I was physically exhausted, my mind was wide awake and spinning frantically. Stopping to rest would allow it to wander into territories best left alone. So I rode, on and on, focusing on my breathing and the road ahead. Onward 'til dusk.

Boston, here I come.

***

In case you're wondering, I never made it. I didn't become a crabber and live happily ever after, decked in a fisherman's cap with all those little hooks—or whatever the hell crabbers might wear. I didn't get to stand on a dock, tethering the boat I was renting or had earned with all my savings. It sounds like a nice enough life, and I'd be lying if I said it wasn't good enough for me—to the contrary, I could never want anything more—but it's not how things turned out.

***

Eventually, with the sunset burning out into a cool midnight blue, I quit pedaling and rolled off the single-lane road onto the grassless lot of an unattended warehouse.

It wasn't really massive, but enough of a mansion for me. The windows were covered with tarp or something, and the front door was boarded up. There were no other buildings for at least a half-mile in every direction. It was the perfect place to hang out for a night or two before hitting the road again. I guess I could've stayed in Katie's house once she'd left, and even vandalized it to my heart's content, but this was better. At least it would keep me out of trouble, and I could cool down a little. There was a door around back that was unlocked. I leaned my new bike against the building and entered.

I couldn't see anything inside when I first walked in, but I could sense a lot of stuff in there. I imagined it was just that: stuff. Boxes of junk that never got shipped to any place, perhaps. I carefully stepped around piles of unseen objects with my arms outstretched, feeling my way deeper into the storage room. I'd have liked to knock out the windows and let in at least a little light so I could've known whether I was about to step in something putrid or not, and whether there was a nice little clearing to sleep in, but I was too tired to be bothered with that.

Not finding anything that felt soft or cushioned, I curled up against what I imagined to be a stack of crates and dozed off. If anything about my fling with Katie crept into my half-awake thoughts during that time, I can't remember it now. But I am certain that at one point I fell asleep, because I clearly remember being ripped from the depths of dreams into a state of blind panic.

At first I thought maybe I'd twitched awake or had awoken from a terrible nightmare, but I lay silently waiting, listening. Then I heard the unmistakable sounds of people creeping around from within the warehouse. My heart skipped a beat. I prayed for it to quit pounding so hard, if only so that the intruders didn't hear it and follow the sound. As I tried to force my eyes to adjust to the darkness, the barely-audible sounds of shuffling feet and whispers grew closer. I could not lie there and allow myself to be caught by whoever was lurking around.

I rose to my feet slowly and retraced my steps to the exit as best I could by memory. I squeezed my eyes shut and took shallow breaths, slowly shuffling to the right with my back against something hard and wooden. I stopped every few feet to listen, focusing all of my attention on trying to differentiate between the smallest of sounds echoing down the corridors of junk and the drum roll of my frantic heart. I strained to hear what might have been just the squeaks of my imagination.

The things that go bump in the night.

I started to move on again, but knocked something to the ground as I brushed against it, and it clattered loudly at my feet—the perfect facsimile of an alarm ringing out to those who stalked me in the darkness of the warehouse.

I swore quietly to myself and broke into a run. I pictured men rushing toward the sound, weaving through the maze with ease like soldiers with night vision goggles. I ran faster, shielding myself with my arms raised at eye-level to keep from running head-on into something. I made it a few more yards before an explosion sounded off somewhere behind me, and I leapt to the side, falling against a wall of garbage.

They were shooting at me. Literally taking shots in the dark. Whoever they were, they were dead set on catching me. There was another loud crack, closer this time, almost immediately followed by a calling of orders.

"Don't move!" shouted a male voice, but whoever was calling out to me was audibly younger than I expected. I was imagining full-grown men, possibly cops, firing at me as a means to take me down and charge me with whatever crimes they deemed appropriate. This was different. Was my life in more danger than I thought? Would they kill me?

"Stay where you are and don't move!" The voice shouted again. "Who are you?"

I didn't respond. I pressed my back more firmly against the pile and slid slowly into a crouched position, opening my mouth wide enough to quickly inhale and exhale without being heard. My left hand fell softly to the cold ground, and I probed about with my fingers in search of some object, whether blunt or sharp, to defend myself with. They wrapped around something fairly large and round, and when I lifted it, it felt hollow and filled with some liquid. I hoped that, whatever it was, it would be effective. The voice yelled again, barking orders for me to show myself and announce who I was and what I was doing there. The guy threatened to shoot, but I doubted he knew where to aim. If I was stealth enough, I could either crawl to the exit and escape or come up behind him and smash his skull with my newfound makeshift weapon.

A bullet buried itself in a nearby pile, and another ricocheted off the floor, shrieking out into the emptiness of the building as if the whole place was a functioning black hole. I spun my head around quickly, looking for a sliver of light to lead me to a back door, but it there was no light to be found. Still, I had a vague sense of where it was, so I made a run for it. I stumbled and ran directly into walls of junk before finding my bearings. It was impossibly dark, and I could barely make out the shape of my hand mere inches from my face. I hurried forward, guessing that I was at least a little less than halfway there when someone tackled me. I had no sense of where the figure had come from or how big he was. All I knew for sure was that there was no safe way of escaping. I swung my weapon wildly through the air as I fell, but struck nothing but empty space before hitting the ground. Then he was on top of me, pinning me down and gripping my wrists tightly.

"I've got him!" he called out between grunts, and I could tell by his voice that he was not the first guy who had shouted at me. There were two of them then, maybe more. I couldn't imagine this ending well.

A beam of light bloomed from my periphery, growing brighter and jittering through an aisle. I tried in vain to fight him off before the stranger with the flashlight—and very likely, the gun—approached. His footsteps fell like the hammering of a gavel, sentencing me to eternal imprisonment. Then he was standing a few feet away, shining the beam of light at me. I stared up at the guy who—lit from behind—remained a silhouette. I could see glints of reflection in his eyes as he glared back.

"Where do you think you're going?" he asked. It was an odd question, and one I didn't really know the answer to. "What are you doing here?"

"I'm sorry!" I replied nervously, and apparently a bit too loudly, because he squeezed my wrists tighter and shushed me.

"I asked, what are you doing here?"

"I...I was just sleeping here for the night, I didn't know anyone was in here. I'm sorry! I was going to leave...I-I'll leave now! Please!" I cringed and turned to the side, sure that he planned to at least strike me, if not put a bullet in my skull. He aimed the light at my pitiful face while I begged for my life.

"He's got the Magic 8 Ball," the figure with the flashlight said, laughing. I stayed frozen, trying to make sense of what he'd just said, then realized that the round object I'd been wielding in my defense was, in fact, the novelty crystal ball. Those things had always entertained me as a kid, but of course there was no level of accuracy associated with them. It's guess was just as good as mine when it came to whether or not the two guys hunched over me would spare my life. "What's your name?" he asked.

"Tom," I answered, peering up at him. I knew the information would neither help nor hurt me anymore than they already planned to. "Please, I'll leave..."

"Tom," he said, crouching down. "What's the hurry, Tom? This place is as good as any to take a little nap, don't you think? Whaddaya think, Jeff? He seems harmless to me."

"Should we send him on his way, then?" Jeff asked. His black eyes bored into mine.

"Let's keep Tom around," the other said, still looking me over. "We could definitely use him. I'm guessing you're a runaway?"

I nodded wordlessly.

"How about you stay with us? You'll have money, food, a place to crash... all you could ask for."

I wanted to decline, and I should have, but he was offering everything. There was no way of knowing whether I could trust him, but there was also no way of knowing if I'd ever get another opportunity like this again. There was no immediate downside to accepting the free ride he appeared to be handing me, so I took it. Whether bait or gift, I took it.

"Sure," I said hesitantly, and he stood up in approval. Jeff stood, as well. Then the guy with the flashlight extended a hand out to me, revealing at least a part of himself in the light he kept focused on me.

"I'm Sam, by the way," he said as he helped me to my feet. "Sam Dover. And this is Jeffrey Dollinger."

I nodded to them in the darkness as Sam shined the light on the floor, guiding us back through the piles of junk towards where they had been sleeping, or more likely, resting wide awake shortly before they chased after me with firearms.

"We've been living here for about three years now," Jeff explained as we walked side by side, following Sam.

***

And just like that, everything changed. A one-night stay transformed into a months-long stay. Guns pointed in my face quickly found their way into my hands, and two castaways unknown to the world became what I can only describe as my two best friends. It wasn't instantaneous, but it might as well have been.

I would've liked to have gone back to sleep that night and waited until morning for a proper introduction to my newfound home and roommates, but obviously there was no reason to expect I would be granted such a luxury. They fed me a decent-sized slice of their shared biography, of which I'll paraphrase here. No need to bore you with the unabridged version—which spans four years—here, and anyway the minute details aren't what's important. Mind you, I was still pretty tired, but the momentary jolt of adrenaline I'd experienced only minutes earlier kept me awake until they finally let me retreat to a far corner of the warehouse to muse over their story until I finally reunited with unconsciousness.

It basically all gets traced back to Jeff, who was kicked out of his house at lucky thirteen. His parents were a couple of religious nuts: an overbearing mother who swore he was going to hell, and a priest of a father who took it upon himself to force Christianity down everyone's throat, even if you were already the most devout Christian he knew. His mom and dad named him Jacob, but he has since changed his name, feeling that it didn't suit him.

Somehow the faith wasn't exactly catching for Jeff growing up, and he was enough of a misfit that his parents cast him out. They probably expected him to come back crawling on his hands and knees, reformed and ready to behave. If so, they were sadly mistaken. For all they know, they only have one son. I forget his younger brother's name, but it was something like Adam or Michael. Anyway, Jeff and Sam went to the same school and always sat together because the students were seated alphabetically by their last names. Sam and Jeff became best friends, though they weren't really anything alike. Sam's father was more the type who would run for mayor rather than talk about religion, and Sam was the middle of three children.

In contradiction to my assumption on first impression, Sam was also more of a follower, whereas Jeff simply assumed the role of leader. Sam tagged along in whatever Jeff wanted to do, and one day in their early teens, Jeff—who'd already been kicked out of his home—wanted to take a long walk out of town, so they went.

Sam explained that the idea to strike out on their own wasn't so spontaneous. It began as a camp-out. They were testing themselves to see how it would go if Jeff tried to live on his own, and Sam was there to help him through that tough time. Eventually, though, Sam found himself completely detached from his own family. It progressed from Sam returning home each night and letting Jeff sleep unnoticed in the backyard, to Sam coming home every other night and pretending he was sleeping over at Jeff's while they actually roamed the streets together, a two-man pack. They were free to do whatever they wanted and start any mischief they pleased.

He didn't realize that he was walking right out of his life as he knew it, but the further they got, the less they wanted to turn around and go home. Instead, they kept walking, and eventually, without verbally acknowledging it, they found themselves discarding their friends and family in favor of a life on the streets.

They moved from place to place very much the same way I did, until they found a place equivalent to a homeless man's castle. There was a brick schoolhouse in the shriveling heart of a ghost town that caught their eye. With boarded windows, a looming tower on the west wing and enough rusted scrap metal and broken glass in the surrounding yard to ward off most trespassers, there was hardly anything more than a couple of loners could ask for. They haunted the creepy halls for only a few months before a construction crew came to demolish the place and rebuild the neighborhood, chasing the duo off in search of new shelter. Jeff's description of their school stay was a little more colorful, but then again I wasn't there.

When they settled in there at the warehouse, Jeff came up with the idea to gather as much scrap stuff as they could and build stacks throughout the place. It was more than just an attempt to furnish the place; creating a maze proved helpful in keeping out strangers and providing some pretty decent hiding places throughout the building. Meanwhile, as the fourteen-year-olds worked on the redecorating, Jeff devised some schemes to build their fortune. These were a little more complex and riskier than the petty thefts they'd committed while living in the crumbling school. They involved bank robberies, guns, explosives, burglaries and stolen vehicles. They stole souvenirs for themselves from almost every place they broke into in every town they passed through, adding to the quickly growing collection.

They were no longer just best friends. They were a team. And now, with four years living together and even longer knowing each other, they could finish each other's sentences and practically predict the other's every move. In a sense, they were one, though it wasn't anything like what you see with a dating or married couple; they were even more in sync than that. You'd probably have to witness it, or something similar, to really understand. For three years, they'd strengthened their bond there in a place only they truly knew inside and out.

And then I showed up.

They accepted me quickly enough, even though they were two years older than I was. Age isn't so relevant anymore when you're out living on your own, hidden away from the rest of the world. It's especially irrelevant to guys like Jeff and Sam, who looked down on the world from their thrones of stolen junk, devising ways to take what they wanted. They were nocturnal kings. They were modern day Robin Hoods. They were two lost and mixed up kids, astray from the path society paved. I couldn't decide right away whether or not I liked them, but they gradually grew on me, and I attribute that to the fact that they were a lot like me. It was easy enough to associate with them even if I hardly knew them. I can still see their faces in the darkness, lit from under their chins by the flashlight as they each took turns recalling everything that had led up to our paths crossing. Their features were heavily shadowed and ominous, and far more sinister at the time than they were the next morning. Still, when I woke up to find them both standing over me, I was pretty startled.

***

"Get up," Jeff said. "We're going out."

"Where are we going?" I asked, rubbing my eyes and looking around. It still appeared to be nighttime, but after a short while I remembered that the windows were all either covered or blacked out.

"Getting you new clothes, for starters," he said. "Plus, I wanna get some food, and more supplies. Come on."

It was still early when the three of us stalked through the outskirts of town, down back roads and along railroad tracks to Riverville, an area they frequented because it was very well to do—so much so that there wasn't an abundance of law enforcement or security around the shopping areas. In the waxing daylight, I could see my new friends clearly. Jeff was tall, with shaggy black hair that fell in a mess over his gray eyes and a thin black moustache. His exact height wasn't clear; he slouched even while he walked. Sam was noticeably shorter, though still a bit taller than me. He had dirty blond hair that he cut himself. He was lean, while Jeff was skinny. They appeared near-opposites of each other, yet still more similar than I was to either of them.

We didn't talk much except when Jeff would explain something, like where we were going and how often they made such trips. We were even quieter when we walked into the first store—just Jeff and me, while Sam stood out front, leaning against the wall next to the doorway and smoking a cigarette. It was the first time I wasn't working alone during a planned theft, and Jeff's presence was imposing, but I tried to stay focused. He walked ahead of me, around and around racks and shelves and displays. Was I supposed to follow him? Or go in the opposite direction so the store clerks couldn't keep an eye on both of us? Stealing always made me paranoid, and having an extra person involved added to the tension.

Two elderly women ran the shop, a little boutique named Shelly's. The cashier—Shelly herself, I guess—eyed me disapprovingly behind gum-pink half-moon glasses. Her dyed red hair, was thrown up in a nest of a bun. Her lips were painted the same horrid shade as her hair. By the deep crevices that lined her face, I'd have guessed she was a school teacher, or maybe a retired one. Her death stare and old-maid appearance wasn't helping her look as young as she was trying to believe she was.

Her coworker was busy moving shirts around to their proper places in the women's section, which took up two-thirds of the store. I stopped at a circular rack in the men's section, safely hidden from the cashier's view. I quickly browsed the shirts, then turned and snatched up a pair of jeans my size before darting out the entrance and running around the side of the building. Had I been alone, I might not have been so sloppy. I might've passed the store altogether. But I was too intent on grabbing something and getting out, so I wasn't taking my time. The cashier and her coworker squawked in alarm and chased after me. Meanwhile, Jeff took his time inside, unnoticed and alone. The old ladies shrieked and hollered, asking each other where I'd gone and answering uncertainly. They repeated this for about five minutes before deciding to go back inside and call the police. By that time, Sam rounded the other corner and joined me, having bolted as soon as I had sped out through the front door. We stood against the wall, inches away from the emergency exit door, knees bent in anticipation of having to flee. Sam and I waited, wordlessly scanning each other's faces in search for an answer, before he finally spoke.

"Where's Jeff?"

"Still inside," I said. "I don't know what he's doing."

From around the corner we made out the puzzled voices of the store clerks, and a rattling of the front door.

"I'm trying!" one of them exclaimed, flabbergasted and exasperated. "*You* try it!"

Sam raised an eyebrow, glancing in the direction of the voices, then turned back to me.

"I think he locked himself—"

Jeff came barreling through the back door, startling us both. We hesitated a split second before running after him. He was wearing a new leather jacket and a pair of sunglasses, and tossed a small bag of black socks to me as we ran. We weren't running back in the direction we came, but I knew we'd eventually head back. For the time being, I guessed, we would work on escaping.

As we made our way back home in a big circle, we stopped off at a massive grocery store swarming with shoppers and dotted with security cameras. Jeff filled us in on what went down inside the clothing store as we went inside. He'd started near the back, where a new line of jackets hung. While I was busy making a scene, he hurriedly locked the door behind the women and went straight to the cash drawer. Using his knuckles so as not to leave prints, he hit the NO-SALE button on the register, opened the drawer and took all the bills. He took $250 of it and shoved it into the side pocket of a pair of jeans hanging in the middle of the store. Then he snatched a three-pack of socks for me.

"With all the walking you've done, I figured you've probably worn holes in yours," he said as we made our way down the frozen food aisle. He was right. The only new clothes I'd gotten since leaving home was a shirt, a pair of shorts, a beanie and a pair of swim trunks, all of which I'd left on the roof of Katie's parents' beach house.

The new socks were shoved down the front of my new pants, which I'd slipped on in an alley. I'd taken the dollar out of my pants pocket and discarded my old clothes in a Dumpster fifteen or twenty minutes before we got to the supermarket. I would've liked to have held onto both outfits, but it would've looked suspicious if I was carrying the clothes around.

"How much money did you keep?" I asked.

"About as much as I left behind," Jeff said. "I like to see how things play out."

"What do you mean?" I asked.

"Someone's going to buy that pair of jeans," he explained, leading us down the next aisle. "But first, that person is going to try on the pants. Nobody just walks out the door with a pair of pants they haven't tried on—except you, obviously," he gestured to my newly stolen jeans, which hung a little loose on me. I dismissed his comment, agreeing that I needed a belt, and motioned for him to go on. "When she puts them on—*she*, because they're girl's jeans—when she puts them on, she's going to realize there's something in the pocket. She'll reach in and find the money. She's either going to keep the money or hand it over to the cashier. Now, that's probably a fifty-fifty possibility either way. I would say most people would take the money, but judging by the kind of people who live in this town, and how everyone claims to be honest and well-brought-up, she's just as likely to hand it over."

"They'll hand it over," Sam chimed in, shaking his head. "Everyone around here already has more than enough money. And whether or not they go to church, the self-righteous pricks all believe so strongly that they're 'holier than thou.' Nobody lets stuff like that weigh on their conscience in Riverville."

"But you said you like seeing how things are going to play out," I said to Jeff. "How are you going to do that?"

"Tom, we just *robbed* the place," he said, rolling his eyes and smiling. "It'll be in the papers. And that tidbit about the money left behind is going to be in the local newspaper sooner or later, if Sam's right. And if he's not, it won't be. We'll see." He raised his hands in a mock shrug and then nonchalantly swiped a box of crackers off the shelf.

"Yeah, Jeff, real subtle, a big ol' box of crackers," Sam said.

"Relax, I've got money on me," he said. "But feel free to grab whatever you want. Small stuff. I don't wanna blow all my cash in one trip."

It was only September, but the place was already decked out in Halloween decorations, with towering displays of candy and blow-up ghosts and witches. The guys talked about looking forward to the holiday—jokingly, I assumed.

It'll be a nice break, getting handouts at every door.

But it was too early to think about it. It was weird to me, to plan things out so far in advance. Hell, I hardly ever knew what I wanted to eat for dinner each night, or whether I'd be eating at all.

They had me carry the grocery bag all the way home, which was a pain, but if they'd been making trips like these for three years, I could imagine how many times they'd done the same. I took the socks out of my pants and tossed them in the bag, making a mental note to steal some new boxers for myself next time. I'd been wearing the same pair for too long. We dropped everything off at home and then they showed me around, pointing out the local library, where they used the internet whenever they needed; the hot spots to eat out at and the restaurants to avoid; and finally, their secret hangouts.

Jeff and Sam didn't mingle with the other teens in the area because they didn't want to be known. I wasn't always so antisocial, and even as much of an oddball as Jeff seemed, I doubted he would have been considered a loner in his former life. When you knowingly shed that part of yourself, though, you take on a new responsibility: shunning everyone and almost everything you would have held close to you before. So we couldn't make a habit of going to the same stores, malls and eateries regularly. Arcades and movie theaters were generally off-limits, too, but that was primarily due to monetary restrictions.

There were still places to go if you knew how to look for them. It just takes opening your eyes and really seeing the world you live in. Then you'll see it. It's like an unknown city lying right under the noses of those blinded by schedules and plans and boundaries. In that sense, we were unrestricted. The world was our playground. If you tried running away and isolating yourself the way I did at first, you might miss it, because it's not like skipping school for a day to see what kind of trouble you can get into before having to return to the daily routine. Out here, it was easy enough to go insane with the idea that there was nothing to do. There was nobody to talk to, in any case, unless you did run into others you were willing to associate with. My new friends unveiled the nature of our surroundings, and the possibilities, while not quite endless, were not as limited as I'd thought. Any place that was left vacant, abandoned or unused belonged to us.

A park at the edge of the neighborhood had become overrun with weeds, and uncut grass spilled out through gaping cracks in the pavement of the basketball court. Discarded potato chip bags and Styrofoam cups littered the ground, which was covered with mulch in some spots around the jungle gym. It had gradually attracted fewer kids after a newer one had been built in the heart of the community a couple years before I'd arrived. The new park was constructed in an open plot of land with streets on three sides and a row of apartments on the fourth. Oak trees were planted throughout the already beautiful park, and old couples were often seen strolling by, usually accompanied by little yappy dogs. The old park had supposedly been closed down, but there was nothing more than a rusted chain hanging around the perimeter to signify that. One of the two swings of the swing set dangled freely from one chain. One end of the seat hung in the dirt where wood chips had been swept clear from swinging kids' feet. To all the other residents it was dead, but to us it was perfect.

We stayed there for an hour before they led me to their favorite spot: the water tower. I'd been afraid of heights all my life, but felt safe enough in their company to climb the pale green ladder all the way up to a construction scaffold at the neck of the old tower. It was still exhilarating, and I had a mini panic attack once or twice just thinking about how high up I was, clinging to the rungs desperately and hoping against hope that I didn't slip and fall. If I did, I'd probably die of a heart attack before I hit the ground anyway. Luckily I didn't, and the wind was blocked from the tower, so that was one less thing to fight against as I climbed. Once we were at the top, we stood there looking down over our town and the ones around it. Jeff and Sam leaned forward against the railing, while I leaned back a little. Even with a railing there, I wasn't crazy about standing so close to the edge. We stayed like that for a while, just staring out over the expanse below us, until finally I broke the silence.

"Do you guys read the newspaper?" I asked, scanning the land without really looking for anything. "I mean, because you were talking about it earlier…"

"Now and then we'll pick one up and browse the headlines, but Jeff usually reads articles online at the library. Why?" Sam asked.

"You said earlier about how when we stole clothes from that place in Riverville, they'll report it in the newspaper as a robbery," I said, letting my thoughts flow from my lips while I remained partially hypnotized by the view. "I left home almost two months ago, and my dad filed a missing person report. I've been gone all that time… You think I'm in the papers?"

"You've definitely been in a newspaper at least once, probably more," Sam said. "But how do you know your dad filed a report?"

"I saw it on TV when I went into one of the electronics stores not that far from my house. Nobody recognized me, or I don't think they did, but there was a photo of me and my dad and… Do you think they run stories about me being missing every day? Or every week?" Something was weaseling around in the corners of my mind, but each time I tried to will it out, it disappeared. I wasn't sure what I was getting at, but it felt important.

"Probably not every day," Jeff said, "but every couple of weeks, or every month, that's pretty likely. They'll want people to be on the lookout for you. And that's not really good for us, so if we go any place where you're likely to be recognized, you'll have to cover your face or stay in the warehouse or something. Only for as long as they're still searching. No reason to raise any red flags."

"But you'll probably be fine," Sam added. "We avoid the general public just as much as you do, and when we have to be around crowds of people, we just try to blend in." He was silent for a couple of minutes, presumably mulling over how our private lives factored into the larger scheme of everyday life. As much as we could try to separate ourselves from the people who conformed to the ways of society, we were forced to be a part of it in some respects. I hadn't planned on making the front page of a local paper, for instance, but I suppose it was considered newsworthy to the townspeople of Oak Ridge. To me, they were being nosy.

"Nobody would recognize me out here, unless the news has spread this far," I said. "I rode my bike so many miles and then walked. I don't think there's any way I'd run into anybody who would match my face to the picture on the TV."

We talked for a couple of hours like that, back and forth with patches of meditative silence while we observed the landscape from our private retreat in the sky. We talked about breaking into houses unnoticed and robbing stores like we did earlier. Then the conversation turned to some of Jeff's little schemes: heists more complex and dangerous than anything they could have accomplished by themselves. We agreed to gradually work our way up to them once I was at their level, and that meant starting with the easy stuff.

With time it became clear how they'd managed to stay afloat for so long without a real home, and why they were so eager to put a bullet in my skull when I stumbled across their hideout. They'd figured out the key to living homeless, and though we looked down on the men and women who lived by the nine to five, they didn't regard them with disgust; they were grateful for a world run by schedules and advertisements and a middle class. Because those people who broke their backs each day were like obedient, slobbering dogs, and we were the ticks hiding in the tall grass. As long as we knew how and when to strike, we would have all the blood we ever wanted.

I was just grateful for some real friends, and especially ones who understood me and the life I was choosing. Friends who had proven they could make it on their own and were willing to show me the way. My real family had cast me out, and this new family of runaways—my fallen guardian angels—let me in with open arms and open minds.

And together, we destroyed everything I ever was.

The businessman left his house every day at nine Monday through Friday, finally giving me a reason to keep track of the days. The only exception to his departure time was when he forgot something in his house and ran in to get it, leaving the driver side door open and the engine running. The car was tempting us to steal it, but we kept still. He would reemerge from the doorway, lock only the handle lock and hop in his car and drive away. He was tall and tan, with short-cropped hair that looked black but may have been brown. His suits all looked the same, save the tie, which was a new flashy design each day. He had an all-chrome car that grumbled loudly to remind the world of his importance, and I suspected he bragged about it to his coworkers while secretly not caring one bit about it, just as he cared little for the women who sometimes stopped by in the morning before he left for work. Just like he cared little for the wife he was cheating on, because she went to bed too early to screw and woke up for work too early to bother making his breakfast.

We didn't make a move for the door right away, even on downpour days when we crouched, shivering as the rain soaked through our clothes. We waited long enough to be sure he wouldn't come back for something, but we didn't wait too long or else the mailman would catch us as he made his rounds. As long as the world ran like clockwork, we would, too.

We targeted the businessman's house because it was ideal. He left later than anyone on the street, so there would be no witnesses to our actions. He was clearly wealthy, and therefore would have things lying around that were more valuable monetarily than sentimentally. Lastly, he was an organized mess. He liked to live fast and didn't have time to worry about things such as padlocks, alarm systems or guard dogs. He was forgetful and reckless. He presumably came from money, judging by his obvious unconcern for blowing it on luxuries, and he was unafraid of being robbed because his neighbors were either too proud or too rich to need to steal. He'd had it made—custom-tailored, if you will—and we patiently waited in the shadows, ready to take it when the time was right. We refrained from making a single move until we could predict every move of his and match ours accordingly. This might sound simple enough, but we took our time, which added up to weeks of observation, timing and planning. Nothing could be left to chance.

We huddled together behind the man's neighbors' hedges, pushing up against them enough to peer through the leaves and watch as the slick silver coupe sped down the road. Anticipation built up with each passing minute Sam counted off from a stolen, wind-up wristwatch. I kept crouched, making sure not to kneel down so I wouldn't get dirt or mud on my pants. It wasn't just because I hated to get my clothes dirty, though that was an equally good reason. If I tracked any dirt into the house, the wife was sure to notice, and she would suspect that either her jackass husband did it or her house had been robbed. I could live with her hating her husband, but I didn't want to encourage her to buy an alarm system. By that point, the first day we were ready to break in, it was around early or mid-October, and the cool air hardened the muddy soil into a putty-like consistency with a surface that reminded me of the crust on a pan of brownies. Still, if one of us pressed a foot against it hard enough, the crust would crack and the somewhat damp earth would cling to our shoes or clothing. Otherwise, we'd chosen the perfect time of year to break into someone's house. Spring was too rainy, and we couldn't sneak around without leaving too much evidence behind, and a snowy winter meant leaving tracks. Summertime was known for an increase in criminal activity, as Jeff had explained one day while we camped out across the street from the businessman's home, and if police were going to patrol those streets at all, they were bound to be there then.

After forever, we left our hiding place and approached the house cautiously. We crossed a well-groomed lawn that had recently been raked clean of colorful dead leaves. We'd scoped the property out completely from all angles on our previous trips, so we were absolutely positive that we wouldn't be visible to anyone in town through the various windows or by the front yard, but we wholeheartedly believed it impossible that we could be too careful. We were also aware of the disadvantage of not knowing the fine details of the inside of the house before entering, but that first venture inside was more to introduce us to those details and give us a better understanding of the layout of the place.

A row of tiny stepping stones that were neither square nor circular, but vaguely both, formed a walkway to the two steps leading up to the wooden porch. Sam and I acted as lookout while Jeff checked the screen door, which was left unlocked, then picked the lock to the front door. As we stepped inside, we pulled plastic bags from our pants pockets and tied them over our shoes to leave no shoe prints on the linoleum floor of the entranceway. I shut and locked the door behind me, and we split up. I started upstairs while Sam checked around on the first floor, and Jeff found his way into the basement. The stairs were carpeted and didn't creak. Photos of the couple and their families lined the ascent on the right side, and more dotted the walls in the upstairs hallway.

One in particular caught my eye, and I stopped to study it a while before entering the master bedroom. The businessman's wife stood alone in the foreground, bundled up in a large, pale pink, winter jacket. Curly brown locks cascaded from under a cloth hat and over a knitted scarf that wrapped around her neck and tucked under her chin. She smiled warmly at the camera, posing in front of a breathtaking backdrop of snowcapped mountains. Her nose was pink from the cold, but she looked truly happy. The scenery was beautiful on its own, but without that glow that emanated from her, the image would have been less stunning. Empty, even. Her husband had to have felt the same back then, whenever he shot the photo, so why did he stop feeling it? How long did it take before she became just another part of his life and he went chasing the women he didn't yet know inside and out?

I imagined that she still loved him, even if she wasn't blind to his act. Maybe he didn't put on an act at all. And maybe there was no love left in that home, and they stayed together simply out of respect for their vows. In time, they would grow accustomed to the resentment that brooded between them. On the weekends while he went out with the guys, she'd call the few friends she still had left and confide in them all the things she hated about him. They'd half-listen and pretend to sympathize, and when they hung up two hours later, she'd cry a little to herself. Then life would go on. Nothing would change. After a while, you just go with it.

***

There's neither a female in my life right now, nor was there then, when I stood in a stranger's hallway in the middle of a heavily-planned robbery. I think it subconsciously dawned on me then that I had officially turned my back on my mother. It wasn't something I had actually figured out in my head, but I'm sure that if someone looked me in the eyes then and there and said it out loud, I would've had to agree. I'd snuck out my bedroom window with the idea that she was out there somewhere and I could find her and be her son again, and she'd be my mother, and I'd once again have a parent who actually cared enough about me to take care of me before I really had to find my own way in the world. But I was growing up in the company of two others, and they weren't so much raising me as they were showing me the ropes. Pushing me out of the nest and telling me to flap my damn wings already or I'd be dead before I could fly south for the winter. This was never just a means to escape, but it wasn't a long road in search of my lost mother, either. What was I looking for, then? People who understood, like Jeff and Sam? Was it some long-winded soul search within myself? I don't think so. The journey wasn't over yet, and heaven knows if it'll ever end.

***

I tore my eyes from hers and went back to work, exploring the bedroom and pocketing a man's gold watch from the dresser and a pair of diamond earrings from an old white and pink wooden jewelry box. The watch was nicer than Sam's, but that wasn't the point. We'd discussed pawning what we stole, but that was out of the question. Instead, we would wait long enough or go far enough out of town to the point where any valuables couldn't be traced back to that home, and then we'd sell them for as much as we could get.

Just as we couldn't continue to steal from the same places repeatedly, we couldn't be seen too often to become recognizable or referred to as a "regular" in any shop or restaurant. It was dangerous enough living in one location, and if the police discovered that there were people living in that warehouse—and discovered *who*—we would lose everything we were working towards. Until we no longer had to worry about money, or getting by from day to day, we had to remain unseen and unknown. Jeff's plans were clever, but they could only make us so much money at a time, and it wasn't enough to live off for too long. I mentally scrambled around for the solution, but each time I thought I had it, it was gone.

After memorizing the layout of the second floor, I was on my way back down when I noticed a string dangling from the ceiling. It was a pull-string to the attic door. I kept in mind to check it out the next time we broke in, hoping something expensive—or at the very least, interesting—might be found up there.

"Did you check the medicine cabinet?" Sam called up from the foot of the stairs, just loud enough for me to hear. Nobody on the street would've heard him, but we were quiet anyway. I turned to face him, shook my head and held up a finger to say "just a second." I stepped into the upstairs bathroom and turned the vanity on its hinges to reveal an assortment of pain relievers, ointments, contact solution, tubes of aloe and other travel-size necessities. I nearly knocked over a tiny container of diamond cleaner as I reached for an Advil bottle. I popped the lid and shook a small handful of tablets into my palm, then popped the lid back on and put it back on the shelf, facing it exactly the way it was facing when I'd taken it. Then I shut the cabinet and headed back downstairs to meet up with Jeff and Sam.

Their findings were more practical than valuable. Sam laid his out on the dining room table before us: a bunch of needles and some string, three spoons, a steak knife and a couple pens.

"Come on," Jeff said, motioning towards me. "Let's see what you've got."

I put the watch, earrings and tablets on the silk tablecloth, and watched Sam and Jeff closely to gauge their reactions. I'd be hard-pressed to guess the value of diamonds regardless of their size, but the watch was certainly worth $300 or so.

"Diamonds?" Jeff asked, scratching the bridge of his nose.

"They're real," I remarked, though that wasn't what he meant with the question.

"And they'll be missed. Not that I don't like your taste, but most thieves would go right for the pricey jewelry. And most thieves would pawn them within the week, and they'd be caught not long after that. But we're not most thieves. We're smarter than that. Put them back. We can take them another time, but not right off the bat. If something that noticeable gets stolen, they might go looking and realize there's a whole lot more missing than just those diamonds. The watch is good, though. He probably won't even tell her he lost it. Not bad."

He wasn't scowling or chastising me for the selection, just correcting a misstep I'd made. I nodded and scooped the earrings up, ready to run back upstairs and return them to the little wooden box where I'd taken them from, but he had me wait until he was finished detailing his venture into the basement.

"I unlocked the two basement windows," he explained as he placed a tennis ball on the table, "so I don't have to keep picking the front door lock every time we come here. I don't want to scratch up the doorknob, and in case he actually bolts the door next time, this'll make it easier to get in. They probably don't check the window locks down there anyway, so we'll have access anytime we want. I'll open a window," he went on, laying a thin, black flashlight on the table next to the tennis ball, "slide down into the basement, and then have one of you close it shut behind me while I go to the front door and unlock it from the inside and let you in. There's a broom and dustpan down there, too, so if I spill any dirt from the flowerbed out back into the basement, I can sweep it up and dump it into a plastic bag. *Not* their garbage, because I don't want to leave any evidence.

"He's got a gun in a case down there, with these," he said, laying a tiny canister of bullets next to the flashlight. "We can take the gun at another time, like the diamonds, but for now the bullets will do. They should fire from the pistol I've got back home. That's all for now. Anything else before we go?"

Sam and I shook our heads, and though the attic door caught my eye a second time as I hurried up the stairs to return the earrings before heading back to the warehouse, I didn't mention it. We were to explore the house in rotations, meaning that I'd search either the downstairs or the basement on the following visit, and I wanted to be the one to make whatever discoveries were to be made up there. I wasn't being territorial; I wanted to impress the others and make up for the lapse of judgment I'd made with the diamonds. There was a personal victory in being seen as an equal among experts like them.

Jeff met us in the deserted park one day that week after a quick visit to the library. The park was one of the few places we were willing to ride our bikes to. Three teens on bikes were easy to identify when recalling the scene of a crime, but when we were just riding around and minding our own business, we were just as easy to forget. I was lost in thought and ankle-deep in a carpet of crisp, rust-colored leaves when he came into view. Sam took one last long drag on his cigarette and stomped it out as Jeff approached. He was wearing Jeff's leather jacket and pair of crimson-tinted aviator sunglasses. I had on a new pair of high-tops and a thin gray hoodie. The sun was a faint yellow smudge in a sky full of clouds, and a light breeze tore dead leaves from branches until the cold limbs were bare. It was a typical autumn day, but by the smirk on Jeff's usually emotionless face, I could tell he had news.

"The police are investigating a robbery at Shelly's," he informed us when he rolled to a stop a few feet from our park bench and stepped off the pedals of his dark gray Diamond Back. "Apparently, about half of the money that was supposedly stolen was recovered from the pocket of a pair of jeans. No word on whether they think the store owners were trying some sort of insurance scam or what, but their robbery claim is being scrutinized."

"Ya think they'll install security cameras in there?" Sam asked.

"It's possible." Jeff gave a slight shrug. "Maybe we should swipe the rest of their savings just in case."

Daydreams of hacking Katie and her boyfriend to pieces vanished with the discussion of our first robbery. I was grateful for the distraction. It was becoming more and more difficult not to think of everyone who had mistreated me over the years. My abusive father. My negligent mother. The typical assholes in school. And then Katie. While I sincerely enjoyed spending time with my misfit accomplices, the world was starting to look strange and bleak, and more so every day. I was infected with the idea of how impermanent everything was, and my many failed attempts to come up with an answer to the overbearing question of my life were leaving me as increasingly bitter as the weather. Jeff's news momentarily allowed me to forget all things long-term, both past and future, and focus on matters at hand.

"After we get our costumes," Sam said, in a way that was only half-joking, as he got up and swung a leg over the seat of his bike. "Who are we going as this year?"

Jeff had gone to the library earlier on to use the computer lab there for the sole purpose of looking up what Halloween costumes were popular. Ordinarily we couldn't care less about trends, but in this case, the knowledge would work to our advantage. We would dress in the three most common costumes and thus blend into the crowds, unrecognizable and impossible to pick out of a police lineup if something were to go awry. I didn't know why they cared so much about a kids' holiday, but I understood their reasoning and the necessity of not sticking out like a sore thumb. I'll tell you, these guys were methodic, if a little shady.

"Movie characters mostly, as I expected," Jeff said. "And they're all pretty simple. The big ones are pirates, vampires and the guy with the machete and hockey mask...uh..."

"Michael Meyers?" I guessed. We were all back on our bikes and riding side by side down a broken side street. We sent sprays behind our wheels from the rivulets of rainwater from the night before. I zigzagged around the larger puddles to avoid soaking the bottoms of by pant legs.

"Jason," he said. "Same thing. Anyway, there's a Halloween store that just opened a few miles away. They should have what we need."

"Yeah, and they'll probably have overpriced costumes," I pointed out. "Those things go for about $40 or $50 each, and we don't have that kind of money to spend, especially when all we're going to get out of them is around twenty bucks worth of candy at most. We'd be better off stealing a big bag from the supermarket and spending that money on real food instead of making ourselves sick." His unusual irrationality was irritating me, and I was already in a crappy mood. I was getting tired of always being the wrong one.

"Tom," Jeff said, "this isn't about candy. Yes, we'll get plenty of that, but it's more for the fun of it, the experience we only really get this one time a year. You'll see what I mean."

"It's really only about the candy," I said. "And sure it's fun, for kids, but I haven't gone out for Halloween in years and I don't see the point—"

"Tom," he repeated, "trust me when I say this isn't going to be anything like the holidays you celebrated as a kid."

"But what about the money? Like I said, we don't have enough to spend." I'd stopped my bike and faced them with a trace of annoyance. I meant what I said, and arguing with Jeff was beginning to frustrate me, especially when it was over nothing, but the frustration was more than that. It was deep inside me, having taken root a long time ago. It had flourished with every passing year in a world that seemed to thrive on idiocy. I looked from him to Sam, who both stopped to turn and return my gaze, and I let my anger dissipate. I wasn't going to lose it on them. Sam's eyes seemed to apologize to me and side with Jeff at the same time, and I could tell he was frowning through his smile. It told me to chill out and lighten up, find some sort of compromise.

"What do you propose?" Jeff asked. Finally, he was asking for my opinion. If I was waiting for a chance to prove myself—and shake off the awkwardness of the situation—this was it. I paused for a moment before putting my two cents in.

"We could try one of those cheaper department stores, if you think it's safe, but even then they'll probably be something like $20 each, and I'm not crazy about spending $60 on clothes we're not going to wear on a regular basis. Or we could steal a credit card." I was just throwing the idea out there, but as soon as the words left my mouth I knew I was opening a fresh can of worms.

"Credit cards are traceable, and department stores are more likely to have security cameras, and then we'd get caught," Sam said.

"Only if we use the credit card for the purchase," I said. "If we take a credit card or bank card that can be used at an ATM, we can take as much money out as we want, ditch the card and never have it traced back to us. They'll never know who took it, and the cashiers at the Halloween store won't know the cash we're spending was stolen."

"What about the PIN number? How do you plan to get any money out without that?" Jeff was clearly getting tired of the argument, as was I, but I wasn't going to give up that easily. I would let him know that I was a valuable member of the group, if only to not get kicked out of my new home. I could live with losing friends, but I wouldn't lose the roof over my head and the consistent three meals a day if I could help it.

"Easy. Steal the card from an older woman, and I mean anywhere between forty or older, and the PIN is going to be either the year she was born or the year she was married."

"How do you know that?"

"Everyone knows that," I said, shrugging and laughing. I started to pedal again, and they rode along beside me.

"All right, we'll try it," Jeff said. "We've got nothing to lose."

We turned and rode home to discuss our battle plan. That was something we didn't do too often, for a couple of reasons. First of all, Jeff and Sam had their own way of doing things, and their ways were ingrained from years of practice. They were essentially through with their trial-and-error days. They'd found what worked for them and stuck to it. They did, of course, have things they wanted to try but had never gotten around to, sorts of things we were gradually building towards, day by day and week by week. Jeff had devised scenarios years ago that he had yet to act out, such as the bank robberies, which would be easier with a third member. It was one of the reasons they'd agreed to let me live with them in the first place. And that brings me to the second reason we rarely came home that early in the day.

Home sucked.

Tucked away mostly out of sight, the warehouse was just a giant storage room, with the added bonus of being a place to sleep when we needed to. It was pitch black inside even on the brightest days because they'd blacked out the tilt-open windows when they first moved in. They did so by piling junk up against the walls so they could climb up and reach the windows and paint them so not a single ray of light could shine through. Then, like a crew of sociopathic hoarders, they kept bringing in more junk. Baubles and knick-knacks were thrown in with tools and tires, creating mountains of useful and useless stuff. Climb one, and you might find something worth thousands of dollars. Climb another, and you might need a tetanus shot. Live in the place long enough, and you could find your way to your mattress just by feel and memory—though you would be happier with a flashlight, just to check your mattress and ragged quilts and sheets for mice and mouse crap. Or spiders. That sort of peace of mind is always nice. And you'd probably want to wear a fresh beanie to bed every now and then in case your sad sack of a pillow starts to feel damp and moldy.

But who knows? Maybe after a while you'd get used to the dusty, musty smells and the creeping darkness and the creaks and squeaks in the night and the lack of a shower or bathroom the way I did. I just had to remember to keep anything I always used in a place where I could easily find it—like the pair of scissors Sam and I shared to cut our hair. We went to the bathroom wherever we had to, but never inside the warehouse. We showered outside on rainy nights, or took turns using the showers in the homes we broke into. It's fair to say—embarrassingly so, but we had no need for dignity when we lived alone as thieves—that we were filthy, and our living conditions were comparable to prisons. Being in there, you really couldn't even call it living. It fulfilled its functions as a warehouse and sleeping space, and we spent as much time as we could away from it when there were other places to be. At times we even stayed out late enough to appear suspicious, had anyone been around to see us wandering the empty avenues. On those nights, like the days spent looking out from our perch of the water tower, the town belonged to us—not just one abandoned building surrounded by fields of concrete, dead grass, rusty box springs and litter, but the whole town. Every acre as far as the eye could see.

We rode alongside the railroad tracks, which cut a straight line right through suburbia and led trains past our home about twice a day. Once shortly before noon, and once in the dead of night, the thundering mass of metal chugged by carrying loads of who-knows-what. Some nights I pictured myself rising from my bed, sneaking around the maze of junk-mounds and out into the night, laying myself down on those rails and waiting as the train charged towards me with bone-crushing speed, ready to decapitate me and spray blood and brains everywhere. It would either lug on into the night or come barreling off the tracks and crash against the ground. Cars would break free and shoot up into the air, then come ripping down into discarded pallets of wood, or stacks of cinder blocks, or through the warehouse walls, maybe crushing Jeff and Sam beneath them and pinning them down in a wreck of twisted metal until they slowly bled to death. Other nights I imagined hopping onto the train and being taken far, far away into a new life and new beginnings. Then I'd tiredly push those waking nightmares away and force myself to sleep. Occasionally those fantasies of my messy suicide would follow me into my dreams.

It's hard to shake those morbid thoughts when you wake up to utter darkness, but I found comfort in eventually growing used to it enough to familiarize myself with my unseen surroundings. Plus, I had my good days. That day, riding our bikes right through the back door and shutting it behind us, I had a feeling things were beginning to look up again. I was set to impress Jeff and Sam with my cleverness and show off my intellect. My deadbeat father may never have been proud of me, but these two would see I wasn't just another sack of meat and bones.

We came to the conclusion that the most sensible way to get our hands on a bankcard was to jump a woman and snatch her purse. Then we would have to find the nearest ATM and use it immediately, before she called the cops or the bank. It sounds a lot simpler than it was, and we knew that going into it, but what we got out of it would be worth it in the end. It felt wrong to go to all that trouble just to be able to afford some silly costumes for a night of trick-or-treating, but Jeff clearly had something more in mind, and anyway we would get more than enough money to cover the cost of the costumes. We would be able to live off the money for a couple months or more.

"It has to be somewhere there won't be any witnesses," I said, staring at them in the flickering light of the small fire we lit in the back right corner of the massive, cluttered room. There was a pocket of empty space there where we would light fires and gather around to see each other's faces while we talked. It created a lot of smoke, but it was better than wasting flashlight bulbs and batteries. And it was kind of cool. It worked especially well as a hangout spot when we'd spent more than enough time in our other hangouts and didn't want to cause suspicion. "We should try to do it later in the day, around nighttime, so we can jump out of the shadows, steal the purse and run off before she knows what hit her."

"Jeff and I have gone people-watching enough to know that women don't travel alone in the dark very often," Sam pointed out. "They're smart enough to know to avoid scenarios where they could get raped. Not that I blame them—I'd do the same thing in their shoes—but that makes our job harder."

"And it'll be hard enough to find someone walking alone in a place where there won't be any witnesses," I added. "We can't exactly wait in the park, or the shopping district, or any street with a lot of houses or cars."

"So I guess we're not going through with your plan, then?" Jeff asked, raising an eyebrow.

"No, we are. We just need to think of a place that's secluded enough to pull it off," I said.

We sat quietly thinking it over. I stared into the flames leaping out of the floor, a blindingly stark contrast in the void around us. Where had I walked alone? No, that wouldn't work. I'd walked alone with hardly more than a dollar in my pocket, and basically *because* I had no money. I couldn't try to picture wealthy women walking down the same road I'd gone. I had no place to go out with friends and to spend my paycheck. I had no car to drive around in to get there. I had no job to leave late at night and walk from all alone to my car in the poorly lit parking lot...

"Parking lot," I muttered, still staring almost hypnotically into the fire. "Or a parking garage. That'd be ideal. It's *perfect.*"

"What's perfect?" Sam asked.

"Where's the closest parking garage around here?" I asked, turning my gaze back to them.

"I like your style," Jeff said. He had an evil grin on his face—or at least that's how it looked with the reflection of the flames burning in his eyes. "Straight out of a horror film."

That afternoon we played a round of golf at the local landfill a mile or so down the road. As strange as it might sound, that landfill is probably the one thing I miss the most. The bag of golf clubs we used was always right where we left them after our previous round. The balls we used were collected from the homes we robbed or found littered about the place. Sam and Jeff had dug the holes in the uneven ground a year earlier one day when they were bored. It was a full eighteen-hole course that wound back around in a full circle. Each hole was lined with a red plastic cup. The holes were hard to find sometimes, so we left sticks poking out of the ground beside them like marker flags. My golf skills were a joke, but it was a fun way to pass the time. Once in a while we'd break from our game and push each other around in a wheelbarrow that sat at the bottom of one of the large hills. It was the most fun I'd had since leaving the beach. It might be the last time I ever truly felt that free again.

A few days later, the ride to the parking garage was long, but I was grateful to be crossing the distance on bike rather than on foot. The first trip was uneventful because everyone who'd parked there during the day had already left, but it offered us a chance to get a feel for the layout of the garage. The downside was that it was located in the middle of what would ordinarily be a busy street during regular business hours. The upside was that the place was practically a shadow within a shadow. The fluorescent bulbs lining the seven floors of parking buzzed and flickered. Dozens of cement support beams, elevator doorways and darkened corners offered hiding spots. For all I knew, there could've been a much closer lot to stalk around and seek out our target, but that was all right. The police would have a hard time finding their culprits; we lived so far from the scene of the crime.

Three nights after our first try, we went for round two. Our timing couldn't have been better. We left earlier in the afternoon and didn't have to waste time searching for a garage. Jeff had an amazingly good memory and could find his way back to any place after being there only once. His sense of direction never faltered, either. He was like Vinny in that sense. I could follow Vinny anywhere without paying attention to which streets we were taking or turning off from, and even if we were just wandering around with no specific destination in mind, he'd always manage to get us back home by whatever time our parents wanted us back. There were differences, though. When Vinny and I hung out, we never packed a gun.

Jeff kept his pistol, among other weapons he'd stolen, found or built from scratch—the latter being primarily homemade explosives—in a trap door he and Sam had installed in the warehouse floor over the course of a couple of years. The trap door was under their beds at what was technically the front of the warehouse, but what we came to know as the back, because we used the actual back door as our regular exit. The front door had long since been blockaded, and a wall of junk a few feet thick stood between the true front door and the space where they slept. Due to the fact that my addition as a fellow roommate was completely unplanned, the closest space for my own sleeping area was on the other side of one of the countless piles.

Before our departure on the first night of the attempted theft of a bankcard at the parking garage, and right after we agreed on the plan, Jeff unveiled their trap door to me by flashlight. It's not that they really needed to hide the weapons; if anyone was to discover our hideout, we'd be screwed anyway. The trap door was mostly a convenient place to keep them so we could find them easily and not accidentally shoot ourselves, or worse, while we stumbled around in the dark. And I suppose you can't really call it a 'trap' door, because it wasn't a trap, just a little alcove three or four feet wide carved out of the foundation of the building. There was a handhold roughly two fingers wide cut out on one side that Jeff used to lift the lid, which could have passed as a worn-down crevice in the floor if someone was really looking for some reason. And that would have to be some meticulous searching, under a couple of mattresses at the end of a maze in an abandoned warehouse that appeared as dark inside as the furthest depths of the ocean.

The pistol was loaded and packed into a small, black, pull-string backpack Jeff wore as he rode. Sam rode between us, and I brought up the rear, pedaling along on my newly painted bike. Specks of neon green showed under the black spray paint we used to make it less eye-catching. The specks were okay, just as long as it looked entirely black from a distance. I also had a weapon on me, though it was small enough to carry in my front pocket. Sam had stolen it for me the day before from the businessman's house, and more specifically, the man's bedside table. I would get a lot of use out of the pearl-white Swiss Army knife, though it surprised me that Sam hadn't kept it for himself. He told me I needed it more than he did, and he was right; I didn't have any sort of weapon in my possession, since I'd left the knife behind with the rest of my things on Katie's beach house roof. Sam wasn't empty-handed, anyway. He was working on crafting an easily concealable weapon of his own all that day, and it was finished by the time we set out. When I asked what it was, he smiled.

"You'll see," he said, "if I end up needing to use it."

A part of me hoped he would need to. That part of me had hardly showed its face since the day I'd had half a mind to butcher the girl who'd cheated on her boyfriend with me. But that part of me certainly wasn't a stranger.

We were dressed all in black, which was essential, if not especially inconspicuous. Two ski masks and a black beanie with eyeholes and a mouth hole cut out were packed into Jeff's bag. Go on, guess which one was mine. And on top of how tired my legs still were from our previous several-hour-long bike ride, I was getting a cold. Honestly, that was more annoying than my sore leg muscles. I attribute that to the fact that I'd been riding and walking constantly for months on end, building my strength and endurance. I was more fit than I'd ever been. At the same time, spending so much time outside and in inadequate living conditions in that warehouse, I was bound to get sick. I was lucky to only have a runny nose, and a mild cough.

A gust of wind beat against us, drying the snotty residue that crusted my upper lip just under each nostril. I sniffed hard and sucked more snot into my throat. The phlegm threatened to go down the wrong pipe, and I gagged. I coughed painfully and hacked it up, spitting it to the curb as I rode. Disgusting, I know. Just imagine how I felt. It kept on like that for literally the entire way, and more than once I wanted to just hop off my bike and give in to a fit of rage.

Calm down. It's just a cold.

Sure, one that was giving me a migraine and a half. One that opened the door to all the bitterness building up over the past months, gathering into a storm of fury that was growing closer with the impending weather. I held my ravenous inner-self at bay and reminded it that soon we would have what we were coming for. I didn't want to be out at all, but it would be worth it in the end. Just a handful of hours, that's all. Then I'd be back home.

Home, in your warm cozy bed, right? Your warm clean bed in your brightly lit room with your television and video game console and not one single little spider crawling up your arm, because it's clean as a whistle, right?

I'd be the first to admit it wasn't paradise, but at that moment it was a place to sit and rest for a while. And things weren't all bad. We were on our way to being Hell-knows-how-much richer.

We arrived just as the sky was darkening, and about a dozen vehicles were visible from the entrance to the parking garage. Instead of heading straight in and waiting around for most of the place to clear out, we rode over to a fried chicken shack and grabbed a quick dinner. It was almost comical: the three of us decked all in black, nonchalantly sitting around eating a bucket overflowing with chicken. We must've looked like we were up to no good, or like we'd just returned from a casual-attire funeral. I tried to imagine what the other diners were thinking when they watched us make our way from the counter to a side booth and start in on our meal. Could they tell we weren't locals? Did they know we were planning to attack someone who, for all we knew, might very well be sitting a few tables away? I blew my nose into a thin brown napkin and covered the soggy mess with a clean napkin, both of which I tossed into the empty bucket. We'd made quick business of the chicken.

"Real classy," Jeff said. "If I hadn't already finished eating, I would've lost my appetite."

"I'm stuffed," Sam said, patting his stomach. "We might have to sit around and digest before we…"

"Yeah," Jeff said.

I sipped my soda and bore a hole in the greasy, crumb-covered table with my eyes. My stomach gurgled and churned, and I wasn't entirely sure that it was digestion I was feeling. The more we prolonged the attack, the more nervous I became. There were too many witnesses looking at our uncovered faces. Our bikes were resting against each other in plain sight out front. Any excitement I may have been feeling about our soon-to-be fortune was immensely overshadowed by the guilt and worry burdening my chest, making it harder to breathe. There was not even the slightest possibility that someone would catch on to what we were about to do and apprehend us before we could make a move, but it played out in my mind's eye as more than probable. It was guaranteed. We were going to slip up somehow, and in the blink of an eye a swarm of policemen would emerge from the front door, and the kitchen at the back of the restaurant, and maybe even a few from the nearby tables, all with guns drawn and handcuffs at the ready.

"You feeling all right?" Sam asked me, looking concerned.

"I'm fine," I lied. "Got a cold."

"We noticed."

"I'm fine," I repeated.

"All right," he nodded, though he didn't appear convinced. "You guys ready to go, then?"

We stood, tossed our garbage in the bin and stepped out into the chilly autumn afternoon. A sickening dread followed close behind me.

The garage was nearly deserted when we returned. The street lights that hadn't long since burned out were glowing faint green and yellow. Jeff led us once again across the ground floor to the stairwell. We stepped quickly and quietly, doing our best to not slide our sneakers across the smooth ground and cause loud, echoing squeaks bounding off the walls and low ceilings. I sniffed twice, too loud, and then resolved to wipe my nose on my sleeve.

As we reached the landing of the second floor, Jeff slipped the bag off his back and handed out our masks. He took the gun out, too, and shoved it into his back pocket. I pulled the beanie down over my face and adjusted it until I could peer easily through the eyeholes. My hands were clammy, and my face grew hot and itchy as we snuck towards the ramp leading up to the third floor.

We froze in place upon hearing a low rumble, and then the high-pitched squeal of tires peeling out. I hurriedly retraced my steps, with Jeff and Sam close behind, just in time to take cover behind the side of the ramp as a pair of headlights sliced through the darkness. An SUV shot into sight and turned sharply away from us, squealing all the way as the driver turned towards the exit. And that would have been that, and I was prepared to follow Jeff the rest of the way up to the third floor to find our target. But Sam had a better idea.

"It's a woman," he said. The announcement made no impression on me at first, but clearly it was of some importance to him. Then he ran out from our hiding spot and into the red glow of the car's taillights, removed something small and shiny from his pocket and threw it hard at the back window. It glinted off the glass without breaking it, but the act didn't go unnoticed. The driver jammed on the brakes hard and paused for nearly a full minute. I remained crouched and still, wondering what the hell was happening. Then it clicked. Jeff stood as the driver threw her car in park, and my two partners in crime ducked down low, moving around to the passenger side. She opened her car door and looked back in my direction, inspecting the shadows for some clue as to what had struck her vehicle. She took a step closer, then another. I couldn't make out her features, draped in the red light as she was, but Sam had been correct in identifying her sex.

My heart was racing full speed ahead, but I didn't move. This wasn't part of the plan. We hadn't discussed this. It had become an impromptu attack, and I was caught as much unaware as our victim-to-be. Was there someone else up there, walking to her car in the poorly lit upper floor? And worse, would they stumble upon our haphazard armed robbery and interfere? If this woman before me was a deer in her own headlights—or taillights, rather—I was a rabbit frozen in terror.

The cloud of butterflies in my stomach rushed up into my throat in panic. Then Jeff and Sam leapt out from behind the woman and knocked her to the ground. My fear became a wave of adrenaline, and in a blur I was at their side, pinning her and patting her down.

"Help!" she cried, face contorting in fear. "Help! Get off of me!"

She was not holding her purse; she'd left it in her car.

"Get her arms!" I growled. It was not as much in anger but more in an attempt to change my voice enough to be unrecognizable to the woman who was by that point kicking and screaming and putting all her might into shaking us off. Our combined strength held her down. Sam and Jeff each grabbed an arm and held them together, and I tore the pull-string out of the loopholes in Jeff's bag and then used it to bind her hands as tight as I could. I stood, wound back and kicked her hard in the head, then sprinted for the driver side door.

"It's in her car!" I said.

Jeff rose from behind me and put a hand on my shoulder.

"Can you drive?" he asked.

I shook my masked head and let him go ahead of me, opting instead for the back seat while Sam charged around and hopped in the passenger side. In an instant we were gone, speeding jerkily to the ramp leading down to the ground floor. I thought I heard her screaming after us as I yanked the mask off my face, but it was hard to tell over the shrieking tires.

"I've got it!" Sam said, pulling a wallet from a small black purse at his feet.

"D'you think any banks around here have open drive-thru ATMs?" I shouted from the back seat. I didn't need to shout, but in the heat of the moment, everything sounded louder than it was.

"I really don't know the area," Jeff said as he maneuvered through the garage. "But we'll find out soon enough."

I could tell the others were either too distracted by our current position or too determined to get out of it to think of taking their masks off. Also, there was one problem left unsolved that could still get us into hot water, regardless of whether we ditched the car and its contents in time to escape the inevitable police call.

"What about our bikes?" I asked.

Jeff jammed on the brakes hard as we came swerving out of the garage, skidding beyond where we'd left them propped against the wall of the entrance.

"Can we load them in the back?" he asked me. Then he quickly resumed speed and shook his head. "No, we don't have time for that."

"But if they connect the bikes to us—"

"How? They don't have our fingerprint records, and how would they find us anyway? Hardly anyone even knows we exist, let alone where to find us," Jeff said as he sped down the darkened streets. "If they knew anything about us, we'd be hopeless anyway, with all the people who saw us today at the KFC. They saw our faces, and I think with the police report that woman is bound to file, they could put two and two together."

"But what about our bikes?" I yelled back. "We're going to have to ditch this car at some point or the cops'll get us, with the vehicle description and the license plates! How are we gonna get home, or *anywhere*? Walk?"

"Dude, cool it," Sam said, turning around to face me. "This isn't helping, all right?"

I gave up and shut my mouth, pushing away thoughts of the bikes we were leaving behind and wondering instead whether the woman we'd stolen the SUV from had gotten herself untied yet. If so, how much time did we have? If not, where was she? We hadn't taken the time to tie up her feet. I knew if I were in her shoes, I'd be running for help as fast as I could. And praying that nobody decided to take advantage of my situation.

After driving nowhere in particular for twenty minutes, we came to a bank with an ATM. It was closed. We drove a little farther down the road and came to an exceptionally cheap-looking convenience store with a glowing neon sign that read "Open." Another neon light next to it read "ATM." It was the kind of place where most people would be uncomfortable to be alone at that time of night. Sam took his mask and black hoodie off and got out, taking the bank card and the woman's driver's license, which would tell us her birth year—and thus, with any luck, her PIN number. I watched Sam through the store window as he walked in and approached the ATM. A middle-aged Indian man with a thick moustache slouched at the counter, wasting away in his dead-end job. Sam slid the card, studied the driver's license, and punched in a series of numbers. I wiped my nose on my sleeve and leaned forward, trying to read his face. He squinted at the screen and pressed a few more buttons. Nothing seemed to be happening.

"Everybody knows that," Jeff said mockingly under his breath.

Sam shook his head—not to us, but at the ATM that refused to cough up the dough—and walked to the counter.

I didn't want to respond to Jeff's comment, but I couldn't stay silent a second longer. I opened my mouth to ask him what he figured we ought to do with the SUV, when just then, a loud, monotonous tune began to blare from the woman's purse.

Jeff tilted his head to the side curiously. "Think she's trying to call her cell phone?" he asked.

I assumed it was a rhetorical question. He didn't trouble himself to fish the phone out of the purse and see who was calling.

"Give me the purse," I said.

"Don't answer it."

"I'm not going to answer it. I'm not even going to touch the phone. Just give me the purse."

"What for?"

"Will you give me the goddamn purse?" I was getting impatient, and he could tell I wasn't going to explain myself, so he tossed it at me. I opened the car door and got out, leaving the door open as I got a running start towards the store and flung the purse overhand as hard as I could. It arced upward just as Sam came out and gave me a funny look. The pocketbook landed on the roof.

"The hell was that about?" he asked.

"We need to go," I said. "They might be tracing her cell phone as we speak, and I don't wanna be here when they find it."

Sam flicked the card into a trashcan at the front of the store and half-jogged back over to the car.

"The card didn't work," he said as we got in and drove off. "Well, I should rephrase that. The PIN didn't work, but the card did. I got a pack of cigarettes with it before I threw it out."

"Well then I guess it wasn't a total loss," Jeff said.

"I don't think we should go much further in this thing," I said. "She's got to have reported it stolen by now, and I don't know how long it takes for the cops to get out on the road and searching for it, but they could already be on the lookout for us. We need to ditch it now."

"The Delaware River isn't far from here," Jeff said. "That'll have them looking around for long enough to give us some time to put distance between us and them."

I nodded, thinking back on my first few days away from my old home in Oak Ridge.

"They'll have a fun time looking for us tonight," Sam said. I was about to ask him what he meant, but I was interrupted by the sound of a light sprinkle of rain turning without warning into a heavy downpour.

We'll have a fun time walking home tonight.

We spent the better part of an hour trying to find the Delaware River through the darkness and tsunami rainfall. Despite the powerfully bright blue headlights, finding our way was next to impossible. The beams of light appeared to simply illuminate the sheets of precipitation like millions of exclamation points highlighting just how totally screwed we were. And though I didn't control the weather, and though I tried everything I could think of to make things right, and though I wasn't the one who'd decided to attack the woman driving out of the parking garage just as we were passing through, I knew they would pin all of it on me. I was the one who had the brilliant plan—which had failed, by the way—and because of my simple suggestion, we were further behind than when we first set out. We lost our bikes, we risked being identified by a dozen or so people, and we were not thousands of dollars richer. With no words and only a few heavy sighs from the front seats, I could feel a tension building.

Eventually we reached the river, but there was a guardrail blocking most of our path to it, and too much traffic coming both ways for us to discreetly smash through it and push the SUV into the water. So we waited. And waited. We sat, angry and antsy, not daring to speak. Each of us was ready to explode at a single word, and I silently wished the night would end and I could wake up with it all done and over with.

We were parked in the grass on the side of the road with our lights out, watching both lanes as car after car drove on, achingly slow. Then the last one slugged by. Jeff slammed the vehicle into reverse, backed up ten feet or so, and lunged forward. He aimed for the too-narrow opening between the guardrail and the rail running along a bridge. The left side of the SUV crashed into the right edge of the guardrail with a *crunch*. We shook violently as we collided with the rail on the passenger side, and then we were through.

The driver side headlight was shattered, and a big chunk of the door was ripped back. The mirror on that side was completely gone, and a deep, long crack ran up the height of the passenger side window, spiderwebbing out into a million other tiny cracks.

I let out my breath, unaware that I'd been holding when we crashed through the barrier. Sam and I hurried out of the car. Jeff threw it into neutral and stepped out. Then we slammed the doors shut, and Sam and I pushed from the back as Jeff steered it into the river. He joined us at the rear in the final seconds before it dove hood-first off the short ledge and splashed dully into the black water. We were drenched from the rain, but we hung around long enough to watch it sink slowly to the bottom and then tossed the side mirror and broken scraps of metal in after it. We turned to leave, and Sam stopped short and cursed, covering his face with a hand and shaking his head as a realization struck him.

"I left the cigarettes on the dash," he said.

"Well, just look on the bright side," Jeff said. "Things can only get better from here."

"It's no big deal, I just forgot to grab them when I got out. I'll get more tomorrow," Sam said.

"Why don't you take Tom along with you when you go?" Jeff raised his voice. "He can come up with another brilliant plan that'll probably get you both killed. What do you think? How would you do it, Tom? Jump over the counter and swipe a pack right off the shelf while everyone watches? Is that how you'd do it? Huh?"

I looked away without a word. I wasn't in the mood to argue. I understood that he was mad—we all were—but it wasn't my fault. Snot began to drip down to my upper lip, but I didn't sniff or wipe it away in case Jeff mistook it as me crying rather than as a symptom of my cold.

"Calm down. Let's just leave," Sam said.

"I wish *he* would leave. He got us into this mess."

Sam tried again. "Jeff, it's pouring, and the cops will be out looking for us."

"Because of him!" Jeff shouted through the rain. "He did this! He's so damn stupid. Just look at him, staring at his feet. He's pathetic. We were better off without him. Tom. Look at me, Tom. Look me in the eyes."

I reluctantly obliged.

"You're a moron, Tom. Sam and I were just fine before you came along."

"I—"

"Why are you still here?"

"Jeff, you're yelling," Sam said.

"Well?" Jeff asked.

"Fine. I'll go."

I turned and walked away, hanging my head to keep the rain out of my eyes. Sam called after me, but I didn't stop. I wanted to stay with them—after all the fun times we'd had, and everything they'd shown me, I'd really begun to think of them as friends—but if Jeff didn't want me around, I wouldn't intrude any longer. I didn't want to bother anyone. I scolded myself for being a constant disappointment. Even if my plan's failure wasn't my fault, it was true that my presence wasn't beneficial to them. It wasn't beneficial to anyone at all. I wished I'd stayed in the stolen SUV as it sank to the trash-ridden bottom of the river. I could think back over the insignificance of my life in the last few minutes before it ended and my body floated lifelessly in the murky water that slowly filled to the roof. Then I'd die anticlimactically and be forgotten. I'd bloat, rot and decay, and when the police finally found the SUV and dragged it up to the surface, I'd be nothing but a skeleton.

A heavy wind picked up and blew the falling rain into a sideways path so that it pounded against me and slowed my progression to nowhere. I was just heading away from the lives I'd supposedly ruined. It was even worse than I'd imagined leaving them would be. I was so far from anywhere I knew. I would have to start over from nothing again. Or I could give up. Sit down in the flooding street and wait to be taken in by the police or run over and killed. I pressed on instead, pushing back against the wind and pouring rain. I covered my head with my soaked hood and trudged through the growing puddles. My feet were sore from walking in my thin-bottomed high-tops, and they were drenched through to the point where it felt like I was walking barefoot. My legs wobbled, and my head ached with every sneeze, but I didn't stop.

I shivered in my wet clothes and wondered how long it would take for pneumonia to set in. A siren blared somewhere, but I didn't care. In my cynicism, I decided that getting arrested would be my last chance of ending the night with a warm meal and a bed indoors. I didn't go looking for the police cruiser, but I didn't have any intention to avoid it if one happened by.

The rain died down after a while. I kept moving. I was breathing through my mouth by then. My nose was inflated like a balloon full of snot. I turned down a road leading into a residential area without streetlights. I was lost and alone, sick and freezing.

"Tom," a voice said quietly behind me.

I stopped in my tracks, unsure if what I'd heard was real. I pulled my sopping hood off to unblock my ears.

"Tom," the voice said more insistently, and I realized it was Sam. I turned to face him, and found Jeff standing silently next to him, arms crossed. "Come on, Tom, let's go home," Sam said.

"Were you following me this whole time?" I asked them.

"Yes. Look, we're sorry. It wasn't anybody's fault that things didn't go like we'd planned it. We're all cold and wet, and things have been rough these past few days, but it'll turn around, right?"

"But he's right, you guys were doing fine before I screwed it all up," I said.

"Tom, I'm sorry," Jeff said. "It was wrong of me to explode like that at you. It had nothing to do with you—well, you know, it wasn't all you. I just took it out on you, but I shouldn't have."

"So we're cool?" I asked him.

"We're cool," he said. "Let's get some sleep and regroup tomorrow morning. What do you say?"

I joined them and we skulked home, too weary and worn out to speak. I drifted in and out of sleep as we walked, only vaguely aware of my surroundings. I put my remaining energy into moving forward and keeping up with Jeff and Sam. The hours dragged on with no end in sight.

I awoke groggy and unable to recall where I was or when I'd fallen asleep. My muscles were boulders weighing me down, refusing to relax. Stiff as rigor mortis. It was even harder to move, and I slowly realized my rain-slicked clothes had encased me in a skin-tight cocoon. The remnants of an awful headache drummed an incoherent beat in the back of my mind, and my jaw popped as I yawned, hinting at the likelihood that I'd been clenching it or grinding my teeth in my sleep. From the pitch black that greeted me when I forced my eyes open, I assumed that we'd made it home, but there was no way of knowing when or how long before I'd woken up. I rolled over, just a smidgeon, and realized too late that I was rolling right off the bed. My arms and legs flailed drunkenly slow and I fell the four inches and belly-flopped onto the dirty floor.

That finally got me moving.

"Hey, Tom, are you awake?" Sam called out, and a halo shined over the pile of junk separating me from their sleeping area.

"Yeah," I croaked.

"We're going to grab some breakfast and then head up to the tower," he said.

After changing into some clean clothes, we went out and bought some breakfast sandwiches and ate them on a wet bench overlooking one of the millions of Main Streets of our lovely garden state. I savored the warm meal and the chance to sit down and relax. My cold had peaked, and so we agreed to stop off at a pharmacy on our way to the tower, but I wasn't in a hurry to get up and go. I could've spent most of that sunny day sitting on that bench, watching the old people window shop and the younger crowd busily power-walk or drive by. Traffic was as busy as ever, and the power-walkers were moving just about as fast as the drivers.

Later, I made the climb up the pale green ladder without any trouble, though my hands were clammy and I had to wipe them on my jeans several times to keep from slipping. It occurred to me that I was intentionally being very careful not to fall to the ground and break my neck, after countless days and nights spent envisioning various ends to my life. It could've been that I was far too tired to bother myself with such nonsense, or that I was finally deciding I didn't want to die. I reached the top and sat between Sam and Jeff on the catwalk that wrapped around the neck of the tower, wondering what would happen if I had met my demise in any of the ways I'd imagined in the past weeks. Would anyone find out, other than these two guys? Would my body be found? Did my father and classmates already think I was dead?

"We need to talk about last night," Jeff said, not making eye contact with either of us. I turned to him, but he was staring at the town spread out below us. I did the same. When he resumed talking, I noticed he was choosing his words carefully, for much the same reason soldiers might step carefully through territory thought to conceal land mines. "We...rushed into things, I think, and we weren't totally prepared for...what resulted. Given the circumstances, I wouldn't say anyone here is to blame. I think we need to regroup and try again. It was a good effort. Sometimes shit just happens."

He went on, and even while he talked and I listened carefully, wheels began to turn in my head. I'd been expecting the worst, especially after our late-night argument under a raging storm, but Jeff was surprisingly positive. I was relieved. More than that, I was surprised. Lately I've learned that periodically blowing off steam is important to staying sane. He'd vented the previous night out of necessity, because if he hadn't, he might've bottled up his anger another few weeks, or months, and exploded. Not verbally, but physically. The way I had at the beach house when I'd trashed the place. We all need an outlet by which to direct our anger and frustration, and as long as I do it the smart way— discreetly, with no incriminating evidence left behind—I'm safe.

"Despite our temporary setback," Jeff continued, "I don't think there's any point in delaying our plans at all. We shouldn't jump into anything recklessly, or without knowing what we're getting into, but we need to get back into it. I'm going to go to the library in a minute and see what sort of things have been reported on what went on last night. Hopefully it's nothing we can't...work around." Then he turned to us, as if punctuating what he was about to say next.

"When I leave there, I'll meet you guys in the park, and we're going to discuss our next move."

We sat around for a moment longer, then climbed down. As Jeff was beginning to leave for the library, I stopped him and pulled him to the side.

"After you're done looking up what happened at the parking garage and everything, could you look up something for me?" I asked him.

"Sure, what?"

I told him and he agreed without a single question. Then he was off, and Sam and I took a stroll around town. He and I were alone pretty often while Jeff went to the library, and though I'd spent enough time at their sides to become comfortable around them, it was awkward even trying to make small talk. I was never the kind of kid who would open up to many people, and it had been months since I'd seen or spoken to the one person who really did know almost everything about me. That was Vinny. More than anything, I wanted to pound on his door and tell him everything that had happened to me since I'd left, but that was out of the question. If I was going to properly start over, I had to learn to trust my friends and talk with them. Talk more than just about where we were going to go and what we were going to do that day. I was curious about who Sam really was before all this and what the world looked like through his eyes. The only way to get inside his head was to let him into mine. Conversation. Is talking to strangers anyone's strong suit?

"Did you have a girlfriend before you left home?" I asked. Had to start somewhere.

"Not right when I left, no," Sam said. "I was dating a girl named Stephanie for three months, but she broke it off about four or five months before Jeff was kicked out of his house. I don't think I would've left if I was still with her. But it wasn't really anything serious, you know? We thought it was serious at the time, but everyone thinks they know what love is when they're that young. No, I was single."

"Do you miss her? Or did you, before all this?"

"I don't think about it too much anymore. I guess I regret having it go the way it went, but that's in the past. Neither of us did anything wrong, we just got to be too much for each other."

"What happened?"

"Well, we'd see each other every single day. Like, literally, every day since we started going out. Her parents worked late, so I'd go over to her house and hang around 'til her mom and dad were about to come home. Sometimes I'd have to run out the back door so they wouldn't catch me alone with her in her bedroom." He laughed and shook his head. "We were dumb, but for most of the time together we were happy. It doesn't matter, though. That's how things go. What about you? Did you have a girl back home?"

I alluded to Leslie briefly, explaining the situation of how she was one of my best friends and the center of my attention at the same time. Then I told him about the girl I'd lived next door to at the beach for a while before riding off and stumbling upon his and Jeff's hideout. He listened without interrupting, laughing a few times until I finished my story. When he spoke again, he surprised me. He didn't side with me and call her a bitch, or a cheating skank.

"That's awesome," he said, still laughing. "I wouldn't be so bugged about it. You had a hot girl in your lap practically every day for a full month, and she was choosing you over her boyfriend? Dude, take that as a compliment. We don't get that kind of action around here, and you got to just hit it and leave and not have to drag that around with you like that jerk she was cheating on. Think about it. By now she's either single or on the rebound and getting called a slut by everyone in her class, or she's back with the guy who made her unhappy enough to cheat in the first place. And here you are, with us! I'd say you got the better deal."

"Yeah, I guess you're right. I hadn't really thought about it that way. I just thought I'd finally caught a break..."

"You did get a break! A pretty sweet one, too. You were *homeless* and she was going around with you all that time? I mean, did you wear the same outfit every single day, that one you had on when you came here?"

"I wasn't always wearing clothes when she was around," I admitted with a smirk.

"She didn't even know! Ha! You could've been anyone, dude. She could have been hanging around and screwing any guy there, and she was with you. That's awesome."

"That's true. It was pretty great."

"And hey," he said, smiling a full face-lift smile, "we're gonna have fun this Halloween. Trust me, you're gonna enjoy yourself. And it's right around the corner."

Our talk gradually changed from topic to topic, but it held up a positive tone that successfully pulled me out of my rut. I was glad to be hanging out with him for the day, rather than Jeff. I didn't have much of a problem with Jeff, but he always seemed so dark and ominous. Sinister. I wouldn't say he was pessimistic, necessarily, but Sam was optimistic to the point where I felt he was the opposite of Jeff. If I was brooding, Jeff gave off a negative vibe that made me more depressed and grumpy. Sam could pick me up and lighten the mood. It was good to have him around.

***

I could use a talk like that now. Because right now, this very second, I don't care about anything. I know I shouldn't feel this way, but I do. I'm right back where I was when I was trudging home through the rainstorm in the dark. I'll never know if you've ever felt this way, but I've felt it a million times, and I'm sick of it. It kills me to think this way, as if there's no point to anything and my death won't change anything. I become numb, and the alcohol doesn't help unless I want to pass out. Or write this all out, which I need. That's the one thing that's got me holding on. Isn't that lovely? I can't live with myself this way, but I can't die knowing my story is unfinished. Sometimes I put my pen down and talk to myself, and Sam's voice of reason leads me back on track just like it did that day. It reminds me that I can get through this, and then if I want to let myself die, I can, but not until it's done. I know I won't kill myself, anyway. It's just nice to know that I can.

***

We went chronologically backwards while we talked, discussing the day we'd each left home for good and working our way back to middle school, elementary school and early childhood, as far back as we could remember. I don't remember all of it, but one thing that stuck in my memory was that he was homeschooled for a while. I told him that would've been a nightmare for me. He said it wasn't so bad because most the kids in his neighborhood lived either on the same street as him or close enough to walk, so he still got to hang out with them after class.

"It's got its charms and flaws," he said. "I wasn't in on all the other kids' inside jokes, and I never got to go to any of the cool field trips they told me about, but I also didn't have to deal with the crappy teachers and projects and all that. My mom taught me up to the end of elementary school, and then she sent me to public for middle school. Partly because I begged her to let me go, and partly, I think, because she didn't want to have to start getting into sex ed with me. Let the gym teachers give 'em the birds and bees talk, right?"

"Was it weird going from homeschooling to public school?"

"Not really. I got used to it. The scheduling sucked at first. They've got the students eating lunch at weird times. We were eating way too late, and I had to wake up earlier

163

than I usually did, and the textbooks always had pages missing. I swear, whoever had my social studies books before me was eating the pages or something. Really, there were big chunks of pages missing; they probably had just as much trouble waiting for lunch as I did."

"It was you eating the pages, wasn't it?" I raised an eyebrow at him.

"You got me." He shrugged and laughed.

All that lunch talk got us hungry, and we didn't wait for Jeff to get back before grabbing a couple of burgers and fries. We took our food to a spot we'd never dared to go before—the park in the heart of town, which was typically buzzing with activity—and sat in one of the enormous white gazebos that were scattered throughout the area. We'd passed the park more than enough times to know what it looked like, but actually walking through it gave us a whole new perspective of how beautiful it was, and how much it improved the town. It was easy to ignore that fact when we spent so much time avoiding crowds and public places. We normally would have continued to avoid the park completely—especially with what had just happened the night before and the possibility that our actions had been widely reported—but it was such a nice day out. Sitting in our park or any of our usual hangouts would have just continued to bum us out, so we opted for a relaxing lunch with a view of pleasant scenery while still secluding ourselves from most of the public eye.

A couple walking their dog happened by and sat down across from us and stayed there, unnerving us a little, but we talked in low voices and did our best to face away from them while we ate. We agreed to not mention any of that to Jeff. It was our little secret of the day, and it was harmless.

The news was better than I'd expected. Police hadn't found the SUV, and the woman we'd stolen it from made her attackers out to be much larger than we actually were. Her shock must have gotten the best of her, exaggerating the incident in her head. Best of all, no witnesses had come forward as of that morning. That was bound to change, but for the time being I was content.

Jeff also filled me in on the goings-on in Oak Ridge over the course of the previous months following my disappearance. What he told me shouldn't have surprised me as much as it did, but in retrospect, I hadn't given it as much thought as I'd thought I had. The news searches took a couple of hours for him to read through, but only five minutes or so to regurgitate in summary. Then he announced a brilliant new plan of his.

"Let's just steal the costumes. It won't be anywhere local, so they won't catch us, and we'll just be in and out and that'll be that. I'll bring my gun, and we'll wear our masks like last time."

Simple. Quick. And, the cherry on top, unscrewupable. There's one glorious word you won't find in your precious dictionaries, but I expect it speaks volumes.

We spent the next week breaking into various houses. We didn't take anything other than the occasional shower, but it was always good to keep up the practice. We were lying low while the heat wore off from the incident at the parking garage, meaning we didn't go steal the costumes right away. Three masked men in one robbery a few days after a similar robbery would be too suspicious. It was nice to take a week off, too. The three of us were getting along better than ever, and we grew closer with every clean break-in. I was a little jealous when Jeff first climbed the stairs into the attic of the businessman's home, but the following day he, Sam and I headed straight up from the basement into the attic and rummaged through boxes and luggage and trash bags. We discovered nothing particularly interesting. There was an expensive-looking globe, and that's about it.

But the old widow who lived seventeen blocks in the other direction? She had a damn goldmine in just about every room of her house. Pristine silverware, crystal chandeliers and gold and diamonds adorning an old hickory bureau. Well, I think it was hickory. That's beside the point. The real treasure was in her rec room: an authentic Claude Monet painting, framed with an intricately detailed, golden, four-inch thick frame. The image was a messy swirl of complimentary colors to a wandering eye, but if you got up close and examined all the detail, you could begin to gauge how many long, drawn-out hours were spent hunched over the canvas.

I wouldn't claim to know a ton about art, but I can at least appreciate it for the beauty and perspective. It was simple, elegant, graceful. Absolutely destroyable. And it was incredible to find it there, not far from our home. Either the hag who owned it had some truly excellent taste, or some truly expensive taste, or both. I was leaning toward both. Who knows what she or her dead husband had done for a living, but whatever it was had made her considerably wealthy. If we were up for a real challenge, that painting would be all we needed. As it was, we took nothing.

***

To be clear, this story isn't about Halloween. I realize I've spent a hell of a lot of time talking about it, and doodling pumpkins in margins on the backs of old balled up pieces of paper I've tossed around the room, but it just happens that a big part of what went on during those weeks revolved around the holiday. Let me fast-forward a bit. On October 28, we finally got the costumes. It was a Wednesday. I remember that because Halloween fell on a Saturday, and that was perfect. We didn't own a calendar, because we had nothing to mark on it and didn't have any other reason for having one, but we kept a close eye on the days of the week so that we didn't make the mistake of breaking into someone's house while they were home or off from work. Off from work sometimes meant away for the weekend, but not always. But I'm digressing yet again.

***

The Halloween store. It was on the left side of a mostly empty plaza on Pinecone Terrace. The whole two people in charge of running the shop that day were hardly surprised to see a group of kids walk in dressed all in black, and they weren't immediately phased by our ski masks. The cashier, a young, skinny, black woman with braids in her hair, insisted that we take them off, though. That's when Jeff brought out the pistol and demanded she and her geeky albino-looking friend lie belly-down on the floor and not make a single move or sound.

Old-school tunes like "The Monster Mash" and the *Scooby-Doo* theme song played in the background as we browsed through the abundant selection. Someone had done a half-assed job at decorating the place with a handful of poorly placed scarecrows, dangling spiders, hanging ghosts, and boogeymen lurking in the corners. I'd chosen to be the machete-wielding psycho with the hockey mask because I wanted to completely hide my face. Sam went with the pirate outfit, and Jeff was the vampire by default. I think it fit him well, considering his dark hair and pale complexion. We took quick shifts holding the gun while each of us tried our costume on to make sure it fit, and while Sam was busy aiming it at the dork's temple, I put on the gloves from my costume and opened the cash drawer. There was a whopping fifty-four bucks, all of which I pocketed before we ran out the door and hightailed it home. It was too easy, but I'm not complaining.

I guess that brings me to the big night, the Night of the Dead. Jack-o-lanterns were already decaying on porches, and real spiders were already adding their contribution to fake cobwebs draped over bushes by the time the day arrived. There was also a fresh coating of eggs splattered on doors and rolls of toilet paper tangled in tree branches from the night before, but most of the aftermath of Mischief Night had been cleaned up and swept away by the time we donned our costumes and set out. The hockey mask I was wearing was not nearly as hot or as itchy as the beanie-turned-ski mask I'd worn on our last two ventures, but it was sort of hard to breathe through. I also felt cheesy lugging around a large plastic machete, but it completed the look, and it was fun pretending to be a murderous maniac. We even took our time spraying fake blood all over my mask and clothes, as well as applying black and white makeup on Jeff's face and more fake blood on his mouth and neck. Then we hit the streets, traveling from neighborhood to neighborhood in a more or less straight line as we knocked on doors and chanted the magic words that put smiles on parents' faces and candy in our grocery bags. In a sense, the routine is almost ritualistic, with the innocent townsfolk making their offerings to the wicked spirits flooding the streets. If only they knew how wicked we really were.

Something seemed to be lacking from the air that night. With everything that had built up to it, I'd been expecting more excitement. I wasn't convinced that this evening was planned to end so anticlimactically, but I also wasn't going to make any comment that reflected boredom or annoyance. The sun crossed the sky like a zipper being drawn on a body bag, setting on a scene of spritely kids and cool autumn colors, until we were cast in an eerie twilight. Leaves crunched as shadows skittered across lawns specked with gravestones and witches. Our bags quickly filled with fun-size chocolates, and I ate half of what I was given as we marched farther from home. Then, when the parents or older siblings began to drag their ghoulish children or younger brothers and sisters to their respective houses, Jeff turned to me.

"Hear that?" he asked.

I pulled my mask up and listened hard, then shook my head, unsure of what he expected me to hear.

"We've got a couple more blocks to go, but I can hear the music. They're having a Halloween party—"

"Wait, who's 'they?'" I asked.

"A group of high-schoolers. Every year they decorate one of the guy's houses like a haunted house and throw a huge bash, and their parents always go away to let them have the party. Tons of food, tons of drinks, and every hot chick at their school, all under one roof. And it's a costume party, so they won't even know that the three guys just now showing up don't go to their school. *This* is why we celebrate Halloween. This is what we've been preparing for all month."

Finally, it made some sense. Unlike me with my month-long rendezvous with the beach bimbo, Sam and Jeff hadn't had much interaction with anyone socially or intimately since the previous year's Halloween. It was a chance to blow off some steam and catch up on a years' worth of partying in one night. We were simply three demons unleashed into an unsuspecting soirée to enjoy one carefree night of fun and a lack of morals or consequences.

"Well, Jesus," I said, "why didn't you say so?"

***

So I suppose it's true: there's a sin in us all. A horror that lies dormant within our soul, if indeed we have a soul, and awakens to the guttural cries of bloodlust and wrongdoing. You know that saying: "Don't let a few bad apples spoil the bunch?" Well, maybe we were bad apples, but we were once green and fresh and pure. It takes time for fruit to ripen and turn, much as it took time for us to become so rotten, but by then we were certainly poison apples with razorblades hidden inside, and we paid little mind to the spoiling we did to the bunch.

***

Four or five girls dressed in thigh-skimming skirts and low-cut shirts—or, in the case of one, simply a decorated bra—clustered together on the front porch.

They were bobbing for apples.

We passed them and went straight inside, as if we couldn't help our need to infest the place. We didn't have all the time in the world, and while a few cute girls walking around in their underwear and dunking their heads in a barrel of water to probe for fruit with their pretty pink lips on a chilly afternoon was all I could ever ask for, they weren't going to bother with us. At least not outside, and not without a few bottles of persuasion.

***

Spirits? A fitting name. Let's polish off a few more here, shall we, and I'll tell you the tale of a night born in hell and buried in this thick skull of mine. There, that'll do. Another never hurt anyone. Drinks all around.

***

Someone thrust a beer into my hand as I entered the party, and I looked at it quizzically for a whole five seconds before Sam took it from me, popped off the cap and handed it back. I'd never gotten drunk, and the loathsome memory of my father's sloppy, alcoholic ravings sickened me, but thoughts like those would only ruin the buzz that was already setting in from the loud music and cheerfully intoxicated strangers. And what was good for forgetting lousy memories? Drinks, of course.

Lights, which flashed green, then purple, red, blue, yellow and so on, pulsed with the bass of the song blasting from the speakers and beamed off the walls. The true color of the walls was questionable. And Jeff wasn't kidding about the Halloween decorations in the place; this was no half-assed job like at the costume store. There were even rats sitting on the arms of chairs, but unlike the rats in our warehouse, these were fake. My busy eyes were flitting from the hypnotic patterns cast from the strobe lights to the bats on the ceiling to a singular beauty chatting and laughing adorably with a small group of her friends on a large, puffy blue sofa. Then the sofa turned red. Her hair was bleach blonde and appeared to be dyed a different color every ten seconds. She might've struck anyone as another temptress in the lot of gorgeous sluts with her deep red lipstick—red delicious?—and sexy attire and all, but at least she was dressed as a vampire and not a nurse or a pigtailed schoolgirl. I took a heavy swig and tore my eyes away, but they found a path back to her.

"Aye, Captain Jack!" a gangly, scurvy-ridden pirate shouted to Sam, wrapping an arm around his shoulder and clinking bottles with him.

"Me? I say you're the captain, eh?" Sam shouted a little to be heard over the stereo.

"Then what's your name, mate?" The swashbuckler asked. He raised an eyebrow over an eye-patch and stroked a beard held on by either a string or heavy-duty adhesive.

I heard Sam insist on being referred to as the ancient mariner, and then Sally of *The Nightmare Before Christmas* took me by the wrist and led me into a dance. I set my drink down on a side table and joined her, following each step and hip-shake. I slashed my machete through the air, partly to be funny, and partly in hopes of catching Draculina's attention. Sally smiled and playfully took it from me, wrapping her arms around me and pulling me closer as she mock-sliced my back.

I did my best not to avert my gaze from hers in search of the girl who'd first caught my attention. At least I was getting some attention myself. Jeff and Sam's whereabouts were already unknown, and I didn't mind at all. I wasn't drunk yet, but the more I danced with her, the more I wanted to kiss Sally, and not because I loved her for her personality. We made some small comments to each other that we washed down with shots.

***

Now the only remnants of our secret conversation are clips of a silent film version in my memory. With time the reels of film will go blank or burn up or unwind, and she'll be lost, except here on this page, and even here, the memory is vague. She was probably great. As far as it concerns me now, she's a ghost.

***

I refrained from taking my mask off for most of the night, but every now and then I'd go out back to get some fresh air and wipe the sweat off my face. Occasionally I'd catch Sam out there smoking a cigarette. I bumped into Jeff twice, and one time in particular. A football player, or a guy dressed like one, suggested Jeff go hook up with his vampire bride in the other room. He was referring to the bleach blonde girl I'd been checking out when we'd first arrived. By that point, I'd danced with a dozen girls throughout the party, including a few who specialized in solo strip-dancing. I would've said something to dissuade Jeff, but I didn't want to come off as possessive, and I was taking that time to finish my third beer and start in on more shots with a group of girls and guys I'd never see again. I'd also eaten a few slices of pizza, some pretzels, chips, cookies and a piece of pumpkin pie.

A marathon of *A Nightmare On Elm Street* was playing on an enormous flat-screen TV in one of the rooms, and I sat watching one of the movies with a cheerleader and a cute mouse, allowing them to cuddle up close on either side of me and nearly bury their faces in my lap each time it got a little gory. Then they'd laugh it off, and I'd half-mock, half-flirt with them while I took another drink. What time was it? Who cared. The name of the girl whose pompoms I was grabbing? I never asked. The credits rolled through, and we got up to dance under the rainbow lights. Someone came bouncing through the crowd, cheering and spraying everyone down with whipped cream.

Then I nearly stumbled out of Jeff and Sam's grip, trying to breathe and vomit at the same time. Somehow we were outside, though I wasn't sure where. My friends had my arms slung around the backs of their necks as they helped me stagger through a deserted street under a yellow-green sky. There was not a single breeze to stir a single leaf. A whisper would have sounded like a crack of thunder in the dead silence. It was clearly early the next morning, but I was lacking the cognitive skills required to explain how so many hours had passed so quickly. So I vomited again and then asked, in a pathetically dumbfounded tone, what was going on.

"You passed out," Jeff informed me, speaking too loudly for that time of day. It was all right, though. Nobody around was awake to hear us. "How much did you have to drink?"

"I don't know," I said.

"We were looking for you all over the house. Sam was dozing off in the kitchen, so I woke him up, and we went looking for you so we could leave before we were too tired to. We can't sleep here; we've gotta get home."

"Yeah," I groaned. I knew he was right, but I wasn't sure I could stomach walking all the way back, especially when the road looked comfortable enough to lie down on and take a quick nap.

"We found you in the basement with that blonde chick in the vampire costume. Looked like you guys were having a good time down there." Jeff gave me a look that told me he knew I'd gotten some, and suspected that I had no idea. I had no idea I'd even talked to her, let alone gone down to the basement with her. Which brought up another question.

"Why the hell were we in the basement? Was I that drunk?"

He laughed. "No, I mean I'm sure you were wasted by then, but they've got it set up like a man cave down there. There're a couple of love seats and recliners and a big flat-screen TV. It's pretty nice. And before you ask, don't worry. You two were alone."

"I don't remember any of that. The last thing I remember is talking to you…wait, no, there was this guy spraying whipped cream all over the place…" Parts of the night started coming back to me bit by bit, but I couldn't even remember Sally until the next day while I tried to piece together what had gone on.

"Wow, you were out for a while then," Sam said. "You missed the fight?"

"There was a fight?" I asked.

"Yeah, maybe you were already downstairs by then. Two guys were calling each other out and swinging fists over this girl. It got pretty crazy, so they were thrown out of the party. Nobody wanted to have the cops show up and bust everyone for under-aged drinking and everything else that was going on."

"Who was the girl?"

"The one dressed like a cheerleader. Well, there were a couple, but the pink one," Jeff said.

I'd had my hands all over the pink one while we watched Freddy Krueger slash sex-crazed teens to shreds. I told them, and they laughed and told me I was lucky the two drunken idiots at the party hadn't seen me or it'd be blood I was throwing up. When we got far along enough down the road to where I recognized where we were, my head began to clear a bit and more questions needed answering.

"When you guys found me, was I naked?" I asked. My cheeks burned while I anticipated the worst. I'd showered naked in the rain just a few feet away from them both numerous times, but that was primarily in the middle of the night, where I couldn't even see my own body, let alone theirs. It would just be weird to see your friends nude, regardless of whether you spent practically every waking minute at their sides. But to my relief, they assured me I wasn't found entirely naked.

"Nah, your pants were around your ankles, but we pulled them up for you, and we didn't see anything. Don't worry," Jeff said. "But I can't say the same about your lady friend. We had a fun time hauling her naked ass off you. She was like dead weight laying right on top of you, I was surprised you could breathe."

"I guess she wasn't that heavy," I said, shrugging. She seemed skinny and light when I watched her in the living room, but beyond that point my memory was a clean slate.

"Not too heavy for a couple of strong guys like us," Sam said proudly, puffing out his chest. "Though a little old for you, don't you think?"

"Probably," I said. "But I'm tall for my age, and with the mask on I probably passed for seventeen or eighteen. Hold on, where is my mask?"

"We couldn't find it. It's probably in the basement, but I didn't see it," Jeff said. "But I doubt anyone saw your face, or if they did, they didn't recognize you from all the missing person posters plastered around Oakland."

"Oak Ridge," I said.

"Oak Ridge," Jeff repeated. "Everyone was drunk anyway, and they think we were people who go to their school. I wouldn't worry about it."

Jeff had told me all about the posters that were plastered everywhere around my hometown, with my beaming face and bold type instructing anyone who saw me to contact the local police. I hadn't thought about it much, except that it was a reminder to stay far away from there and the surrounding towns. Other than that, I had done a good job at keeping my head low and pretending I wasn't a runaway who'd spent the last couple of months living off the bare minimum. I managed to walk the rest of the distance to the warehouse unassisted, and when I was finally inside and found my way blindly to my mattress, I collapsed and slept for most of the day. No claustrophobia set in from so much time spent in the black hole. My back didn't ache from laying on the uncomfortably thin and clumpy mattress for an unknown number of hours. No thoughts of the previous night bogged my brain and kept me from resting. I was at peace with the world, and I savored the eternal darkness that blanketed me.

Sleep came off and on every few hours and finally evaporated late in the day. By then I was too restless to stay lying down, so I got up, stretched my legs and walked out back to find Jeff and Sam sitting against the wall. Sam was having a smoke while Jeff talked about this or that, and they gave me a little wave when I stepped out to join them. I sat on the other side of Jeff so I didn't have to breathe in the cigarette smoke. We tolerated Sam's smoking, but I could never understand why he did it. It was something I never asked him about, and I won't ever know why or when he started it. It was just something we lived with.

"Morning, sunshine," Sam said. He was wearing the leather jacket Jeff had stolen from Shelly's, along with his aviators. His Mr. Cool Guy look was almost complete. All he needed was some gel to slick his hair back. Then again, I guess it was greasy enough.

"Are you guys hungover?" I asked.

"Just a tad. How 'bout you, big guy? First time being drunk, right? How's it feel?" Sam took a long drag from his cigarette and rested his head against the wall, exhaling slowly.

"Not bad. I'm a little tired, and I've got a headache, but nothing unbearable," I said. "I guess I'm lucky."

"There's no such thing as luck," Jeff said. "But considering how wasted you got, I'd have to agree."

I rested my head back as Sam had done and shut my eyes tight, rubbed my temple and then just stared off across the empty expanse that stretched out into a ruddy horizon. It was a perfect spot to sit and talk, but until then we'd never done so. It made sense to stay away, but there was hardly anyone around to see us lingering and loitering. If anything, we were more likely to be seen hanging around the old playground or climbing up the very visible water tower. I needed to stop worrying about it, though. Most people didn't have to concern themselves with the frequency with which they frequented certain territories. And while I wasn't like most people, I deserved a break from my problems just as much as most people. I would've said 'responsibilities,' but that would've been a bad joke. My only responsibility was making sure I didn't drop dead or get us into an unsolvable predicament.

"I'm too tired for any of that existential shit right now," I said, "but if there's no luck and no God and no fate guiding our lives, we're probably more fucked than we think."

Sam grunted and took another drag from his cigarette.

"Yeah," he said. "You're probably right."

"I need some coffee," Jeff said. "You guys wanna come?"

Sam joined him, but I stayed sitting there, too comfortable to get up. I didn't drink coffee, and while I would've been cool with taking a walk through town, I was content with watching the orange sky melt into the horizon over the yellow field behind the warehouse. I picked up a pebble and ground it against the concrete, wondering what my other two friends were doing. Vin and Leslie felt states away. Were they hanging out together right then? Were they wondering where I was, or had they given up thoughts like those a while ago? It was already November, after all, and I'd been gone since mid-summer. I could see them sitting together in her room, Vin's arm around Leslie's shoulder while he comforted her, telling her everything would be fine. He'd say I was in a better place. She'd say she hoped so. I hoped so, too. I scraped my finger and yanked it to my mouth to suck off the blood. The pebble had been worn down to nothing. I got up and went for a walk.

I never went on walks by myself—not since I'd stumbled upon my new friends—and it felt strange to be doing so. It was like returning to the scene of a crime, but that had less to do with my lack of company and more to do with where I was walking: back down the same road we'd taken to get to the party house. It was curiously quiet in the streets, though not as quiet as our early-morning venture home. It dawned on me that the houses seemed lifeless and empty, or at least mostly so, which made no sense. Where could *everybody* be at that time of the day? A faraway voice answered my questioning thoughts, and I followed the sound while taking care to remember which streets I was turning down so I didn't get lost on my way home.

The voice led me through a barren town, using the acoustics of the lined-up houses to bounce off and reach my straining ears. It reminded me of a recurring dream I've had all my life, but which I hadn't had—or couldn't remember having—since I'd left my home in Oak Ridge. In the dream, I was wandering down a long, narrow underground tunnel. I could hear an echo of a voice far off in the distance. And even with the exceptional acoustics of a tunnel, the voice was faint—too faint to understand what was being said, but just loud enough to know that I wasn't imagining the voice altogether. I'd follow it deeper and deeper, but it continued to elude me, and after a while of walking down the straight path, I could see where the tunnel turned at a right angle. I knew if I could get past the bend, I'd be that much closer, or that much more likely to find the person whose voice I was following, but I always woke up before I got there. Sometimes I'd run, knowing that I had little time. It was as if my body wouldn't allow me to find out what it was I was running to. I never turned around and walked in the other direction, never even thought about it while I was dreaming. There was no time to waste, and I had to know whom the voice belonged to.

The strangeness of it all, and the odd similarity to my recurring dream, made it feel like a dream I was walking through; maybe a variation of the dream, with a new setting to match the new life I was leading. But I knew I was awake, and the voice grew louder until I realized it was not a single voice but numerous voices intertwining. The goosebumps on my bare skin multiplied as I approached what I discovered to be a mass of people surrounding some object they obscured from my sight. Many of them were holding candles, and hundreds of little flames burned through the darkness like lights on a Christmas tree.

The chatter that led me there was actually composed of the whole lot of them singing in unison. The song was one I vaguely recognized, but I couldn't tell if it was a church hymn or something else. They sang about angels and heaven and a light. The tune was pretty and chilling at the same time, which can typically only be said about songs of mourning. I hid behind a tree across the street from the hundreds of townspeople who were huddled together in what was unmistakably a candlelit vigil and watched on as the sky darkened and the world grew colder.

I didn't need to hide, but I didn't want to be a part of that weeping mass. I didn't want to be handed a candle and have someone express his sympathy to me. That's how it had gone when Jim Deacon had died in sixth grade, and I wasn't close to Deacon. It was sad when he'd died—run down by a distracted driver while he was skateboarding across a street— but I think I was only sad because he was someone I'd met and known about. I didn't know him personally, so the shock wasn't as painful for me, though it was still there. I knew his friends called him Deacon, or Deeks for short. I knew he literally skateboarded everywhere, and especially the places where he wasn't supposed to. He was one of the tallest kids in the class, and he always spiked his hair. When he died, my father—who was still quite fatherly at the time, even if he was a bastard—walked Vin and me to the vigil. Crying parents hugged me and expressed their deepest sympathies to me like I was Deek's best friend, or brother, even.

I was more comfortable hiding behind the tree across the street and waiting it out until the crowd finished discussing how it was a terrible shame. The cacophony of memories being shared died down about an hour after I'd arrived, and I stepped out of the shadows once the last grieving family slunk back home. I guessed that Jeff and Sam were already back at the warehouse sipping their coffees and wondering where the hell I'd run off to by the time I crossed the street to check out the memorial constructed for Rachel Owens.

A sadness swept over me even before I recognized the girl in the photograph as the one who I'd supposedly slept with in the basement of a stranger's house a few blocks away. When I made the realization, sadness was joined with regret and an impossible longing to truly know who Rachel was. From the first moment I'd seen her, I could tell she was someone special. Had I actually gone to school with her as I'd pretended to the night before, she might have been the focus of most of my attention each week, the way Leslie was.

I examined the picture closely, trying to make a mental copy of it. Her hair was brown, long and wavy. It was probably her natural hair color. Her eyes, which I would've guessed were blue if I was trying to recall her from the night we'd met, were actually closer to gray. She looked happy, but I knew that pretty smile wasn't for the photographer. It was the standard smile provided for every yearbook photo-op—not the kind of smile she flashed for a boy whose face she'd never seen. Or had she? I wished I could have been sober enough to remember walking up to her, seeing that smile in person, just for me. Talking with her, flirting with her.

Getting the briefest glimpse of her outlook on life before hers was taken all too soon.

"Did I kill you?" I asked the photo. "Is this my fault?"

I didn't know the answer, and I was afraid. Jeff said she'd felt like dead weight. Was she lying there on top of me, already a corpse when they found me? What had I done? What had *she* done? I didn't deserve to be the last person on earth to have seen her alive. I shouldn't have even been at that party. It wasn't supposed to end this way. All I'd wanted was to have fun and unwind. No consequences. Not like this. I wanted to know her. And I know, nobody's an angel. No one's perfect. We all want to think the best of someone when they're dead and deny any possibility that they were only human. So who was Rachel Owens?

All the flowers, photos, folded-up notes and burning candles at my feet were becoming too much. I had nothing to place at her memorial, so I stared into her stony eyes for a moment longer and turned away. I retraced my steps and walked home with my head hung low. Thoughts of how I'd enjoyed myself at the party suddenly made me sick. I was disgusted with myself. My eyes stung, and I couldn't shake my confused, pitiful mix of emotions brewing in my heart and throbbing in my head. Of all the girls, it had to be her. It had to be the one who'd lit up the room with her cheerfulness. The girl whose voice made it sound like she was singing when she talked, and whose laugh made you laugh along, even if the joke wasn't funny. And what else? What else would they have said about her while I was hiding in the shadows, oblivious to her lack of a pulse? How would the countless other guys who'd shared her company describe her? Who kept her secrets? A mason jar exploded into a thousand shards of broken glass in my gut, shredding my insides apart. It was wrong to make it about me. Someone's daughter had lost her chance to grow up. Someone else had lost a sister. A best friend. I hadn't lost a damn thing.

"Where were you?" Sam asked when I got back. They had resumed their spots sitting against the wall. I shook my head and walked in, felt my way unsteadily to my mattress and crashed onto it. I wanted to be left alone, but my self-accusing thoughts bombarded me and robbed me of any possible sleep. Sam followed me in and sat down on my mattress, not bothering to ask whether it was okay or if I wanted to talk. He'd decided we were going to talk, and there was no avoiding it.

"Hey. What's up? Where'd you go? What's wrong?" I should've expected the outburst of questions, but I wasn't in the mood for them. Besides, I was already making a hell of a long list of questions myself.

"She's dead," I said, trying not to choke on my words. "The girl you found me with in the basement? She's dead."

I sensed him nodding in the darkness.

"I figured that's what it was. We heard a couple of people talking about it at the café. Guess the news has been spreading like wildfire. But—"

"I think I killed her," I said.

"No, Tom, listen," he said. "She died of alcohol poisoning. You didn't kill her. We heard them say it. I guess it was on TV or they found out from word of mouth after the police did their investigation, but you weren't responsible. She was obviously very drunk, and probably died sometime after you'd already passed out."

The truth was a bit of a relief, but the guilt wasn't entirely lifted. I might've encouraged her to drink more, leading to her death. I might've even handed her a drink. In any case, I was there with her at the end, and we weren't exactly holding a prayer circle down there. But after talking it over with him for the next hour and wishing for most of that time that he'd stop being so reassuring, he eventually did convince me to ease up on myself.

"You being there had nothing to do with her death. She would've been partying anyway—and she was; she'd already been drinking when we got there, right? And she didn't know you. Maybe she thought she did, but you were just a guy in a mask. So a guy in a mask hands her a drink? That could've been anyone in that house that night, and it would have been. She was going to die either way, and you happened to be there when she died. But it wasn't your fault."

"Okay…yeah. You're right. It's just, it hits kind of close. You know?" I said.

"Yeah, I know." He patted my shin, and then stood and left.

Somewhere, miles from where I lay staring up at a blank ceiling—and months earlier—a crowd of people had stood silently weeping at a similar vigil. Some of them were people I knew well. The memories they shared were ones I remembered fondly. The photo at the center of it all was my own. Jeff had relayed the news of my assumed death to me the day Sam and I had eaten burgers in a gazebo in the park and swapped stories of our unimpressive love lives. My neighbors, friends and teachers had long since given up on finding me, and while there were still the missing person posters taped to every telephone pole for miles in every direction from the home I'd left, the overall belief was that I would never be seen again. Not alive, anyway. The difference was that I actually was alive, and I wasn't quite the angel the people of my neighborhood were remembering me to be.

My fading cold took a turn for the worse and became a full-fledged flu virus. I didn't want to eat or move, so I lay in bed for two agonizing weeks in my cold, dark, damp and dirty excuse for a shelter. I had the pleasure of constantly swatting and flicking unseen bugs away and wishing I had the energy to crawl over to Jeff and Sam's sleep area, lift up their mattress, open the secret compartment and unload Jeff's pistol into my skull. Never in my history of illnesses had I lived through a worse fever. I was hot and cold and nauseated and tired. My stomach ached from not eating, and by the end of it all, the little organ I hadn't come close to filling with food every other day had shrunk to the point that a light breakfast would make me stuffed. I was restless from laying on my clumpy mattress for days on end.

Jeff and Sam brought me medicine and sleeping pills when they could. The medicine helped a little. The sleeping pills did nothing, though I was convinced they made my headaches worse. Little by little, my eyes adjusted to the dark. I hadn't thought that was possible before, but a couple weeks without sunlight wasn't normal. I missed the sun, and regular food, and fresh air. Tossing and turning didn't quite compare to my usual exercise routine of constant walking. I urinated in empty bottles I left by my bed and did my best not to throw up. And, for better or worse, I was almost entirely alone during that time. They checked in on me each day to see how I was feeling and to give me what little food and water I would consume, and then they would be out the door. Alone in the dark with my thoughts. What joy. For the first week, those thoughts were of blowing my brains out to put me out of my misery. The second week was a little more productive.

While Jeff and Sam were breaking into houses or playing a round of golf at the local landfill, I was plotting our next big escapade. The idea came seemingly out of nowhere, and almost immediately I was amazed at how I hadn't thought of it sooner. The concept was simple, it required little preparation to execute, and it was bound to have unprecedented success.

I spent most of each day going over it and coming up with a mental list of what could go wrong. If there was a single scenario where the plan could backfire, I wouldn't suggest it to the guys. Everything had to be perfect. To make it perfect, I had to walk through it step by step and take a red pen to any faulty logic, uncertainty or possible misstep that could wind up getting us arrested or killed. And to do that, I had to think like a cop.

Putting yourself in someone else's shoes and trying to think like that person is difficult enough, but attempting to see the world through the eyes of someone who has more training and experience than you can fathom is damn near impossible. My plan wasn't going to be as exact as the clockwork predictability of a mastermind villain in an action film, but with time on my side, I would do what I could with what I had.

***

That sounds unnecessarily vague when I don't lay my plan out for you straight out, I know. But what would be the fun in giving it up that easily? All in good time.

***

I was wrapped up in a personal lesson of psychology and educated guesses when it occurred to me that Sam would have helped move things along significantly faster. He was a smart guy, and though I wouldn't say it about many people, he was definitely smarter than I was. I was willing to bet he'd been a straight-A student and a pretty popular kid in school. Why would he throw that away and resolve to live on the streets? Being there for a friend would be a good excuse to put off a few hours of studying, maybe, but it's not enough to balance out everything else he was leaving behind. He even admitted that he wouldn't have made this choice if he was still with Stephanie, a girl who shouldn't have meant as much to him as his family. My family consisted of one man who hardly acted as a father figure, let alone covering for my other missing parent. My aunts, uncles and grandparents all live in Kentucky, and it'd been years since I'd visited them. My family, then, was not something to stick around for. Jeff was in the same boat, and even worse off because his parents had actually kicked him out of the house. And Sam's parents? They sounded like the kind who were supportive and drove him to achieve excellence. His parents cared about him and encouraged him to look to the future so he wouldn't end up...well, where he was right then. Hanging out in a landfill with a fellow refugee, slumming around and stealing money just to be able to feed himself. Were they the kind of people you run away from to spend your life with your best friend instead?

From his perspective, I could understand why he would answer 'yes.' It was foolish, especially for someone as smart as him, but not without reason. Mr. and Mrs. Dover pushed their son to be better than he was. Their unfair expectations frustrated him, and just as an absence of a parental figure was harmful to me, a constant presence smothered Sam. It must have felt like they were breathing down his neck. Always in his way, and always in his business. They would want to know why he wasn't perfect, and what he was doing wrong, and what they could tell him to do in order to improve in every detail of his life. But his life was a narrow lane, and he was a bowling ball. And they were acting as bumpers lining the sides so he didn't roll into the gutter. They would steer him straight and never let him try another path. If he had no control over his own life, it'd be strangling. During his early teenage years, that could absolutely be enough to set him off and lead him to take a path they would frown upon just to spite them. In fact, it could be said that each of our parents had unfair expectations of us. Jeff's wanted him to follow in their footsteps religiously. Mine expected me to raise myself. That was not parenting: it was slavery.

That's why we needed each other. Sam needed people who would listen to him and appreciate him for who he was. Jeff needed someone who would follow rather than guide him. And I needed two people who could take care of me, and whom I could relate to. I don't mean to sound like I couldn't live independently, but when you're fifteen, you can use all the help you can get. This wasn't a matter of pride, but peace of mind. And I knew I'd find peace if only I could get out of that black hole of a home and into a place where I didn't have to hide or take cover in the dusty old forgotten buildings inhabited by rats and roaches. Everything would be all right once we left.

My knees and joints popped when I finally stood upright sometime in mid-November. Jeff and Sam were already out, but I wasn't going to wait around for them to come back before I ventured out. My restlessness had overcome my sickness, and though I didn't feel one hundred percent better, the need to get out was too strong to ignore. I gathered the bottles of urine, beelined around and passed the looming piles of hoarded items, and pushed the exit door open with my elbow.

Daggers of white light pierced my dilated pupils as the door swung open, and my temporary blindness shocked me into quickly covering my eyes with my hands. In my haste to blot out the sunlight I forgot I was holding the bottles, which fell to the ground and shattered at my feet, spraying pee and shards of glass all over my shoes and up the legs of my pants. I didn't need to open my eyes to know I'd need to change. The warm liquid seeped through my pants and socks and into my shoes. If my feet didn't smell bad already from not taking my shoes off at all except for indoor showers, they reeked to high heaven then.

"You've got to be kidding," I mumbled to myself, standing still in the quickly cooling puddle. I pulled my wet things off and threw them into the mostly empty garbage bin at the back of the warehouse, then trudged back inside and found some fresh clothes.

When Jeff and Sam returned, I informed them I was feeling well enough to move around. I also explained the minor accident, and they laughed it off. Fortunately we were inside while we talked about it, so they couldn't see how utterly embarrassed I was, but whatever.

"It's no big deal, man," Sam assured me. "That's life."

Life, as it happens, chose that point in time to turn around for the three of us. There were no major incidents, no arguments and no dives into depression for quite a while after that. They even agreed with me when I suggested that New Jersey ought to be a place of our past, which was a huge step in the right direction. I had it all figured out, but I didn't tell them what I had in mind immediately. I had to work it in slowly, bits at a time, until just the right moment. Meanwhile, I encouraged Jeff to carry on with his own plans.

"I can't stand this place anymore," I told them one day as we headed out for lunch.

"What do you mean? Are you going somewhere?" Jeff asked.

"No, but I think we should. All of us. I don't know how you lived in this place for three years, honestly," I said. "I think we should move."

"Where to?" Sam asked. "You've got something in mind?"

"Yeah, you noticed that, right?" Jeff said to Sam. Then, to me, "It does seem like you've had something on your mind."

"Not anywhere in particular, but I think we should move out west," I said. "Somewhere warm, and far enough from Jersey so we don't have to keep looking over our shoulders all the time. I think if we landed something big, like a bank robbery or something, we could walk away with enough money to keep us afloat, and then we could skip town and find another place to live. I want us to leave together, and I don't want to spend another month more than I have to in the warehouse. It sucks."

"I know what you mean, but I don't know if we're ready for something like that yet," Jeff said. I knew he meant robbing banks, and not leaving home. For us, running away wouldn't be an issue.

"We're more than ready," I said, with only enough roughness in my voice to show sincerity. "We have to get out of here. I know you guys don't want to live here for the rest of your lives, and I don't want to die in there just because it's moldy and crawling with bugs and rats and all kinds of diseases.

"And I've been thinking… What do you guys want to do with your lives? I mean, we're still young, and we're not going to go out and get jobs tomorrow or anything, but down the line? Did you have goals or dream jobs that you wanted before you left home?"

"Yeah, Tom, I was thinking maybe I'd be a cop, but heading west sounds good, too," Jeff said. "We could go panning for gold in California, or settle down in Phoenix even. I always did like the name."

I laughed at his sarcasm. "But in all seriousness, think about it. I don't know exactly what I want to do, but I know I want to travel. I don't want to be stuck in any one place. And whatever you want, I'm sure you can find it out there somewhere. Not here. I'm tired of it. I've spent too much time in Jersey. I want to leave."

We were all quiet for a minute while they considered what I'd said, and it was hard to tell how they were taking it. I was starting to worry that they'd tell me to set off on my own if that's how I felt, but then they nodded.

"Yeah, I could use a change of scenery," Sam said.

"Sure, all right," Jeff said. I think he hesitated ever so slightly before he added, "If we're going to go ahead with this, I've got just the plan for it. We'll have to do it to a T, and if we mess up, we're dead, but if everything goes according to plan, we could be out of here before Christmas."

"I'm in if you are," I said.

"Let's do it," Sam said.

And so it was settled.

The rest of that month was spent planning for what was to be our big break. We gathered supplies, outlined precise timing of our actions, and discussed it to no end. Or, I should say, to no end until it was absolutely without a doubt completely finalized and ingrained in our heads. You may remember our previous conversation in which it had been noted that winter was not the best time to get involved in criminal activity, but when December rolled around and the crumbling leaves disintegrated to make way for a light carpeting of snow, I felt there was no better time than then to cash in. I was itching to pull it off, and equally as eager to set in motion what I'd been working on during the first few weeks of November, and between the two, I was practically foaming at the mouth with excitement. I kept my ideas secret for a while longer and took everything one step at a time. Miraculously, I didn't lose my head.

Well.

Not any more than I already had.

We were ready halfway through the first week of December. Jeff and I had come to depend on Sam to keep track of the times, dates and days of the week regularly, and he was even on top of adjusting his watch for Daylight Savings Time. Jeff researched operating hours for a chain of banks in Delaware, and we guesstimated how long it would take to traverse the roads, bridges and rivers to get there. I had a pretty accurate internal clock that woke me up five minutes earlier than I intended to no matter what, so I was responsible for waking the others up early that morning so we could get a head start and arrive shortly before the bank was closing for the day. I also had to carry the backpack, which held our ski masks and an inflatable raft that had taken almost a whole day to find among the piles of assorted souvenirs. I'd talked them out of stealing a car to get there, because although it would be faster and more convenient, it wouldn't do to continuously steal cars whenever we needed one. Besides, I knew we would need one later on, and I knew exactly which one I wanted to take. Until then, that car had to remain with its owner.

During my time with Jeff and Sam, I'd come to understand that a lot of what had been stockpiled in the warehouse served some sort of purpose in one or another of Jeff's schemes. He kept a notebook of his ideas, diagrams and schematics. His notes included steps on how to create various homemade bombs, along with footnotes for his own concepts. He briefed me on his long nights spent wide awake tinkering and altering this and that, and then the three of us went around back to watch him test his latest creation.

It was essentially a hand grenade, but was cleverly disguised as an ordinary tennis ball. If anyone inspected it, they would discover it had been sliced in half and sewn back together. If anyone tried to play with it, they'd need a new hand and racket. Jeff explained that he wanted to build one that was remote-detonated, but we didn't have the technology or resources available. A quick trip to an electronics store might've supplied us with such technology, but for the sake of time, we made do with what we had. And what we had was pretty impressive. His tennis ball grenade worked wonderfully, sending clumps of dirt shooting out from a large black cloud of smoke when it hit the ground. We piled three more into a tennis ball container, which we carefully handled while making the trip to Delaware the next day.

Jeff's photographic memory was helpful for more than building things and getting us home after long treks across the state; it also helped direct us to places we'd never been before. All he had to do was stare at a map long enough, and he could walk us through the most direct route to wherever we wanted to go. We didn't make a single wrong turn, which was good because, as always, I wasn't paying attention to which streets we were walking down. My thoughts were occupied by the role I was about to play in the biggest bank robbery of the year.

I cringed against the frigid breeze blowing against us as we passed through town after town and stopped at the riverbed a few dozen miles from where we'd dumped an SUV over a month earlier. The wind was worse down by the water, and I dreaded the thought of tumbling into the icy river. I shrugged the backpack off my shoulders and unzipped it, then handed a tennis racket to each of my blue-lipped friends. We were bundled up as much as we could be, meaning that if we did fall overboard, our heavy clothes would weigh us down and possibly cause us to drown. I pulled out the inflatable raft, and Jeff and I took turns blowing it up. Sam's lungs were practically useless to us; he was hacking and wheezing even as he flicked the butt of his last cigarette into the frosted grass.

When the raft was fully inflated, I zipped up the backpack and slung it over my shoulder, wondering what other goodies we might've brought along with us if we'd had more time to scavenge the mountains of miscellany in the warehouse. The backpack was too old, worn and bulky to fit everything we needed to lug from Jersey to Delaware.

"Only one of us is going over on the raft," I said once we were ready. "Any volunteers?"

For a minute I wondered whether it could hold the combined weight of one of us and a bag filled with thousands of dollars. We stood around, shivering and looking at each other expectantly. This was the part we hadn't planned out, because it was dangerous as hell and a little unfair for the odd man out. One of us would have to ride across the river with the explosives while the other two crossed over the bridge. It was merely a precaution so that nobody saw the three of us traveling together into Delaware, where our targeted bank awaited. We had to pass through inconspicuously until it was time to don our masks.

Or, that's the reason they gave me, though I secretly believed Jeff just wanted to test me. See if I'd agree to such madness. And I did agree, to prove my newfound willingness to accept every part of his plan. It was an exercise in trust.

"Draw straws?" Sam suggested.

I nodded to Jeff and Sam. Jeff nodded back. Sam coughed loudly into his fist, then pulled out a pack of cigarettes and removed three. He tore the filter off one, then shuffled them behind his back and held them out for us to choose.

Jeff wasted no time. He reached out and picked one from Sam's hand, ready to get it over with. His was filtered.

I followed suit, picking the one closest to me. I hesitated a moment, wondering if Sam had placed it closest to me intentionally, then pushed that thought out of my mind. It was up to chance. I pulled it from his grip, checked it, and let out a nervous laugh.

No filter.

"All right," I said, accepting my fate. "See you guys on the other side."

"Good luck, Tom," Sam said, patting my shoulder and replacing the cigarettes in the carton. "And remember, no rush. Be safe."

"Thanks. I'll take my time. The bank's not closing just yet."

I took the tennis rackets and the tube of tennis-ball bombs and then scooted onto the shaky floatation device. They helped me set off, then grabbed the backpack and headed for the bridge.

I used the tennis rackets as makeshift paddles while cradling the canister of bombs in the crook between my legs. I faced forward, keeping my eyes locked on the opposite shore and fighting the urge to look down into the freezing water. The sun peeked through a swatch of clouds and glimmered off the waves that rocked the raft gently from side to side as I drifted slowly across the river. Some minutes passed, and then snowflakes began to drift dreamily down around me. I might've been in awe of the scene if I wasn't trying to block out what would result from the raft tipping over. Of all the ways into Delaware, I hoped this was the best way to go unnoticed. It was obviously neither the smartest, nor the safest. Would I drown, or would the three homemade grenades explode in my lap before I was fully submerged? I swallowed hard and paddled on, toward the rhythmic splashing as I neared the opposite shore.

There was no reason for anyone to assume we were any more than a group of tennis-loving kids looking for a court. We had the balls: bombs that would ruin your day if you stood within a ten-foot radius when they went off. We had the rackets: the heads covered with protective cases to act as perfect paddles to get me across the river. The bag Jeff carried could just as easily be filled with snacks and bottles of water, not a loaded gun and masks. Our ploy was simple. And sure, not many kids skip school to hang around a bank. And if you asked me, the odds that they'd be moseying around in the dawn of winter, walking slowly like they were waiters carrying tall stacks of dishes, were somewhere between zero and zero. But once the *S.S. Flimsy* docked at Port Delaware, and I stepped onto dry land like a surgeon taking care not to twitch with a scalpel in hand and slit a major artery, we did our best to pretend we were exactly where we were supposed to be on a Friday morning.

Jeff took the masks out of the backpack and handed them to Sam and me. We each stuffed ours into the pockets of our hoodies. The anxiety of possibly dying a sudden, terrible death left me feeling both fatigued and wide awake. I was jittery, but I refused to let my hands shake. Caffeine would calm me. It was too early for soda, but I wanted one anyway. I don't drink coffee. I can't even make a pot of coffee without messing it up. I'd gotten up early for some reason one morning, and my oh-so-pleasant father had grumbled at me to make a pot of coffee for him while he put some pants on and went out to get the newspaper. I put the beans in the coffee maker and pressed the right buttons to get it grinding—the thing was as loud as a passing motorcycle—

and then pouring into the pot as it ought to, but in my blurred state of consciousness I'd forgotten to put a coffee filter in. He'd taken a sip and spat it back into the cup. He poured his mug down the sink and yelled at me. Then he poured another and made me drink it. I was not accustomed to the bitter taste of coffee without sugar or cream, and the gritty clumps of coffee grounds gagged me as I swallowed each mouthful.

"Would *you* drink that?"

I hung my head. "No."

"No? But you expect *me* to drink that garbage?"

When he got like that, there was never a correct answer to his questions. If you didn't answer at all, though, he'd raise his voice louder. If you still didn't answer, he'd take off his belt. Sometimes he'd take his belt off anyway, just to make a point. The welts were worse than the coffee grounds.

We talked very little as Jeff led us to the bank, so I went over my part of the plan again a few more times in my head. It was good to have something like that to keep my mind off what I was holding, even if what I was about to do was just as life threatening. I couldn't relax, and my eyes were peeled for anyone who might be looking at us suspiciously. I couldn't stop shaking, either. The freezing air nipped my thighs and calves through a couple small tears in my jeans.

Weeks of preparation still don't really prepare you if you've never seen the place you're about to rob. I had plenty of experience sneaking in and out of the businessman's house, for example, before I had taken a pair of pricey diamond earrings home with me. I'd never even seen a picture of that holy grail of dollar bills before we walked in with a firearm. It was plenty nerve-wracking, then, as you might guess, when Jeff stopped us in our tracks and nodded towards the half-old-school-half-modern structure looming before us. The front end was some classic-looking architecture, with ribbed columns and the whole deal, and around back there was a drive-thru. The three of us pulled our masks on. Then Jeff walked straight up to the front door while Sam and I followed the arrow to our battle stations. As we did, a siren sounded in the distance.

"D'you think they were tipped off?" I joked, hoping my voice didn't betray my nervousness.

"I just hope they're too preoccupied to come chasing us down after this is done," Sam said. He pointed to one of the three vacant drive-thru lanes, told me to take it, and then went to one in the middle. I popped the lid off the tennis ball container, handed a ball to Sam and then carefully—oh-so-carefully—rolled a second one out into my palm. I checked the ceiling of the drive-thru area, hardly surprised to find that there were no security cameras. The place was only partially new, and the bank employees probably felt safe enough with a window of bulletproof glass that looked out onto the drive-thru, by which tellers could clearly see what was going on out there. They believed, naïvely, that any danger to their lives would be found in the lobby. I peered through the window and saw Jeff walk in with his mask on and his gun drawn. I turned and nodded to Sam, who nodded back.

"Time to make our deposit," he said.

I placed the tennis ball into the tube that was meant as an easy and efficient way to carry out transactions from the comfort of one's vehicle, and pressed "Send." The ball was sucked upward into the ceiling. Sam's ball joined it, and together they dropped down on the other side of the window. I didn't stick around to watch that part, though. I'd already set down the container holding the third ball by the entrance of the drive-thru so that when I dove out of range of the imminent explosion, I didn't have to worry about jostling the last bomb and detonating it.

Sam and I ran around the side of the building just in time before bricks and glass and stone blew out the backside in a ground-shaking *bang*. That took care of the security cameras above the counter as well as the tellers who manned the front desk, and it caused the kind of distraction necessary to confuse both employees and customers while Jeff did his thing.

His thing involved leaping over the counter, grabbing as much cash as he could fit into the backpack, and climbing out through the gaping hole we'd created for his escape. I heard yelling and screaming as I went back around to the backside and picked up the container that held the third ball. Jeff's masked head poked through the hole, the sides of which were charred and lined with broken brick. The entire bulletproof pane had blown out.

I didn't waste any time by asking how everything went inside. I hurried to the front side of the building and tossed the container at the entrance to the bank, where it exploded and destroyed both the door and any fingerprints I'd left on the container itself. Then Jeff, Sam and I stripped our masks off and ran like hell, and we didn't stop running until we came across a DART bus about four blocks away. We boarded the bus, paid our fare, and took our seats in the back row, where we glanced out the back window to see if we'd been followed. We weren't. I turned to Jeff and Sam, who were seated next to me across the aisle, and Jeff gave me a thumbs up. I allowed my heart to slow to a jog and slumped into my stiff seat, closed my eyes and basked in our collective victory.

The back of the seat in front of me appeared to have been ripped or cut open, then patched over with duct tape. I picked at a corner of the tape, peeling threads of it off as we rode through a state unfamiliar to the three of us. Even Jeff didn't know where we were going. He hadn't memorized any bus routes or paid special attention to any of the streets we were passing down, because we hadn't expected to hop on a bus as a means of escape. It was noted as a possibility, but if the bus wasn't there as we were fleeing from the scene of the crime, we would've kept running until our legs gave out.

We did it. We'd robbed a bank and had gotten away with it. The DART smelled of rancid body odor, but I didn't care.

I stared out the window at all the passing homes and stores and restaurants and cafés, and I caught the reflection of my own toothy grin. In a few months we would never have to lay eyes on any of those places ever again. We were free men, and we were wealthy men, and we would be leaving our warehouse and our pasts behind. We'd get a place to live that smelled good, with a shower where we could wash the scents of the bus off us.

A half hour passed, and we got off the bus and stretched our legs once more. The sun wasn't quite on its way back to China yet, but the day was more than half over, and we had to find a place to spend the night. We settled for a dirt-cheap inn and got what we paid for. The single room had a single bed and a double coating of grime. No pictures or decorations hung on the walls, and the room was furnished to the bare minimum. A roach darted under the lonely dresser when we turned the light on. The place was barely a step up from what we were used to, but at least there were lamps.

Jeff unzipped the backpack and dumped the money onto the bed. We stared at it for a second, dumbfounded by our prize. Then we divided it up into three piles, counted it out and added the total together. It didn't look like a whole lot there, but I wound up giggling like an idiot as I thumbed through hundreds, fifties and twenties.

"They were just about to put all these stacks into the vault when I came in," Jeff was saying as I counted. "A few minutes later, and I would've just been stuck with whatever was in the registers."

I had $6,000 in front of me. Combined, we'd stolen $15,300. To three homeless teenagers, the number was staggering. We bundled it back up in neat stacks and stuffed it back into the bag, then hid the bag under the bed and lounged around like kings for a while. Sam and I agreed to let Jeff have the bed that night, and we slept sitting in desk chairs.

The next morning we discussed our new possible living arrangements. I refused to return to New Jersey, so we debated staying put for the time being versus moving west. It was a mild-mannered debate, but I wasn't making it easy.

"I thought you said you wanted to travel?" Jeff said.

"I did, and I do, but…" *But I have unfinished business to attend to.* "Here's the thing. I know we made off with a lot of money—thousands—but I think we can get more."

"I'm not hitting the same bank twice," Jeff said. "And if you want to hit other banks farther west, that's fine, but we're not doing it the same way or the police will make a connection between—"

"No," I said, interrupting him. "No more banks. I've…got something else in mind. We could keep going the way we've been going and stealing thousands of dollars at a time, and eventually get caught, or we could land one final score and disappear for good. I'm thinking a million dollars, maybe more, but it won't work if we're halfway across the country."

"Can you stop beating around the bush and just tell us?" Sam said. "You already persuaded us to leave, and now you want us to hang back. What could be that big that it would keep you here *and* get us millions of dollars?"

I stared into the darkness under the bed before answering, my thoughts lingering over the bag of money and the thousands more I had in mind. A million, even. He was making a good point, and it was hard to argue with him, but the dollar signs were too enticing to ignore. It wasn't just about the money; I wanted to tie up loose ends. It's been said that living well is the best revenge, and I planned on living the life I'd dreamt about every day of my miserable existence in the confined walls of my bedroom in Oak Ridge, but I sought another sort of revenge. The life I'd dreamt about was one where a certain someone was buried in a shallow grave deep in the woods where no one would find him.

"A ransom," I said.

"Oh, of course, a ransom!" Jeff said, hardly concealing his amusement. "And who is it that we're holding for ransom? Charles Lindberg?"

"Me," I said. "I didn't even think about it when I ran away from home, but it's perfect. Everyone in my whole town pulled together to try to find me, right? They all grieved together when they thought I was dead. But I'm still a missing person, and there's no reason not to believe I'm alive, and that I disappeared because I was kidnapped. We'll leave the town a ransom note demanding however much we think we can get—a million, million-five, whatever—and they'll all pull together to get me back. Then we'll take the money and run."

"Okay, but why hold a ransom against an entire town? Don't people usually demand ransom money from the kid's parents? And what about the police?" Sam asked. His eyes were fixed on mine. He looked interested, yet tentative. He wouldn't budge unless my plan was unscrewupable. I was glad we were on the same page.

"My mother might hear about it and decide to come back to make sure my kidnappers release me unharmed, but I doubt it. As far as my father's concerned..." I paused, thinking about how I wanted to say what I wanted to say. I was getting excited just thinking about it. "We're going to use him to get through to everyone, to prove that we're not messing around. We're going to kill him, and leave the ransom note by his dead body. My neighbors probably won't discover he's dead right away, so that'll give us time to drive back up to the warehouse and get everything ready for when the cops come with the ransom money."

"Hold on. You're going to drive all the way back to the place you swore you were leaving behind, so you can kill your dad?" Jeff asked. "You were torn up when you thought you killed that girl, Michelle, and it wasn't even your fault. How the fuck are you going to kill *family?*"

"Her name was Rachel. And that was different. She was innocent, and my father's the biggest scumbag on the face of the planet. He deserves it. He deserves it after all the times he hit me, and for driving my mother to abandon me. And for giving me no other option than to leave home to find some sort of happiness rather than wait around for him to beat me to death. As long as he's alive, I'll never really be free. I need him to die. Besides, we killed those people at the bank, didn't we?"

"Yeah, but you didn't watch them die," Jeff argued. "For all you knew, they could've been badly injured at most. You think you can really hold a gun to your own dad and pull the trigger?"

"We're not going to shoot him. That would be too loud, and attract too much attention. We'll have to do it quietly, and sneak up on him and surprise him, but quickly so he doesn't have time to scream for help."

"What about the cops?" Sam asked. Jeff opened his mouth to ask another question, but Sam held a hand up to signal him to wait. "Even if we succeed in walking, or driving, all the way down to your house and killing your dad like a bunch of ninjas, and then leaving a ransom note and coming all the way back up to the warehouse, and setting it up to whatever specifications you think we need to for when the cops come, then what? Do we just walk out, take their briefcase full of money, and shoot them all and take their cars and drive off into the sunset, a million dollars richer and happily ever after? 'Cause I don't think that's gonna work, and a car chase will definitely get us all killed."

"Not exactly," I said, getting up from my chair and taking a seat next to them on the bed. "We're going to lure them in and pick them off one by one. You know the term bottlenecking? Like, making the entrance narrow so that only a few people can get in at a time, instead of all at once? But then once they're in, we'll have them trapped. The police won't be able to retreat fast enough, because they'll be stuck in the bottleneck with other cops crammed in behind them, so they'll have no choice but to come in to try to make the swap: the money for me. Then we'll shoot them down one by one until they're all dead, and then we'll take the money and run. We'll leave in one of their cars, or in my father's car, it doesn't matter. We'll leave, and no one will ever know what happened." I balled my hands into fists and then moved them apart, fanning my fingers out in a vanishing motion. "Happily ever after."

"I still don't think you have the guts to do it," Jeff said. "Even if it did make us millionaires."

"I can do what needs to be done."

"All right. Then you'll have to prove it," he said. "All of us will."

"Fine," I said. "Whatever it takes. But we should lay low for a while, just long enough for people to forget about the bank robbery. Let's hang out here for a couple days, figure out where we go from here, and then we—"

"Can practice killing people," Sam said. Jeff and I stared at him curiously for a second, and he shrugged. "What? That's what you were getting at, right? By proving that we can? We'll have to numb ourselves to killing so that, when the time comes, we don't back down."

"We don't have to kill any innocent people," I said. "There's no reason for them to pay for my father's guilt."

"Then what are we going to do?" Sam asked. "Run into a prison and shank a bunch of convicts?"

"No…" I said.

But someone out there deserves it. Katie. Her boyfriend. All the selfish, sinful, rotten bastards who are nothing but wastes. The ones who live to make our lives hell.

"We have to take this seriously, guys. Because this is serious," Sam said, looking back and forth between Jeff and me. "Can we bring ourselves to take the life of a total stranger? Because that's what you're asking of us, Jeff. To prove that we can kill not only Tom's dad, but a dozen or two dozen cops, maybe more, we have to tear down our mental and psychological walls and forget right and wrong. We have to accept that we're capable of murder, and go through with it. This isn't hypothetical shit. It will seriously fuck us up in the head."

"I don't think that last part is going to be a problem," I muttered.

"I'm serious, Tom. You said we don't have to kill innocent people, but as much as you want to believe cops are the bad guys, they signed up to *protect*. They are innocent. I'm asking you, can you kill an innocent person?"

A heavy silence fell over the room. I considered his question. I thought about how badly I wanted my father to disappear. I imagined the three of us driving west, with more money than we'd ever dreamed of and a wide-open road ahead of us, filled with endless possibilities. When I left home, I'd gone with the certainty that I'd do whatever it took to make things right for myself. Whatever it took. And if it took ending someone's life just to make mine a little easier? It wasn't right. It wasn't decent. It was beyond unfair. But let's face it; I'd given up on humanity when I'd learned everybody else was only out to help himself. I was ready to take their immoral code of ethics and throw it back in their faces. It was time for me to stop obeying the rules that the powerful always broke and take what was rightfully mine.

"I'll do it," I said. "If you're both in, I'm in. All the way."

Jeff nodded. "Right, then. I suppose if we're going to stay here a couple days, you can fill us in on your plans?"

I walked them through it twice and answered every question they threw at me along the way. I even offered them a chance to make alterations to the plan, but they seemed content with how it was. I was surprised and relieved by their seal of approval. They should have shot it down, called it crazy and left me to curse them behind their backs while I followed them through their lives like a shadow of past mistakes. I was immensely proud of myself, and that's saying something. I'm not the kind of person who's accustomed to pride.

***

The electric company cut the power to this place today, so I guess that's my cue to wrap it up. That's fine, though, because I already finished five six-packs and two bottles of wine, and the well is running dry. Pretty soon I'll have to pick up and leave. It's a shame. This place was really starting to feel like home. Oh well, *c'est la fin.* Or *c'est la vie*—however you say it.

***

Treading back and forth from the front door to the sidewalk for three days left a slushy path that put our overlapping shoe prints on display. It snowed a little the second and third days, and the prints froze. Someone really should've shoveled the walkway, because a senior citizen could've slipped and broken something. A detective would've matched the prints to those left at the warehouse, or the house where Rachel had died, or the parking garage or the flowerbed that sat in front of the unlocked basement window of the businessman's house or a thousand other places we'd been. All right, I don't actually believe that last part, but I can honestly say I was a little paranoid about it at the time. I was glad when we left the inn the afternoon of that third day and went off in search of a new, temporary home. I was getting sick of spending all our crisp, ill-gotten twenty-dollar bills and praying we wouldn't have to start breaking fifties and hundreds.

I felt more comfortable in the decrepit glass factory with its crumbling smokestacks and soot-covered brick walls. The barbed-wire fence that surrounded the perimeter looked more dangerous where it lay on the ground, hidden under a blanket of vines and moss. Every window was broken or barred. Paint peeled away from the walls and doors, and rust ate through the pipes. One of the staircases inside had collapsed and hung from a grated-metal landing that led to a lightless room with no door. With all the side corridors and hidden ventilation ducts, the place was even more of a complicated maze than our old wasteland. Where the ceiling had caved in, shafts of light shone through and illuminated the gloomy chambers. Pillars of dust crept dismally into the light and retreated into the shadows like a macabre dance to the morose, inaudible song of the dead men who once worked there. It was exactly what we needed.

Winter winds whistled loudly in the night and clawed through my layers of clothes. I shivered and hugged my legs against my chest, curling into a tighter ball on the freezing factory floor.

And how's that for alliteration, Aunt Josephine? You always did love poetry, almost as much as all those silly old proverbs.

Needless to say, we only spent a few hours exploring the building before hitting the streets for a round of much-needed hot chocolate on that first full day there. We filled a closet with canned meats, soups, fruits, vegetables and sodas. We piled some discarded blankets and sweaters into a corner of the room we'd chosen as our sleeping quarters. It was about as homey as we could make it, and while the walls were still cold and bare and lifeless, and the interior looked like a psychopath's nightmare, I was pleased with our new address.

"This place is a deathtrap," Sam said one day, observing the dangling staircase.

"Then it's perfect," I said.

"There are plenty of places to hide the bodies," he said. I couldn't read his tone, so maybe he was already dead inside. The thought had had enough time to linger in our heads and rot our spirits, but I was optimistic about the future. If a few people had to die for me to live comfortably, then so be it. Jesus supposedly died for us, and how did we celebrate that gift of death? Trampling each other for the last Cabbage Patch Kid the day after Thanksgiving. I didn't think I was being unreasonable.

***

Do you hate me yet? I wasn't always a bad person. You might not believe that, but it's true. It's just all that nature-nurture garbage, and the hell I've been put through. And the warehouse. A place can poison your mind, you know? It can make you cold and heartless. People can do that, too, but not people like Jeff and Sam. We had our squabbles, true, but they were good people. It was that damn warehouse and the flu. Weeks spent in isolation, without food or light. I take full responsibility for my actions, but you've got to understand that I wasn't myself. Maybe I'm bad at explaining it. How the hell could you understand? You weren't even there. They were good people. We all were. Sometimes you just have to do things you don't want to do, and it's worth it in the end.

***

We were coming down the street one day after eating lunch at a place that specializes in every kind of sandwich imaginable, and Sam stopped us and subtly pointed out a guy across the street. He was an older man, but his age was impossible to tell. His face was unshaven and his beard grew in a white tangled mess that offset his black skin. He was ringing a bell for the Salvation Army. The few people passing him on their way to run errands didn't pause to drop a quarter in his bucket. They went on with their day, ignoring him. I imagined them returning to their warm houses with their fireplaces and their smiling children, and they'd be happy as could be with what great sales they'd gotten on all the gifts they'd bought. They'd go to sleep in their big, comfy beds, tucked in tight, and they wouldn't dream about the man with the bell. They'd forget about him as soon as he was out of sight. They wouldn't feel bad at all.

"Wanna make a few extra bucks?" Sam asked us.

"From him?" I whispered, tilting my head toward the soldier of salvation.

"Not from him," Jeff cut in. "I doubt if he even has a dollar in there. He's wasting his time out here. He'd do better in the city."

Sam didn't say anything, but raised an eyebrow at us expectantly.

"We don't really have anything else going on," I said. "I could go for a trip up to the city."

I had New York on my mind. From what I've heard, it's a real winter wonderland that time of year. Lights everywhere, enormous Christmas trees, families ice-skating in open-air rinks. My mother walking hand-in-hand through the snow-covered Time Square with a man I'd never know. Then again, she could've been sledding down glaciers in Alaska for all I knew. But the city that called my name was too many miles away, so I settled for Philadelphia.

Philly was pretty far, too, and two full days passed before we got there, but I didn't mind. It gave me time to think, talk to the guys, and just walk without the pressure of some burglary or theft. My hair was longer, almost to the point of shagging in my eyes. The skin on my knuckles was cracked and bloody from the cold, dry air. I thoughtlessly bit off the chapped skin from my lips and chewed it as we wandered through unknown territory, taking turns lugging the backpack full of cash because we didn't dare leave it in the factory.

We came across a terrible car accident on the way and stopped to check it out. A car and a pickup truck had collided head-on and the car had caught fire. There was glass everywhere and a body on a stretcher covered by a bloody white sheet. The hood of the truck was smashed in, and the headlights were gone. The car's entire front end was a mess of twisted metal and tubes leaking fluids. Two ambulances, a fire truck, police vehicles and a couple dozen people blocked most of the scene from view. Officers were asking questions and writing notes, a man covered his tear-stained face, and passersby pointed and rubbernecked. We stepped around a tire that had somehow wound up separated from the car, and moved on.

When we made it to Philly, we did see a few Salvation Army posts, but we couldn't figure out an easy way to steal a bucket and bell, so we roamed around for another day and then turned around and made our way back to the factory. On our way back, we slept in alleyways huddled together, so nobody could steal the money. On one of the nights I dreamt I was running through an underground tunnel. The echo of a voice reflected off the narrow walls and led me deeper into nowhere, and I woke up thinking I was back in the warehouse. Reality set in when I looked up and saw the full moon glowing above me, and then the sounds of a jazz band floated down the street and lulled me slowly back to a dreamless sleep. It was warmer there than the factory, but we'd also never slept with our heads resting on each other's shoulders before.

***

There was no sign of the accident on our way home. It was like it had never happened. I didn't really think about it at the time, but I guess so much goes on these days that no one has time to think about all the accidents they find long after they're gone. It's different for the people involved, of course, because they've got to live with it. But if you weren't in the accident, and neither was a friend or relative, you'll likely forget it happened after a couple days. I'm not sure why I remember it so vividly. I guess it was just so much like everything going on in my life at the time. Or maybe it was the corpse the EMTs were wheeling into the ambulance. I'd been half expecting to see the sheet slide off the body to reveal my mother lying there, returned to me at last.

***

The legs of the metal folding chair scraped against the cement floor, screeching in unison with the girl's muffled screams. Jeff warned her not to scream, but she had no real options. There was no way she was going to escape, and nobody in their right mind would just sit there and take it without a struggle. The girl was in her early to mid teens. It was hard to tell, especially with the duct tape over half her face. The other half of her face was bright red and blotchy from crying, and her makeup was running down her cheeks. It was surreal to see someone like her look back at me wide-eyed and terrified, but it was no time to start feeling sympathetic. I was the first one up to prove that I could kill someone in cold blood, and I couldn't back down. I opened the longest blade of the Swiss Army knife Sam had given me. I watched her flinch as I stepped toward her. She tried to protest, and Jeff yanked her ponytail hard to quiet her. She grunted in pain and wailed.

"Just do it already and shut her up," Sam said.

I wasn't sure how I wanted to do it, though. It's easier to imagine killing someone hypothetically. When you're standing a foot away from your victim—and she's mentally willing you to stop, and you're mentally willing yourself to get it over with—then it starts to really set in. I was about to cross a line from which there's no coming back. I'd already made the decision to kill her, and I wouldn't know how I'd feel about it all until I'd done it, but I could still stall long enough to figure out what I was feeling while I stabbed her to death.

"What are you waiting for?" Jeff asked.

"Move aside," I said without thinking. I hoped they would believe my nervousness about killing the girl was more over getting blood on myself than ending her life. In truth, it was her eyes. She knew that I knew right from wrong. She also knew I was deliberately choosing to ignore my instincts. Her eyes begged me to put the knife down. Jeff stepped away from behind her, and I took his place, holding my blade against the curve of her neck. I inhaled deeply and pulled her ponytail back and down to expose the area I was about to cut. I clenched my jaw and yanked the blade across her throat.

***

I forgot to mention how nice it was in Philly. I mean, it wasn't exactly the way I imagined New York would look around Christmastime, but it was absolutely spectacular. There were huge wreaths decorated with big red bows, ornaments hung on the corner of every block for miles, and almost everyone was smiling ear to ear while it snowed. The kids, and a few adults, caught flakes on their tongues and laughed honestly under their snow-flecked hoods and caps. It was a very pleasant time in the city, and I was glad we went. What a relief not to be standing around ringing a bell for hours and hoping some of those smiling faces would take a second to drop some pocket change in a bucket for us before resuming their holiday shopping.

***

A thin line of blood bloomed from her jugular, and she moaned and shook violently in the chair she was bound to.

I'd done her no favors in slitting her throat. She was in pain, but she wasn't dying. I cut her again, pressing harder, and she let out an agonizing cry. Sam and Jeff rushed to either side of her to hold her down as she writhed in the chair, and I began to stab her in the chest. I raised my arm and thrust the knife into her again and again while my face flustered from the struggle of the kill. She was supposed to die quickly, with a jet of blood spraying out in a sudden wave from her artery and gurgling shortly in her throat before she collapsed lifelessly from bleeding and a lack of oxygen. I blamed her stubbornness to live, but it was my fault for not using a larger blade.

***

Girls about her age had passed us on the Philly sidewalks, giggling to each other and occasionally glancing our way as we pretended to window shop. They were bundled up in scarves and long jackets and boots, but I wasn't interested in their winter fashion. I wanted to see them bouncing around on the beach playing volleyball in their tiny bikinis, or diving into an oncoming wave on a hot August day. Winter's all right, too, though. I could pull one of them close—*how about you in the hood lined with fox fur?*—and watch her breath spill out like smoke right before I kissed her and wrapped her up in my jacket. She'd hold my face close to hers with her mittened hands and stare into my eyes and wonder where I'd been all her life.

***

The girl's shirt was covered with tiny, bloodstained slits by the time she rocked with a final violent convulsion and lay slumped and motionless in the chair. Crimson drops ran down the sides of her neck like a tattered Christmas bow dangling loosely over her collarbone. Some of her blood had splattered against the side of my hand as I'd stabbed her, but most of it was slowly oozing out of her from the many holes I'd punched into her flesh. When it was over I dropped the knife on the floor and stood bent over with my hands on my knees.

***

The girls on the city street passed out of sight and out of our lives. It was better for them that they did, because a week later we began our search for people who looked easy to kill. The smaller and skinnier the better, because they were the easiest to capture, haul back to the factory and tie down. Girls made it especially easy, because they couldn't fight us off as well as guys could.

***

"Are you all right?" Sam asked, putting a hand on my shoulder.

"Yeah…I'm good," I answered, unable to avert my gaze from the corpse Jeff was untying from the chair.

"You did good, man. The first one's got to be the hardest. Do you want to sit down?"

Not in that chair.

"I'm gonna get something to drink," I said. I went to the room that served as a pantry and grabbed a root beer, popped the cap, and headed back into the murder room. I sat down on the dirty floor and sipped the soda, staring at the girl I'd stabbed to death. Torture is probably a better word. I focused on convincing myself she was just a sack of bones and organs. I could deal with what I'd done if I didn't imagine her as a living, breathing person who used to have friends, family and plans for the future. I didn't want to think about how she might've been just like me. And those terrified eyes of hers.

Just like mine.

I balled my free hand into a fist and only relaxed my grip when I realized my long nails were digging half-circle indents into my palm. Sam was right; it would get easier with time. Eventually I'd be desensitized to killing, and the remains wouldn't bother me. And she might've been a preppy, stuck-up bitch who deserved what she got.

No, that's not right. She was nobody. She was nothing. Just forget it. Don't even say 'she,' because all it ever was was just a sack of bones and organs. A waste of space.

I chugged half the bottle, raising it high enough to block the body from my view.

You killed her you killed her, oh God, and you made it last, you dirty boy, you cut her up and killed her slow.

"You'll get used to it," Jeff said, lifting her by her armpits and dragging her into a large trash bag Sam was holding open for him. "After a while it'll just come naturally. And next week you can help me pick one out for Sam."

"Yeah," I said. There was nothing else to say. He made it sound like we were going to go shopping. Sam said something that I didn't quite make out, but it sounded like "Easy, Jeff," or "He's in shock." Either way, I didn't care. I was watching my two friends roll the legs of a corpse of a girl I'd killed into a garbage bag and tie it up, and I didn't care. The small red smear on the floor meant nothing to me. I finished the bottle and told them to untie the bag.

"I've just got to throw this out," I said, holding up the empty root beer bottle. I tossed it in the bag and they retied it, then lugged it over to the other side of the room and sat down on either side of me.

"You did good," Sam repeated.

"I'm starving," I said. I wasn't, but I wanted to get out of there. My limbs were heavy, like I'd been working out for hours. The voice in my head was disgustedly mocking me, or indulging in the vulgarity of the situation, or both. It was the vile voice of the monster inside me. It was the voice of my father.

I stood up without warning, ran across the room to the garbage bag and kicked it repeatedly. The limp body didn't resist my fury. I wanted to obliterate it.

"Tom, stop!" Sam shouted. "She's dead, and if you break the glass in there, and it rips the bag open, you're gonna get blood all over the floor."

It was a nonsensical excuse to stop, seeing as how there was already blood on the floor, and none of us were worried about keeping the place sanitary, but I ended my outburst and hung my head.

"Come on, let's get some food," I said. They stood and joined me for some dinner.

The next day we went out to a toy store and bought a few board games and a deck of cards. We wasted time in one of the control rooms of the factory, sitting on the floor and playing poker and Monopoly. Those times were almost therapeutic for me in a way. We didn't talk about our problems. Instead we talked about whatever was on our minds, or some anecdotes of our past. We all had peanut butter and jelly sandwiches sitting on napkins next to us and a can of soda or iced tea. It had taken a week and a half for Sam to find a place that would sell him cigarettes without asking for identification, and he smoked them relatively sparingly throughout the day. Our lives were never going to be the same as they once were, but we acted like nothing was changing. I learned Texas Hold 'Em on the floor of a building where hundreds of people once worked to make ends meet years before. We looked around to see what we could find, but mostly just for something to do. I thought about the strangeness of our time spent together and how temporary everything felt. This wasn't an entirely new concept to me, but I found myself increasingly unnerved about moving from place to place, through the homes and halls where others had gone before us. It made me doubt the path I'd chosen.

Then I'd remind myself that we were still kids, and we deserved to build ourselves the proper childhood our families had denied us. We were no longer innocent, and we'd seen and done things no teenager should, but that's life. I'll learn from our mistakes. I think I already have, and I know everyone makes mistakes no matter what age. I decided to just play with my friends. Some days we played checkers, other days we played capture-the-girl. I'll admit there's no victor in the latter.

Jeff and I hit the streets alone to find a victim for Sam's first try at murder. I wore Sam's watch so we could time our progress through one of the nearby towns. We found a high school girl standing alone at a bus stop, but her bus pulled up just when we arrived. I considered suggesting another parking lot or garage, but I knew our odds were, ironically, better out in the open. Even in broad daylight we looked like we were up to no good, but it was easier to find people out and about. I brushed my shaggy hair from of my face and looked Jeff over, trying to see him through the eyes of someone who hadn't spent the previous three months with him. His hair was longer than mine and just as matted with grease. He had a full moustache that grew into his scruffy beard. His red, tired eyes appeared to rest on purplish-black beanbags. His clothes were frayed and tearing in spots, and the cuffs and knees of his pants had dirt stains, which I assumed had come from sleeping on the unswept floors of our homes. We were thinner than most people, but our baggy clothes hid that detail. I didn't think we looked like killers. Heroin addicts, maybe, but not killers.

"It's been weeks since we've been in the warehouse," I said. "The place is probably a pigsty."

Jeff gave a surprised laugh and shook his head at the ground. "Yeah," he said, "we'll have a lot of cleaning up to do when we get back."

"What we're doing out here is gonna make an even bigger mess at home in the factory," I said. He didn't respond for a couple of minutes, and when he did, his words had nothing to do with killing girls in an abandoned factory in Delaware, or killing my father in New Jersey, or ransom money. It had nothing to do with anything we'd talked about over the past months, and thus it gave me a complete shock.

"Next week is my birthday. What are you gonna get me?" he said.

"Really? So you'll be eighteen?"

"Yeah, I'll be an adult. I'll be allowed to vote, and get arrested, and everything."

"Well, you can't drink yet."

"I guess that means you're not going to buy me a six-pack for my birthday?"

"Hey, I'm not giving away the surprise. You'll have to wait 'til your birthday to find out," I said. "It's exactly a week from now?"

"Christmas Eve," he said, nodding.

"Then it'll have to be something extra special."

"I'll hold you to that. How about her?"

"Huh?" I followed his line of sight and spotted the girl he was watching. She was slowing to a stop at a red light in her cherry Mustang. The convertible top was up, but I could imagine how fun it'd be to take that thing for a drive in the spring or summer. "How will we get her?"

Jeff picked up a rock and hurled it at the Mustang. I winced when it hit the driver side window and bounced off into the grass by the sidewalk. It was the same trick Sam had pulled in the parking garage, and one that clearly worked like a charm. The girl threw her car into park and got out, slammed the door shut and stomped over to us.

"Hey, what the hell is your problem?" she yelled. I wasn't thrilled with her vociferous articulation for several reasons, and I'm sure they are all pretty obvious. The biggest problem, though, was that she would draw attention to the three of us. The thing we disliked the most was attention. "What do you think you're doing, throwing—"

Jeff ran at her and caught her by the wrist. She yelped, and I leapt at her and knocked her to the ground. She was a little pudgy, and she made for a soft landing. Her bratty face would've been the perfect punching bag. The problem was that I knew I'd only knocked her over by surprise; if she'd braced herself, only my sheer muscle strength could make her wobble, and she was sturdy enough to stay standing. She'd be pretty heavy, especially when we planned to lug her down multiple blocks back to the glass factory.

"Get off of me!" she wailed.

She was almost up into a sitting position when Jeff gave her a series of swift kicks to the head and knocked her unconscious. We hurriedly grabbed her arms and legs and dragged her into the backseat of her car, where I sat with her while Jeff drove us back to the factory. It was hard work lifting and carrying her, and all the while our heads were on swivels, keeping an eye out for anyone who was keeping an eye on us. When we were seated in the Mustang, Jeff floored it, turned us around, and sped home.

"I know it doesn't help to say it, but that didn't go as well as I'd expected," I said.

"We got her, didn't we?" Jeff said.

"We did, yeah. All I'm saying is we should probably have a better plan than that next time."

"How's she looking back there?" he asked.

"Not well, but I'm sure she's always this ugly," I said. "By the way, how'd you get my girl home?"

"You don't want to know," he said.

"Try me."

Red and blue lights flashed in the rearview mirror, and I looked out the back window to find a police car blazing a trail about a quarter mile behind us.

"Dammit," Jeff whispered. "Oh, crap."

"Maybe it's not for us," I said.

"Maybe it is." He turned right at the corner. "Someone must've seen us. We need to hide her."

"Quick, pop the trunk."

"What if *he* tells me to pop the trunk?"

"Well, where else are we going to hide her?" The unmistakable whine of a siren blared and drew closer. I looked down at the unconscious girl on the seat next to me and panicked. The police would see her, arrest us, discover who I was, contact my father, and release me into his custody. Four long months wasted, and I'd be forced to confess all I'd done and explain to all the residents of Oak Ridge that not only was I not dead, but I was the reason why others were. I'd have to face my devil of a father. *Unless...*

"Pull over," I said. "We need to get her out of the car."

"Shit," Jeff replied, and pulled up to the curb. We both got out on the driver side and pulled the heavy girl out by her arms and legs. "This isn't going to work."

"Yes it is. Now, bring her over to the front and line her up with the car," I directed. "Keep her legs together. Steady, steady. Lay her down. Don't block the wheels."

We lay her down on the ground, and I pressed her arms to her sides. I checked to make sure no part of her was blocking the path of the Mustang's tires, and then Jeff got back in and pulled forward. When the car was directly over her, I signaled Jeff to put it in park again, and then got in the passenger seat. My door had no sooner swung shut than the police car turned the corner. Jeff rolled down the window, and the cop pulled up behind us. We waited for longer than I thought was necessary before he stepped out of the car.

He was a tall, broad-shouldered man with a beer belly and cropped hair. He spoke with a tone that told us not to bother screwing around.

"License and registration?"

"I forgot them both at home," Jeff said.

"We just pulled over to check the back seat for my wallet, but I can't find it. It must be on my—"

"Where's home?" the officer asked. Clearly he also didn't have time to waste on excuses.

"Nineteen Shakespeare Drive," Jeff said.

We're dead.

"You're Nelson's kid?" the cop asked, raising an eyebrow and his tone a bit.

"I'm Connor, his nephew," Jeff said without missing a beat. "I'm staying with him for the week while my parents are up in the Poconos."

"I didn't even know Nelson had a nephew."

"You're not going to tell him about this, right?"

"That depends," the officer said, leaning partially in through the open window. He looked me over for a second, noticing me for the first time, and then glanced at the empty backseat. He returned his attention to Jeff and said, "Pop the trunk for me, Connor?" It was not so much a request as a demand, but the edge in his voice was mostly gone.

"Sure," Jeff said. He pulled the lever between his left leg and the driver side door.

The officer went around to the trunk and checked it for a whole five seconds before slamming it shut. During that time I stared at Jeff.

"Relax," he whispered to me, and smiled. I smiled back.

"All right," the cop said when he returned to the driver side window. "I want to ask you a few questions. Some witnesses on the street said they saw a couple of long-haired fellows in black jackets beating up a woman and driving off with her in this car." He stared at both of us for a minute with wide, probing eyes. The steel blue of his irises stood out from his gray, lined face. We waited for him to get to the question. Finally, Jeff spoke up.

"They said this car?" he asked.

"This car. Do you happen to know anything about that?"

"I didn't see anything," Jeff said, and turned to me. "Did you?"

"I wasn't paying attention," I said, shaking my head.

"There was another red car up ahead of us before," Jeff pretended to remember. "I don't think it was a Mustang, though. I think a Charger. Maybe that was it?"

"Which way were they going?" the cop asked.

"That way," Jeff said, pointing in the direction we'd been heading before we turned right and pulled over. "But that was five or six minutes ago, now."

"And this is your car?" he asked.

"My sister's," I said. If he ran the license plate through the system, as I suspected, it'd come up registered under Chubby Bitch's name. It wouldn't make sense for Jeff to say he owned the Mustang, and it wouldn't work for him to say it was his uncle's. I didn't trust him to make another airtight lie. But I could be Chubby Bitch's brother.

"He's driving your sister's car?" he asked.

"Yeah," I said, shrugging.

"What's her name?" he asked, testing me—and a pretty damn good test at that. I hadn't checked her ID. Jeff's license might've been at home, but her registration wouldn't be there—it'd be at my home, supposedly in Chubby Bitch's possession. He would cut through our bullshit and discover we were the guys he was looking for, and then he'd start looking a bit closer for the girl we'd kidnapped.

"I'm sorry, officer, but are we in trouble?" Jeff asked, saving me from making up a name. "We just told you we saw the car you're chasing, heading in a different direction. No offense, but you're only wasting time talking to us, and it sounds like a woman is in danger."

He looked from me to Jeff. I swallowed. He seemed to want me to answer his question, but I held my tongue. I waited him out, and finally he gave up.

"You boys stay out of trouble, and go straight home and get your license and registration. I don't wanna see you out here on the road without them again." The cop turned to leave, but he paused mid stride and called back, "And get a haircut, what do you say? The both of you." Then he hopped in his cruiser and drove off with the siren sounding again.

We stayed put until he was out of sight, and then I got out to haul the girl we'd kidnapped back into her car. She was already waking up and beginning to crawl out from under the vehicle as Jeff backed up.

"Hell no you don't," I said, and slammed her head into the ground with my foot. She groaned and reached for my leg. I kicked her again, and she went limp. I motioned for Jeff to help me, and he got out and grabbed both her legs. Together we lifted her up and stuffed her back into the backseat and then drove back to the factory.

The girl's face was a little bloodied up. By the time we dragged her into our killing room, pulled her into a sitting position and tied her to the chair, she looked like she'd already been through her first round with us. Fortunately for her, Sam was much quicker and more precise with his methods, and she didn't suffer long. She tried to scream and get out of her bondage, but her struggles ended the same way the first girl's had: in vain.

I had to hand it to them. The girls. At least they tried. Her face blanched and she cried through squeezed eyes after glimpsing the sharpened pole in Sam's hand. He'd broken it off from some piping in the factory and had worked on it all week after my incident with the inadequate knife. His spear inspired Jeff to carve a silencer for his pistol out of the same piping, but because of the intricate shaping required of the silencer, it took over a month to complete.

Sam wound back and impaled her with the metal spear, piercing her heart. She died almost immediately. Blood squirted out in a stream through the hollow center of the piping and drained until she bled out. It was a far messier kill than mine, but much less painful. He left the spear sticking out of her chest and walked to where I'd sat the week before and squatted down, nodding to himself. He looked from Jeff to me, back and forth, with a blank expression.

"All right," he said, sitting down. He lit a cigarette.

I went to the pantry, pulled a large trash bag from the box on the shelf and helped Jeff untie the cadaver and lift it into the bag. We brought it over to the far side of the room and dropped it onto the first corpse, beginning a pile. Then we changed into fresh clothes and tossed our bloody clothes into the body bag and tied it up. The three of us played Monopoly for the rest of the night into the following morning, drinking sodas and eating crackers. I gave Sam his watch back before we went to sleep shortly after two o'clock.

It didn't take long to start seeing everyone around us dying. I couldn't walk down the street without seeing a man or woman walking by and wondering what he or she would look like in his or her final moments. It drove me crazy, but I let myself picture it. Here a corpse, there a corpse. Everywhere a corpse-corpse. Blood would fill the streets and run into the gutters. Guts would squish under our worn-out shoes. Screams and squeals and shrieks would fill the air like the blaring sirens of cop cars. It consumed me during every waking minute. It haunted my dreams. I daydreamed about how easily my blade slid into her flesh, slicing through her lifeline. It muddied my mind. It sickened me, but for some reason I wanted to feel that sickness. Gradually it got to the point where just thinking about it wasn't enough.

***

The next day we went to the movies to take our minds off it. Normally we wouldn't go near a movie theater, but we were content in the knowledge that our identities—and mine specifically—were completely unknown in Delaware, and thus we were safe. We took a bus to a small independent theater and sat there for a couple of hours watching an unadvertised film called *Trigger*.

You've probably never heard of it unless you're well-versed in underground indie films, and it was actually pretty interesting, so I'll describe it a little here.

The main character is a writer named Nick who is working on a mystery novel. The opening scene begins with Nick waking from a dream he can't remember. He feels like it was something important, but the harder he tries to recall it, the more it falls apart, so he gives up and sits down at his writing desk. He pulls out some scraps of paper and freewrites for a while, and then when something strikes him, he pushes away his notes and slides his typewriter in front of him and proceeds to type away at his novel.

Days pass, and the more Nick becomes engrossed in the book he's writing, the more he feels that what he is writing is correct. That's the way that he describes it to his wife: correct. As if he's living through it, or has already lived the events that he's writing about, and is now working on accurately portraying what he remembers. Some nights, he'll lie down in bed, just to jolt awake a minute later and flick the light on and jot down some sudden thought or idea. He has no idea where these thoughts are coming from, but something about the fact that they come to him in the hypnotic state of semi-consciousness, or in the process of thoughtless freewriting, clicks with him. It is as if the memories of the events in his novel are lying dormant in his subconscious.

Here's where the movie takes a crazy supernatural, yet very cool twist. After pondering this and simultaneously reading some very realistic books from other authors, Nick discovers that he—as well as possibly a handful of authors around the world—has a special ability to recall the events of previous lives after dying and being reincarnated. He finds that writing, or letting his mind roam free, can occasionally trigger a memory from another life he's lived. Dreams might provide occasional glimpses of memories of past lives, but they are too disconnected and mixed up to make sense.

Nick thinks it would explain why writers often feel the need to repeat or recreate certain stories, or remake movies. There is something within the stories, tugging at their psyches, begging to be remembered. He also thinks it could explain the excitement he feels when a story he's writing begins to unfold, as if he's onto something. Furthermore, it could make sense out of *déjà vu*, funny feelings, and possibly even hunches. He begins to wonder if he can somehow use his discovery to predict the future, or find out more about who he used to be.

Towards the end of the movie, Nick gives up trying to finish his novel, because he's been trying to force himself to remember how it goes, and he can't. Instead, he tries to make his wife understand his theory, and tells her that being reborn might be the key to remembering who he used to be, or what he is supposed to remember. His wife asks him to calm down, saying that he's not making sense, but he simply responds by telling her to find him when he's born again. Then he shoots himself in the head, and that's it.

I know it's just a fictional story, but it stuck in my head for a while after we stepped out of the theater and made our way back to the factory. It was a pretty interesting psychological thriller, and I've always been fond of those mind-bending movies, but it also sort of freaked me out. The whole thin-line-between-genius-and-madness thing, and the paranoid conspiracy theory aspect to it, and the question of rebirth. Maybe it was just because I'd been in an unstable mental state while we watched it. In any case, I thought I'd mention it. It could be part of the reason why I'm retelling this story in the first place. The story of the past year of my life, that is. It's been nagging at me ever since I came here and holed myself up, to the point where I actually picked up a pen and notebook from downstairs and started the long process of putting it all down on paper. I know there's nothing to it, and it was just a clever movie, but...well, like I said. It was interesting.

***

Two days later, Sam and I chose a rainy afternoon to peruse the streets for Jeff's victim. We huddled together under a large black umbrella and followed people around town. The uncanny semblance to a funeral procession marching along the sidewalks wasn't lost on me as I eyed faces half-hidden under similarly large black umbrellas. I was grateful for the casual yet efficient way we could hide in plain sight. And to top it off, everyone was too busy going about their lives to suspect that the perpetrators of two missing girls walked among them. The fliers stapled to telephone poles and taped to shop windows were either ignored or turned to a soggy, illegible pulp that dreary day.

"Even if we jumped this woman ahead of us—and besides the fact that she'd scream for help and get us caught before we could knock her out—there are people walking behind us, too, and they'll see what we're doing and call for help, or call for the police," I whispered into Sam's ear. It was a loud whisper so he could hear me over the rain, but low enough so that anyone not walking under our umbrella couldn't hear. "I think instead of sneaking up behind someone and grabbing them, we should get someone who's behind us."

"They still won't see us coming," Sam whispered back, nodding. "The only thing is, we have to make sure there's no one behind *them*, and we have to do it so that nobody else around us sees. If there were alleyways or something, that would help, but I don't see any place that would give us much privacy, and we can't knock them out in plain sight. Or, at least, it would be hard to."

"We should've planned this out more," I said.

"We've done fine so far," Sam said. "And we don't have all the time in the world to plot a bunch of murders. It's taking long enough just doing this once every week, and then we've got to go back to the warehouse and set everything up before we send out the ransom note. I'd like to get all of this over with and get out of here sooner rather than later."

"How long do you think it's going to take before we leave?" I asked.

"Honestly, even if we leave after Jeff kills whoever he's going to kill, we're already basically through December, and if we work all day every day to get everything inside the warehouse situated for the collection of the ransom, that'll take three or four weeks. That brings us to February. And then another week for us to drive down to…Oakland?"

"Oak Ridge."

"About a week for us to drive down to Oak Ridge, kill your dad, leave the ransom note, drive back, and wait for the cops to show up at our doorstep. You know, this isn't going to be easy," Sam said. Then he smiled. "Are you sure you don't wanna just try to win the lottery or print counterfeit money?"

"I know what we're doing is dangerous, and it's going to take a lot of time and effort, but it's going to be worth it in the end," I said.

"I really hope you're right." He squatted to tie his shoe, and I stopped in my tracks to keep the umbrella over his head. When he stood again, there was a glint of mischief in his eyes. "Don't look now, but there's a girl walking past us. She's alone. She's perfect. We'll follow her and see if we can get her."

I tilted the umbrella back away from my eyes so I could see her clearly. She was only a little shorter than I was, and she had a small enough frame for me to guess that Sam and I would have no problem forcing her to the ground, beating her unconscious and carrying her home.

***

That was a normal assessment for me to make, but it sounds ridiculous and crazy to my own ears now. How could people think that way? How could I? I used to wonder what a girl might look like without her clothes. I'd become a boy who wondered what a girl might look like sawed in half. I had a serious mental health problem, but I justified my behavior with the idea that I would benefit from it all in the long run.

***

I kept my eye on the short, thin girl as she wove through the mass of pedestrians and increased or decreased my pace accordingly to keep up with her while still hanging back at a reasonable distance.

"How did you and Jeff catch the girl I killed?" I asked him. I'd asked Jeff the same question before, but he'd refused to answer. Sam opened up about it, but by his tone I could tell that he wished I hadn't asked.

"Jeff and I had gone around the back of the factory and went in a straight line from there," he said. "After walking a few blocks, we were passing this alley when we saw a couple of guys messing with this girl—your girl. I'm not sure what they planned to do with her. Rob her, or hurt her, or...rape her, I don't know, but we stopped them before they did anything to her. She was scared and crying, and Jeff yelled at the guys. They were acting tough and threatening to beat us up, but they didn't fight us. Jeff pulled his gun out—well, just the handle, but they saw it and ran off. She didn't really say anything to us, because she was so shaken up.

"We told her we would take her to a safe place, so she came with us. Then we led her back home."

"So you saved her," I said, "just for her to wind up killed anyway."

"Yeah," he said.

I wasn't sure how to feel about the information. Had the torture she endured from me been worse than what she would've faced? I couldn't be sure. I just had to stop thinking of her as a person. Somebody like you or me.

We continued to follow the girl Sam had spotted for ten or fifteen minutes, but she reached her destination before we found a suitable place to attack her. Her path led us to a young guy traveling alone. We went after him instead, and caught up to him just as we were passing a church. No mass was in session at the time.

"Excuse me, I think you dropped this," Sam said to him. We were about a foot away when he turned around to see who was speaking to him. Sam and I closed the gap between him and us within a matter of seconds, and Sam pressed my knife against the guy's throat while I held our umbrella at an angle so nobody could see what was going on. To any passers-by, the three of us appeared to be having a friendly chat. "Get in the damn church, and don't make a sound or I'll slit your throat so fast you'll be dead before you hit the ground."

He gaped at us behind his oval, wire-rimmed glasses and then obediently climbed the stairs to the church. We stayed close behind him as we followed him in so he couldn't run out of our grasp. I set my open umbrella down inside by the entranceway and ordered the guy to do the same. He closed his umbrella slowly, as if considering whether to try and use it as a weapon to fend us off, then thought better of it.

He looked back at us nervously every few seconds. He appeared to be the quiet, bookish type. His orange hair was parted to the left. A million freckles spotted his otherwise pale face. I practiced looking as menacing as possible as we marched him out of the lobby and downstairs to a hallway in the basement. The basement level of the church was filled with classrooms, closets and offices. Sam nodded to an office door, and I tried the handle while he held the blade against our captive's throat. To my surprise, the door was unlocked. I opened it wide and flicked on a light.

Sam shoved the guy into the office and then stopped before walking in after him. There were footsteps somewhere above us, followed by voices. Our assumption that churches were empty when not in use was apparently false, and we were trapped down there with a murder-victim-to-be standing frightened in a small room filled with Jesus statuettes, religious texts and Christian memorabilia.

"Please don't hurt me. I won't tell anyone, I swear. Just let me go. I don't even know you. Please!"

"Shut up," I growled at him, quietly so as to not let the men or women upstairs hear us. Then, to Sam, "What do we do now?"

"Stay here with him. Keep him locked in there, and don't leave the room unless...unless it's absolutely necessary. I'm going to go back and get Jeff. We might have to take care of this here."

"Here? Jesus," I said. No pun intended. "All right, here, give me the knife. I'll watch him. Hurry back and don't get caught."

I went into the room and locked the door behind me, then leaned against it and pointed the knife at him casually.

"You might as well sit down and make yourself comfortable. You're not going anywhere," I said.

"What are you going to do? Why'd you bring me here?" he asked. His voice had changed from his previous pathetic, whining tenor to a more cautious, questioning tone. His words still held an inflection of worry, but less so. I was both glad and disappointed. His pleading reminded me of my first encounter with Sam and Jeff, which was embarrassing, but hearing it come from someone else and directed at me gave me a small boost of pride. The sudden confidence, no matter how weak, was not something I wanted to encounter alone. As bad as it sounds, I needed the advantage of strength in numbers. My bloodlust was the only thing that helped me keep my cool.

"Me? I'm not going to do anything to you. I'm not the one you have to worry about. Just keep quiet and…" I looked around the tiny windowless room, counting the hanging crosses, "…pray for your soul."

He sat warily on the desk and stared back at me. I smiled viciously. I knew how he was feeling, and what he was feeling. I could imagine seeing the events unfold from his perspective, and it was nothing short of terrifying for him. He'd gone from going about his daily business to being thrown into deadly circumstances without an ounce of control. I felt like I'd been there before. But I wouldn't let him know that I could relate to him. I stood there silently, listening for the voices upstairs and watching the guy on the desk sit there helplessly.

It had taken Sam and me roughly forty-five minutes to wind up in the basement of the church, but that was because we'd been creeping along the streets and lurking among the crowd. I hoped Sam would be able to run back to the glass factory and lead Jeff to the holy office in less time. He had his watch on him, and there was no clock on the wall to time his progress, but the wait felt unbearably long. We were locked together in a windowless room with no sense of time. The word "limbo" crossed my mind. The footsteps continued for a while overhead, and at one point the voices rose in song, but soon all sounds from the first floor ceased.

Ten minutes or more had passed when the guy—who I guessed was about the same age as Sam or Jeff—rose from the desk and surprised me. I hadn't even realized that the décor of the room had distracted me long enough for him to doubt the seriousness of the situation.

"I have to leave," he said matter-of-factly, and made an attempt to brush me aside and walk out the door.

"You have to stay and wait," I corrected him. "You're not getting out of this room alive."

"You're wrong," he said. He glanced warily at my blade hand, and swung at me. He was holding a pencil he must've taken from the desk while I wasn't paying attention. I lifted my left arm defensively and caught the pencil's point between my wrist and elbow. The pain only infuriated me, and I slammed by entire body against his while thrusting my blade into his stomach. He fell against the desk and lost his footing, and I jumped on top of him. He caught my arm mid-swing and struggled to throw me off him. In the process he knocked to the ground a reading lamp and a mug containing various writing utensils. We wrestled there on top of the desk. He pushed, trying to knock me off. I held fast and brought my blade inches from his face. He managed to push it away. We stayed like that for one very tense moment, glaring at each other, knowing it was a fight to the death. Jesus frowned from his places throughout the room, watching as I grappled with a kid not so unlike me. The graphite tip of the pencil had broken off in my arm, but I hardly noticed.

"Give up," I barked through clenched teeth. "Struggling is only going to make this worse."

"No!" he shouted back, and pushed. We toppled over, and he landed on top of me. He didn't try to kill me, but for his sake he should have. Instead he pounded on me a couple times and then scrambled to run away before I could get back up. One of his blows struck me square in the face, knocking the canine on the left side of my jaw loose. I spat it out and grabbed his leg as he jumped over me. He landed with a heavy *thud*, and I climbed on top of him again. I jammed my knife hard into his exposed neck as he tried to turn around. He jolted, gasping, as if electrocuted. Then he lay still. Blood trickled from his mouth and neck wound. I sat upright against the wall next to the desk and caught my breath.

Jeff and Sam arrived much later.

"What the hell happened?" Sam asked.

"He got tired of waiting," I said, shrugging.

We snatched his wallet and hid the body under the desk, and I picked up my tooth and stuffed it into my jeans pocket. My tongue habitually probed the bloody gap where it once sat snugly against my other teeth. We left the church without bumping into anyone on the way out and headed straight home to regroup. I was frustrated with myself for having been unable to hold the ginger in the office alone without letting him get away or get killed, but Jeff praised me for taking care of the situation as best as I could. The truth is I could've done better, and I knew it, but I let it go. The past was in the past, and we had to deal with the present accordingly.

"Can we just consider this your birthday/Christmas gift?" I joked.

"Oh, no, you're not getting out of it that easily," Jeff said, smirking. "You've got to get me something. And wrap it with a bow."

"Okay, fine," I said. "But in that case, once we bring someone back for you to kill, that's it. We're done. We're going straight back to Jersey and setting everything up for the ransom collection, and then we're going to go and kill my dad. No more of this, no more delays. Deal?"

"Deal," he agreed. "Now let's head back to the factory."

"Actually, I'll meet up with you guys. I've got a little birthday shopping to do," I said.

"Right now?" Jeff asked. "Are you sure? You'll get back all right?"

"I'll be fine. Run along. I'll meet you guys back home in an hour."

We departed, and I headed to the toy store where we'd previously gotten a few games to occupy ourselves on the days we weren't killing people. I passed crates of balls, shelves of books and boxes of action figures and then went straight to the counter and pointed to a remote-control helicopter behind the desk. It was twelve inches long and looked pretty easy to disassemble.

"How much for the chopper?" I asked.

"It's $89.99," the cashier told me. She waited for me to turn away disappointed.

"How much more for it to be gift-wrapped?" I asked her.

"I don't think you'll have enough," she said.

I laid $150 on the counter.

"And slap a bow on there for me," I said.

An hour later, Jeff tore the wrapping paper off the large box and beheld his new toy. He took one look at the remote control and shot me a knowing look. I'd never seen him so happy.

"You shouldn't have," he said.

"I hope you like it," I said. "I figure you can take the transmission receiver out of the helicopter and wire it into a tennis ball grenade, the way you always wanted."

"I love it, Tom. This is perfect," he said, and patted me on the shoulder. Then he held up the helicopter itself. "But I've got a better idea for this."

Two days later, Sam and I tried once again to find Jeff a victim. We came up with a new plan and bought three pairs of rollerblades, two of which we strapped to our own feet. The third pair was in our backpack, which I carried as usual. The icy, slushy sidewalks were not ideal for skating, but it was the best we could come up with, so we slid and stumbled and sped through town after town. When we found a girl walking alone down a mostly empty street, we picked up speed and held hands, clotheslined her, then quickly turned around and beat her unconscious. We tossed her handbag into a sewage grate, strapped the third pair of rollerblades on her, and stood her up. It was hard to keep her balanced, and it was completely obvious that she was not fully awake, but we held her hands and pulled her along with us with only a little trouble. No one stopped us, but several people called over to us, mostly to let us know that we looked like imbeciles for rollerblading on icy sidewalks. We dropped her a couple times, but we got her to the factory alive. She had a split lip, but she was no worse for wear.

Jeff was sitting in the lone, bloodstained metal chair in the center of the room filing his silencer when we came rolling in with her. His face was hidden in the shadow of his long, black hair. As we dragged the girl into the room, he stood and set the silencer aside and then took up Sam's spear. We sat her down and began tying her up. We exchanged no words, just got right to work. After our first time, with my girl, we didn't talk anymore when it was time for us to kill. It helped us to focus on the task at hand and ignore what was about to happen. I can't really explain it, but it made it less real somehow. It made it feel like what we were doing was just a job. Something necessary.

She groaned and shifted in the chair as Sam and I worked on tying her hands behind her back. I was nearly done with the knot when she pulled her hands loose and leapt forward. She stumbled out of the chair and fell hard to the ground. She kicked at the ropes binding her ankles, screaming as we raced forward to stop her. She was almost free, and trying to escape. She got one foot loose and ran, dragging the chair behind her.

Then Jeff charged at her and stabbed her through the back. She toppled over, and he tugged the spear free and stabbed her again through the lower back. The second stab wound likely ruptured a kidney. We watched her crawl out of the room and into a long hallway leading to the main entrance, leaving a trail of blood behind her. It spilled down her back and arms, but she kept going, determined to make it. She shook and cried with every inch she crawled. Jeff stayed a few steps behind her, watching how far she'd get before she died. The girl hardly made it halfway before letting out a final exhale. Sam and I untied her foot from the chair, dragged the body back into the room and pulled her into a garbage bag, glad to be finished with all the capturing and killing.

We spent the night there, wrapped up in blankets and extra clothes. I hardly slept. The wind howled through the holes in the walls and ceiling. Corpses rotted together in a room on the other side of the building. Birds flitted in and out through the broken roof, and mice scurried about in the shadows. I got up and walked to the pantry in the hall for a late night snack. My bare feet pattered quietly along the cold floor. I reached the pantry, but it turned into a classroom, and all my classmates were sitting with their hands folded. In the center of the room, a projector displayed horrifying images on the white pull-down screen built into the chalkboard. I took a seat at the back of the class and watched myself on the screen. The me in the movie pulled a cross off a wall and plunged it into my mother's pregnant belly. Her screams could have shattered glass. I had to stop her screams. And more importantly, I had to prevent her from giving birth to the demon inside her. I couldn't see it, but I knew it was no human baby. I knew it had wings and horns and cloven feet and a tail. I kept stabbing her over and over, covering us both with more blood than her body alone could hold. It splashed over my face and in my eyes. It flowed out from the huge gash in her belly. The blood at the pointed tip of the cross sizzled as I mutilated the unborn devil in my mother's womb. The devil was me. The movie me howled a bloodthirsty war cry, and the film in the projector caught fire. The images on the screen turned black and burned up. My classmates all turned to me in unison. Their glowing red eyes accused me. Their glowing red eyes damned me. Their mouths opened wide to reveal rows of needlepoint teeth.

I awoke in a cold sweat, relieved to find myself lying beside Jeff and Sam as they snored and mumbled nonsense in their sleep. I stared at the ceiling for a few hours and willed my heart to resume a slow, normal pace. The silence—save for my friends' noisy sleep—calmed me. Or maybe it was their company that calmed me. Eventually I fell back into a dreamless sleep and woke again much later to a dull golden light flooding the wide, empty room.

That morning we packed up what we were bringing back to the warehouse with us and left behind anything that didn't fit or wasn't necessary. We stuffed as much of the food as we could into my backpack. We carried some of our clothes with us and stuck some drinks in the pockets of our spare pants and hoodies. Jeff wrapped his toy helicopter in a blanket. The rest of a loaf of bread and a box of crackers didn't make it, so we spilled the contents onto the floor for the rodents. We also decided we weren't taking all the money with us. Jeff was the mastermind behind that bit of insurance.

"We should leave some of the money here," he said. "That way it's less to carry home, and we don't risk having to leave it behind in the warehouse when we're running from the cops."

"There won't be any cops to run from if we kill them all," I said, "but you're right. It's better if we only take some of it with us, for food and necessities."

"How much is there?" Sam asked.

I checked the notepad I'd kept to balance our funds.

"We have $13,218.63," I said.

"Okay, let's leave an even ten here and take the three-thousand-whatever with us," he said. "That should be more than enough, and if we split it up three ways, I think we can each handle a thousand without losing it. Right?"

We put the ten grand in the empty bread bag, tied it off and walked up to the second floor, where we broke open a small vent and stuck the money inside. With that done, we gathered everything we were taking with us and left. We had to tread carefully so we didn't slip on the icy patches or step on the tangled barbed wire hidden under the snow. I crossed over the deadly threshold and took one last look at our crumbling safe house that concealed a small fortune before heading out on our final adventure.

Flurries drifted through the air. Crows cawed at us from their perch on a telephone wire, their voices shattering the still silence of the winter day. Somewhere, families were decorating Christmas trees and wrapping gifts. Policemen searched for four missing people. I imagined a phone ringing in the police station. Was there someone to answer it and receive the news? Would they slam the phone back down in its cradle, grab their coat and hurry off in their cruiser, racing for the church? And there, bordered with a lot of yellow tape and accompanied by a nervous preacher, would they see what I'd done? A crow ruffled his feathers and took flight, circled us twice, then flew over the treetops to our right. I hugged my extra hoodie and pants against my body for warmth. They didn't help much.

We traveled north in search of an unfrequented bridge. We passed graveyards, banks and sewage plants, and the miles stretched behind us. We stopped occasionally for quick meals and bathroom breaks, but mostly we walked. Day turned to late afternoon, and finally night. We continued through the darkness for a while and called it a day.

I stood next to Sam as we looked out over the river from behind a metal rail. A rainbow of lights shimmered on the black water like stars in the night sky. In the background of our picturesque view, drivers rolled on home. My teeth chattered from a late December breeze.

"I think the Tacony-Palmyra Bridge is gonna be our best bet," Sam said. He took a drag on his last cigarette and scratched the stubble on his jaw. "I don't know how much farther it is, but unless you guys wanna get hit by a car or freeze to death trying to swim across, that's it."

"No, there are plenty of bridges across," Jeff said, hoisting himself up onto the rail and sitting on it with his back to the river. "We'll probably reach Route 40 early tomorrow and be back in New Jersey in no time. Actually," he said, then rubbed his weary eyes and yawned, "it kind of sucks that we didn't already bottleneck the warehouse entrance and set up our supplies. If I remember correctly, we'll pass Oak Ridge on our way home. We could've been getting this over with a lot sooner. And there's no way in hell we're walking all the way into Pennsylvania to get back into Jersey."

"Is there a walkway along 40? Or will we be running through traffic?" Sam asked.

"I think there's a walkway," Jeff said. "You know what? I think it runs parallel with 295 there, and that should be closest."

I could hardly keep up with the conversation.

"How do you guys remember all that? Streets and bridges and everything," I said.

"You're not too keen on geography, are you?" Jeff said, laughing. He leaned back, hooking his feet under the lower rail so he wouldn't fall off. "And you want to be a travel agent? Have fun with that."

"I never said I want to be a travel agent, just that I want to travel. And I know about as much about geography as anyone else my age."

"Which isn't saying much," Sam chimed in. "Don't worry, Tommy-boy. We'll get you home."

We chatted for a little while longer, and then we climbed over the rail and slept on the frosty ground. I knew we were setting ourselves up to catch a cold, but we had nowhere else to spend the night.

***

There was a time when I used to think I'd do some great things with my life, but if I had caught pneumonia that night and died, it would have been just as well. I hadn't done a single decent thing since claiming to be independent. I was doing terrible things. We hadn't left the warehouse for good, we were returning to it, and then I'd return to my father. It felt all backwards. It was the last thing I truly wanted to do, but something I felt I had to do. I couldn't get what my father owed me unless I became an orphan and inherited it.

This is what I'd amounted to. I remember someone asking me where I saw myself five years from then. I was right to say I didn't know. I'm not a damn psychic. If you asked me now, I'd tell you that in five years I'll either be six feet deep or climbing my way up the corporate ladder. How's that for opposite ends of the spectrum? Death or success. No one knows for certain. It's not in the hands of fate or a holy supernatural entity. Knocking over one domino doesn't always lead to a chain reaction, because sometimes the dominoes are spaced too far apart. What the hell am I trying to say? I guess all I mean is that I stared up at the few stars I could see that night, and I knew in my heart that things don't always go as planned. You knew that since the beginning of all this, didn't you? Of course you did. I wish I'd known.

Out of everything I've learned thus far in my life, this might be the most important, the most depressing, the most sobering and the most unwavering fact: We will never win. We will never be fully and completely happy. Bliss is unattainable because, as so many people love to point out each miserable day, perfection is unattainable. You can't always get what you want. There will always be death; there will always be desires. When you look away for just the briefest moment, something will happen and you'll miss it. Will it cause an accident? Will it give a crooked politician just enough time to work in some backdoor deals or fraudulent actions before you can blink? Not always. But still, sometimes. There will always be a need for lawyers and cops. There will always be that yearning to break the law, to speed a little bit faster or cut corners. There will always be the fakes who buy in and sell out. There will always be hate, deep-rooted and laced with evil, waiting to prey on those who believe so naïvely in good will and respect for all.

Some will fall into apathy and indulge in their misery, wasting away as death slowly creeps in to consume them— and some may have sons like me who are willing to kill them for torturing and neglecting them, for failing to provide for them a path more likely destined for success. Greed and envy will always dance hand in hand through the streets of the poverty-stricken cities, spreading like a disease through the festering heart of this country. And all for what? Religion tries to strike fear in our hearts against all of this, to warn us to strip ourselves of these things or else we'll burn eternally. Just another lie to confuse us and make us second-guess our every thought and action. I've gone through hell, and I've glimpsed heaven, and they are both manmade constructs binding us in a permanent limbo in our own chaotic world.

We will live for the moment, and we'll plan for the future, and we'll riddle ourselves in that paradox. We'll get ourselves caught up in the politics of daily life, a never-ending stream that doesn't make sense until you're too old to make a difference before you're ready to hang up your hat and die. And then someone new will step in to take your place, just as confused as you were, and so the cycle continues. There is no progress, because there is not enough time for progress. There is no end to the change, because time dictates that change, and there are far too many people with far too many differing viewpoints, leaving us with nothing else but bickering until we fade into the void. This life of madness is simply a prelude to nothing, dotted here and there with successes and achievements and milestones and passion, which will eventually wilt and disintegrate with age. The tiny details that go forgotten within the larger story. This we have to understand and accept. If we are ever going to look anyone in the eye and attempt to explain the meaning of this life— that we are each meaningful on the smallest of scales unless we affect others on the largest of scales—we must realize that everyone is unique, everything is circumstantial, and all will eventually end.

Time's running out. I can feel them getting closer. This could be it. I'll get on with it.

***

We got home two days later. Jeff was right about the bridges. We were all pretty frustrated at not having our bikes, and we hadn't moved the chubby chick's car since parking it behind the glass factory. Those two days could've been cut down to a few hours, or a day at most. As it was, we could've run a damn marathon with the overall distance we'd covered from all our walking.

It took two long months and an unthinkable amount of backbreaking work in the dark to get the inside of the warehouse looking the way we wanted it. The work took my mind off wanting to butcher people, though, so that was good. We bought a cartload of flashlights to light up the place while we worked at knocking over towering piles of garbage and combining them into a huge U-shaped wall. The extensive work redecorating the warehouse was only part of the reason it took an extra month longer than we'd expected. The other part, which sort of goes hand in hand with the first, is that we realized halfway through that we didn't have enough junk to finish the wall. We'd gotten it into a U-shape, but we needed to make it about a foot thicker and narrow at the opening for the full bottleneck effect.

I hadn't realized that the warehouse could possibly be under-cluttered until the center of the room was completely cleared out. We couldn't spend another year gathering odds and ends to cram into our makeshift bunker, so we hiked up through the landfill where we used to play golf. At the foot of a hill filled with tons of garbage, there was the wheelbarrow we occasionally pushed each other around in. That day was not spent on childish games. We took turns pushing the wheelbarrow to haul junk from the landfill to the back of the warehouse where the exit of the building was still unblocked.

When it was Sam's or my turn, Jeff worked on transforming his toy helicopter into a flying bomb. The landfill was nine blocks away, and we had to take a back road for most of the way there so people didn't see us suspiciously hauling garbage from the landfill to the warehouse. After seven weeks, we finally had all that we needed. We practiced climbing up and down the wall we'd built to test its sturdiness. When it was done and we were confident that it was structurally sound, we lined the narrow entranceway with the flashlights.

Then we loaded up on guns.

Jeff had his pistol, so all he needed was a spare and more ammo. We staked out the businessman's home that weekend and broke in when we were positive nobody was home. Jeff went in through the basement, sweeping up after himself as always before meeting us at the front door, which he unlocked from the inside. He handed Sam the gun from the basement, locked the door, and we left.

Next, we planned to hit the rich old woman's house. She'd apparently decided not to meet with any of her elderly friends or go out by herself, as she sometimes did, so we were stuck rummaging through her shed rather than breaking into her house. Luckily, that probably saved us from hours of searching in vain. There was a rifle with a locked box of ammo in the shed. Handguns would have served us better, and were easier to conceal as we trekked home, but the rifle would help in the war against the cops if they got too close.

It was too big to carry around with us, so we left the rifle in the shed, where we'd pick it up on the way to my old home. We crossed from the old woman's backyard into the yard of her neighbor. Looking in through the back window, we spotted an older sister or babysitter watching TV with a small boy.

By this point in our plans, I didn't care if anyone saw us snooping around. Soon we'd be either dead or states away with enough money to get us through at least another ten years. And after that—if we were long gone, I mean—who knew? I thought we'd stick together—three friends who'd gone through hell and back for each other. But there was that other possibility, too. We could go our separate ways in search of whatever it was we wanted for ourselves. We all had different dreams, and disbanding would make it more difficult for the police or FBI to track us all down and pin the murders and my faux-kidnapping on us.

We moved on from the neighbor's house and found an empty house. Jeff picked the lock to the side door, which led into a laundry room. I ran up to the bedrooms on the second floor while Sam searched the first floor, and Jeff checked in closets. I yanked open drawers, searched under the beds, looked through the closets and even checked for secret safes, but I didn't find anything. They didn't own a gun.

I was about to leave the bedroom when I heard a car out front. I ran to the window and, sure enough, found a car parked in the driveway. The driver's side door swung open, and someone got out. I ran out and alerted the guys, and Jeff and I stormed down the steps. We followed Sam out through the laundry room, slammed the door shut behind us and then ran through a few backyards until we hit a fence.

***

It's kind of funny in a weird way, now. On our last adventures before heading back to Oak Ridge, we were like kids, just getting into trouble for the thrill of it. Sometimes I could imagine that we weren't on a mission to arm ourselves with the intent of killing—like the whole world really was ours, just as we'd pretended when we were younger. Breaking into places one by one, we knew the consequences of what we were getting ourselves into, but we put it out of our minds for the time being. And even though I knew we weren't—that I wasn't—I felt free.

***

After breaking into a few more places and stealing two more pistols from a box on the top shelf of a closet of a retired cop's house on the corner of Willow and Sunfield Road, we headed back. We made a pit stop at a burger joint to grab some lunch before completing the long walk. Standing in line there felt like the most mundane thing in the world after stealing weapons we planned to use to kill cops who we expected to deliver a million dollars to us. Most fast-food customers probably don't think about such things while they wait to be served. I tried to clear my head and ignore the bulky weight of the gun in my pocket. A man ahead of us told someone on the phone that he'd see him or her the following week. A mother ahead of him asked her son what size fries he wanted and then told him he was getting the medium instead of the large he'd asked for. Nothing had changed in the world, but I seemed to be looking in on it from the outside. I recognized it the way you recognize someone you meet up with after years of absence.

"What does that one on the left say?" Sam asked me.

"The double cheeseburger?" I said. "You can't see that?"

"No, it's blurry from this distance," he said. "I'm supposed to wear glasses, but they broke almost two years ago when I fell off a pile in the warehouse."

"I didn't know you wore glasses," I said, suddenly staring at his face and trying to picture what he'd look like with a pair on.

"Yeah, well you weren't around back then. I'm hoping to get new ones when we leave," he said.

"Next?" called a girl behind the counter. "Can I help you?"

I turned to her and choked on my words before thoughtlessly ordering a double cheeseburger. I didn't even look at the menu before making my decision. It was the first thing that came out, which I was thankful for, because I almost said something that definitely wasn't on the menu.

I'd almost said, "Leslie?"

It wasn't her, but at first glance it looked like her. She had the same hair, the same face shape and everything. I looked away bashfully and told Jeff and Sam I'd grab us a table, then darted down to the far wall and took a seat. I'd even forgotten to grab a drink, but Sam grabbed me a root beer. They brought our food over, and we ate and chatted, but they didn't ask why I'd bugged off the way I had. I was glad, because I didn't want to get into it. All I could think about was the girl I'd left behind so many months before and all the ways I'd changed since I'd last seen her. All the things I'd done, all the reasons I'd never be able to look her in the eyes again.

***

Are you there, Leslie? I've been meaning to apologize to you. About everything. Maybe I didn't know anything about love back then when I knew you, but I needed you, and I think if there's anyone in this world I could ever love, it's you. I know I don't deserve you, though. Nothing I do or say can erase what I've done. Leaving you the way I did and becoming the person I am now is worse than the lie you believed. It's better that I'm alone again. You learn a little about yourself through social interaction, but you need some time by yourself to figure things out. Sometimes people are a distraction, and in their absence, when all that's left is you, your identity becomes clearer. You're forced to face yourself and dive headfirst into the heart of your inner conflict. It's important to keep in mind that life's an ongoing catastrophe, and nobody truly has it figured out. Then you can climb back out from the fiery gates of hell and look into the eyes of your challengers unafraid because you know there is nothing left standing in your way. The past is a memory, the future is unforeseeable, and the present is always changing. I'm not the same person I was once, and neither are you. Regrets are fruitless. All it means is that you can admit to mistakes. Yes, it's far better that I'm alone. That way there's nobody to disappoint but myself. What's life taught us? That we'll all screw up continuously until we die. We'll learn how to exist, yet fail to coexist. I'll strive to live happily, but neither desolation nor companionship can ever satisfy me. I don't want to hate this, or you, or myself, but I think I've been doing it for so long that it's become the only way I know. Not hating you, though—I didn't mean that. If I've confused or angered you, I'm sorry. I still don't really understand it all, but I'm trying to. I want to be a good person. I want to be happy. Normal, if that's possible.

Everyone says they fear dying alone, but it can't be so bad. It's just that it's the last thing we'll ever do, and getting through things is always easier with someone by your side. But I think I'll be all right. If my last obstacle to overcome is letting my life end, I'll spend my final moments smiling in memory of all the good times we shared. I'll die alone if it means not having to see you cry when I go.

I guess I'll get on with it.

***

The next day was March 6th. We hid behind the same hedges as we had a hundred times before, knowing it would be the last time. Through a small hole in the hedge, we watched the businessman start the engine, then throw the car door open and run back inside. The three of us ran out and up the driveway. Jeff hopped in the driver's side, which the businessman had left wide open. Sam took shotgun, and I climbed into the cramped back seat. We peeled out and took off before the businessman could get whatever it was he'd gone inside for, and then his house was out of sight and we were on our way to Oak Ridge. We all had our guns, including the rich old lady's rifle and Jeff's silenced one. He refused to test the silencer at the warehouse in case it didn't work and someone nearby heard the gunshot. It had been all right to test the tennis ball grenades when we were leaving for Delaware because we hadn't initially planned on coming back, but now that we were back for a couple days longer, we didn't want the cops to come earlier than planned, and without the ransom money.

We had our masks in the backpack I was working on shrugging from my shoulders in the small space behind the front seats. My knife was in my pocket. Besides the guns and our shares of the cash, that's all we had, and all we really needed. We stopped only once, for gas, and picked up a road map while we were there. Sam read off the turns to Jeff while I tried to prepare myself for what we were about to do. It's weird. I'd imagined it playing out so many times in my head, but when we were actually on our way to fulfilling those fantasies, I grew tense. I knew what was coming, and I wanted it, but I couldn't help feeling a sense of dread mixed in with the excitement. After almost eight months of being away, my homecoming felt more alien to me than the day I'd left.

Driving into a town where everyone hoped to find me made me feel a little like I was on the list of *America's Most Wanted*, and a lot like a diver wrapped in fish guts swimming through shark-infested waters. We passed my school where I'd wasted so many months doodling in notebooks and not paying attention to my teachers' droning. We passed the comic book store where Vinny and I would sometimes visit with our friend Eric, just to see what we could find. We passed the sewage plant and the firehouse. We passed my entire childhood, and through a neighborhood where I never belonged, but still felt strangely connected to.

I didn't see a single missing person flier, and while that wasn't totally reassuring, it reminded me that most of the residents there already thought I was dead. They'd given up hope that I'd turn up at all, and they would not expect to find me murdering my father on his doorstep.

Jeff put it in park.

"We're here," he said.

Sure enough, there before me was my broken home in all its glory.

"Are you ready?" Jeff asked. He was asking both of us, but I knew he was directing the question to me.

"As ready as I'll ever be," I said. "You?"

"Let's go."

They got out, and Jeff pulled his seat forward so I could get out. Jeff pulled his mask out of the bag and threw Sam's to him and then held the open bag to me. I tossed it in the car without taking my own mask out. I wasn't going to need it. It wasn't enough to barge in and kill the man who'd chased off my mother, neglected me and beat me when he was so drunk he could hardly stand. I wanted him to know it was me. He had to look me in the eyes and see all he'd done to me, and know that I'd come to seek retribution. I needed him to know his actions were not committed with impunity.

I led them up the short walk to the front door, which was now curiously lined with rows of flowers. I took a deep breath and rang the doorbell. I'd hardly pressed the button when the thick wooden door swung in, and then a hand pushed the screen door out. He'd heard us pull in to the driveway, of course. He'd come to see who was parked in front of his house. There, standing before me and catching me slightly by surprise, was my father. I hardly recognized him.

"Can I hel—" he started, looking around at the three of us and then paused on the only one of us whose identity wasn't concealed. The pause was as brief as a hiccup, but it was clear that he didn't recognize me at first, either.

Eight months had changed us both considerably. My hair was long and unkempt. The dark circles under my eyes bulged so much that they could have hidden a second pair of eyes. I was sickly and pale, yet more muscular. My clothes were dirty, torn and stained from weeks of wear without being washed. I glared up at him with a ferocious determination.

"Thomas?" His voice was filled with relief, confusion and surprise.

I lunged at him, my blade hand outstretched, and caught him under the chin. He groaned and swung at me instinctively, throwing me down and out through the doorway. Jeff and Sam caught me and charged forward, pushing all four of us inside. One of them must've shut the door. Everything from that point happened so fast, and somehow so slow at the same time.

I spun around, picked my knife up off the floor and turned back around to see Jeff aiming his gun at my father's head. I felt a pang of jealousy that Jeff would be the one to kill him, but it was short-lived. Jeff squeezed the trigger, and his gun appeared to explode. The silencer's hollow inside was maybe a millimeter too small, causing the bullet to rip it in half as easily as a sheet of paper. Jeff bellowed in surprise. He dropped the gun and held his bleeding hand. My father caught some of the blow because of his proximity to the malfunctioned weapon, and wound up with a nasty gash on his head. Some of his hair—which, I noticed, was partially gray—looked to have been singed or blown off from the sudden eruption, leaving a bloody chunk of flesh behind. He tried to stand, shouting something. I ran over to him and stabbed him in the scalp where he'd already been wounded. He howled in pain.

I sensed that this was not the same man I'd known growing up. Something had changed about him. Was he slowing down? Growing soft? It could've been that since I'd left, he didn't have a child to use as a punching bag, but I wasn't sure that was it. It was difficult to pinpoint while I was scrambling to kill him.

Sam tackled my father as he was trying to get up. The two fell to the ground and I stooped next to them. I wrapped my hands around my father's thick neck and pressed down as hard as I could. He thrashed about, kicking and squirming. He couldn't snake out from underneath Sam, but he came close. With us tag-teaming him, his size and experience were still outmatched. He coughed and gasped as I choked him. I squeezed harder. I didn't take my eyes off his. He turned his eyes to the side to stare back into mine. He let me know that he knew why I'd come. He also let me know he wasn't going down without a fight. I wouldn't have had it any other way.

I suffocated my father, and Sam sat on his chest, wailing on him and holding him down as best as he could. Jeff came up behind us and stomped on his shin once. Twice. Three times, but it didn't cause as much pain as he'd intended. He stooped a few feet away from me and twisted my father's foot hard, grunting in pain from his injured hand as he did so. My father shut his eyes and exhaled involuntarily from the jolt of agony. I held my grip and dug my fingers into the back of his neck. My thumbs—covered in blood from the stab wound under his chin—pressed down firmly on his Adam's apple. He gurgled, flapping his lips but unable to speak. Then, forcing out a long, struggling whimper, he writhed for a few seconds. His kicking faltered. After a moment, he stopped fighting back altogether.

We stayed the way we were for another minute before confirming that he was dead. It had all happened so fast. Maybe it was Jeff's smart call on having us kill a bunch of other people first, but I really didn't feel anything one way or the other. I mean, I was glad that it was done, but that was because that's what we'd come to do. It hadn't gone as smoothly as we'd hoped, and if any of my neighbors had heard the gunshot or any of the screaming, the police would be on their way any minute. But I wasn't scared, and I wasn't excited. I was just glad it was over with.

"Jesus, are you all right?" Sam asked.

I turned around and found Sam rushing to Jeff's side. Blood trickled from a wide diagonal cut on the back of Jeff's hand from his wrist to the space between the knuckles of his index and middle fingers. The rest of his hand was bruised and swollen.

"Yeah...yeah, it's okay," Jeff said, breathing heavily. He clearly wasn't okay, as he winced and clutched his injured hand. "Stings like hell, but I'll be all right. Get me some wet paper towels and tape...please..."

I was already running into the kitchen. I tore off more paper towels than necessary and ran them under the tap until they were damp without being soaked through to the point of uselessness. I wrapped them around his whole hand and told him to hold it in place while I looked for tape. I ran to the pantry in the hallway, subconsciously taking in how unusually neat and tidy the whole house seemed to have gotten since I'd been there last.

The phone rang.

My first illogical impulse told me it was the police. When the absurdity of that notion crossed my mind, I knew it had to be one of my neighbors calling to ask if everything was all right. I stood still, as if the caller would hang up if they couldn't see me moving around inside. Eventually the ringing stopped and the voicemail kicked in.

"Hey David, it's me," a woman's voice announced from the answering machine. "Just wanted to make sure we're still on for tonight. I can't wait to see you. Call me."

I grabbed some masking tape from the shelf and ran back to the other room where Sam and Jeff were sitting next to my father's motionless body.

"How about it, Oedipus?" Jeff said, looking up at me. "Wanna hang around a while and meet your old man's new lady?"

"There's no time for that," I said, slightly perturbed by the suggestion. "Here, hold your hand out. We need to make the ransom note and get out of here. He should be fine where he is, so we can just prop him up and lay the note on him so they'll find it. The sooner we get out and back to the warehouse, the better. How's that?"

Jeff nodded to both my words and the tape that held the damp paper towels securely in place. They stood and joined me in my search for supplies for the ransom note. I discovered that my bedroom had been made into an office. The whole house had been renovated and redecorated, presumably thanks to the woman who'd come into my late father's life. He was visibly thinner, but at first sight I'd taken that to mean he'd stopped eating so much. It was possible that he'd started exercising and dieting for her. That thought struck me as more absurd than the possibility of the police calling to check on us. My father? Exercising? *Dieting*? Was I going to believe he quit drinking and smoking, too?

"You didn't tell me your dad smoked," Sam said, walking into the office holding a pack of cigarettes. "Or did he start after you left him?"

That answers that question.

"No, he always smoked," I said. "And unless he slowed down, you'll probably find more around the house."

I pulled a blank sheet from the printer and selected a large pair of scissors from a cup filled with writing utensils, paper clips and markers. Then, deciding a traditional ransom note was too time-consuming of a project, I stuck the scissors back into the cup, returned the sheet to the printer, and turned on the computer. It was password protected, but my first guess—simple and sickeningly sentimental—worked. I typed THOMAS and hit enter, then waited as the screen loaded a desktop mostly bare of icons. I expected to find a photo of me set as the wallpaper. Maybe even the one used for the initial television reports of my disappearance. Instead, I saw my thinned-down and somewhat aged father with his arm around a woman I didn't know. They smiled like long-time lovers. From the way the photo was cropped, it was impossible to tell where they were, but they looked to be seated together at a bar or restaurant.

I found a word processing program and began typing. Jeff walked in, and the two of them helped me figure out the precise wording of the note:

> *We have Thomas Rollins. He is alive, for now. Bring $1 million to the abandoned warehouse on Vienna Road in Lakewood on March 8 at 10 a.m. sharp. No guns, or he's dead. One deliverer, or he's dead. Come on time, or he's dead.*

It was exact and concise. It left no wiggle room for the cops, and only enough time to comply with our demands without setting us up for an ambush. I printed it, and we walked out of the office, propped my father's corpse up against the wall, and laid the note on his lap. I took one last look around the house before we left. I was leaving for good.

I wondered if the woman whom my father was seeing would find him first.

Does she have a key?

He'd changed more than I'd imagined. To be honest, I really hadn't thought he would've changed a thing. If anything, I thought he'd look worse. I wanted him to look worse. Instead he'd moved on with his life, and he was happier than ever. He was actually happy. He scared off his wife and son, and believed his son was dead, and had wound up a new man. Unfortunately for him, his son had risen from the alleged grave and ended that happy life.

The engine roared, and we were gone.

***

Have you ever stared out a window and been unable to really focus on what you're seeing, because you know the end of something is near? And no matter how hard you try to put those thoughts out of your mind and really see what's in front of you, you can't. All you see is the end. Or, more precisely, the shape of it. You probably won't really know what it looks like until it's crashing into you. I felt that way on the drive home, staring out the porthole of a window in the back of the businessman's car. I feel like that now, staring out the almost-opaque window installed at an awkward height in his attic. The view is uninteresting, but then, the architect never meant for this window to look out at something breathtaking. I never knew of anyone to stand around in an attic, looking out over the backyards in deep reflection over an impending end.

There's no doubt they're closing in now. I'll have to run soon, before they discover my current hideout. It's all right, though. I've got somewhere to go where they won't find me.

***

When we got back, we played poker behind the warehouse until the sun set. Then, knowing it would be our last chance to, we crossed the two miles to the edge of town and climbed the pale green ladder up to what I'd come to think of as the crow's nest of the water tower. It was the only time we ever went up there at night. It would've been nice if all the houses were lit up, but most of the families below appeared to be asleep. The street lamps glowed their dull yellows and blues across the town. I looked up to a brilliantly starlit sky. That's what we lose in the daytime. No matter how beautiful a day can be because of a bright, cloudless sky, it can't match the stunning beauty of billions of tiny orbiting balls of light. The poets call them diamonds. The astronomers can spend years staring up at them. The world around us isn't all that ugly, it's just that it's nothing compared to the untainted art of nature. It's humbling to think that the image of something can last years after it's gone.

"Do you think anyone has found him yet?" Sam asked.

"I'm sure his girlfriend did, unless she's too mad at him for not returning her call," Jeff said.

"Ironic," I said.

"Yeah," Jeff agreed.

"No, I don't mean about that," I said. "This whole thing is ironic. They're going to find him dead and call him a martyr. Maybe even a saint. They'll say he died so that I could be returned to the town safely. Nobody knows that he deserved it. They won't know that this is all his fault. If I really did go back, they'd tell me how brave and strong he was, and how his angel is watching over me—never mind that he drove my mother to abandon us and abused me in the privacy of our home. He's a goddamn hero to them now."

"That's true, but so what?" Sam said. "It doesn't mean he won. He's dead, and we're reaping the benefits. In a day and a half we'll have the ransom money, and you're already the orphan you dreamed of being since you left. You might be the villain, but you're the one who's coming out on top."

"It wasn't the way I wanted it to be when I ran away," I told him. "I just wanted a better life. I was angry and depressed all the time, and I needed to get away from him and that house and start over someplace new."

"Isn't that what you got?" Sam asked.

"I guess," I said. I hadn't thought of it that way. "Yes, it is what I got. I got more than I wanted, actually. But not the way I intended to. I've just always wished I could've been a part of a normal, happy family. One that wasn't so screwed up."

"Dude, every family is screwed up. That's how it is. You either make do with the one you've got, or..." Sam trailed off for a moment, staring up at the stars with me. "Or you run away and join a new family."

***

Thirty-six hours from then, we would be in the most tense, uncertain time of our lives. But thirty-six hours felt to be years away, a far-off point in the future. There were a million things to be said between the three of us, but the rest of our conversation was inconsequential and irrelevant. In hindsight, I don't know if I would've changed that. I watched blinking red lights soar past the twinkling constellations, and I was happy. I was finally convinced that I'd made the right decision. I don't think I could trade that half-hour of small talk with my second family for the hours of conversation we might have had otherwise. So, in hindsight, I'm glad I didn't know the truth.

***

We spent all of Ransom Eve inside the warehouse. The preparations were complete, and all we had left to do was wait. If we took a step outside, we ran the very likely risk of being seen, and we didn't need an internet connection to know that the news of my father's death—and thus the ransom note—had been made public. At least one helicopter hovered around the area, sometimes daring to get within a stone's throw away from the roof of our hideout. We preferred to not let our enemies get any clue as to what they were dealing with, so we stayed in and killed time until night fell. We'd built the inside wall high enough to peer out the blacked-out windows when they were swung open, and a couple times we climbed the wall to get a glimpse of the chopper. It was definitely a news chopper. When we became uninterested in the helicopter circling overhead, we lit a fire and played a bunch of different card games. We ate our canned food and went over the plan again, though we'd gone over it a hundred times.

That night we took shifts staying up and listening for anyone who might attempt to break in for a late-night rescue while we slept. The guns and ammo were laid out like milk and cookies for Santa. The remote-control helicopter bomb sat against the far wall where Jeff would take his post in the morning. We set our mattresses up on the wall opposite the entrance. Sam and I rested first, but I could hardly sleep. Thoughts raced through my head and kept me from dozing off. I lay in bed, silently listening as Jeff shifted around on the wall and kept lookout. I stared up into the darkness where I imagined hundreds of little spiders dangling from the ceiling. Where had all the time gone? It passed like a dream while I searched for an answer to a question I didn't understand. It was an incoherent dream of a thousand scraps of memory from the thousands of lives I had lived before. Had I made it out of the tunnel? Had I finally reached the end? Could I move on and stop dwelling in the past?

Jeff climbed down from the wall and tapped my arm. I got up and took his spot on the wall as he lay down to rest for a while. The window facing the entrance was open just enough so that I could look out. By the light of the moon, I searched for any movement, but the world outside my window was still. I didn't dare take my eyes off the dirt drive that led up to the warehouse until I was certain there was no one hiding out there. Then, bored, I used my blade to hack off my long hair. My shift ended uneventfully. I shook Sam awake and returned to my bed, where I actually managed to fall into a dreamless sleep.

Sam woke us up the next morning just after eight.

"They've been out there for a couple hours," he said through the darkness as we rubbed our tired eyes and got ready to take up our positions. "They're keeping their distance for now, so we don't get nervous and do something stupid."

"Like killing me?" I said. All the irony and joking was gone. We'd led the police to our door with a dead body. Things were serious now.

"Exactly. We didn't give them much time to plan your rescue, so they're probably discussing it now," Sam said.

"We've had this planned for over a month," Jeff said. "Nothing they come up with will catch us off guard. They don't have a prayer."

"My guess is they've already taken that into consideration," Sam said. "Whatever they do next, they'll do with extreme caution. They have no idea what we've got up our sleeves, but they can bet that there's no simple way of handling this."

"Let me see where they're at," I said, and climbed the wall towards the front of the warehouse. I couldn't open the window without alarming the police, so I used my knife to scrape off some of the black paint. Then I pressed my face up against the window and looked out through the small eyehole. Orange cones lined the foot of the dirt road leading up to the warehouse. Behind them, a whole police force awaited orders. Despite the warning in our ransom note, I saw quite a few of them holding machine guns and automatic rifles. Vienna Road appeared to be closed off. I watched them for twenty minutes or so, but they didn't budge. Occasionally an officer would say something to the others, or another would shift his weight. Other than that, they were still as statues. I couldn't see their faces from the distance, but I hoped they were more nervous than they seemed.

"What's it like out there?" Jeff asked me when I climbed back down. He and Sam were shining small flashlights between the three of us so we could see each other while we talked. In the harsh yellow light, I could see Sam was wearing Jeff's leather jacket.

"Not much going on. Maybe twenty or thirty guys standing around with guns at the entrance of the dirt road," I said. "Everything's blocked off. That's it."

"We should get into position," Sam said. "I'll stand by the door and keep an eye on my watch. When it's time, I'll turn on the big lights, open the door, and back up to the far side of the room. You guys stay up on the wall and be ready to fire. Tom, you've got your spot at the window. Use it, but cover me too. I don't think they'll come on heavy, but if they do, we need to be ready. If I yell duck, we all get down. All right? Then they should have no choice but to come in. Let them in only so far and then unload on them. The bottleneck will slow them down enough so they can't get in or out fast enough to escape. If it gets bad, break the window and shoot out at them, but be careful.

"Again, it shouldn't get that bad, but just in case. If they do like we told them, there should be one unarmed officer coming through to hand over the money. And if we're lucky, we won't even have to kill him. I'll tell him to close the door behind him and then slide the money over to me. You two grab him, and you'll both hold him hostage while I clear the exit. Then we're out. Ready?"

"Ready," Jeff and I said in unison.

In my peripheral vision, I saw Sam checking his watch every few minutes, so I knew he hadn't lost track of time when the first man to break from the pack headed our way. He wasn't carrying a briefcase or a gun. Just a megaphone. He strode to the entrance of the warehouse purposefully, though I could tell he wasn't being cocky. He knew he was in the danger zone.

"Someone's coming," I warned Sam.

Seconds later, the man paused a few hundred yards from where Sam stood and announced himself.

"This is the New Jersey State Police. Release the boy and come out with your hands up. You have nowhere to run. We have you surrounded. Your only option is full cooperation with the authorities."

He sounded like a robot spewing police formalities at us, but I understood the serious danger of the situation as much as he did. But we weren't going to back down that easily. We'd expected some resistance in the beginning. Eventually they'd come around, and then we'd strike. I probed the back of my pistol with my thumb and flipped the safety off.

The man who was acting as a spokesperson for the state police waited silently for five minutes. Seeing that he hadn't gotten through to us, he tried again.

"I repeat, this is the police. Let the boy go. Come out with your hands up, or we will use force."

Another fifteen minutes passed uneventfully. By that time, according to our ransom note, they should have already delivered the money to us. I was getting antsy, and I could tell the man with the megaphone was losing his patience and temper, but the officers lined up far behind him were more reserved. As far as I could tell, they were focused on the warehouse through the viewfinders of their weapons as they hid behind police cruisers. It could have just been my eyes playing tricks on me, though. The man with the megaphone pulled a walkie-talkie from his belt and said something into it that I couldn't hear. It was unclear whether he was having an argument or just barking orders. After a moment of communicating with some unseen person, he clicked on the megaphone once again.

"This is your final warning. We know you're in there. Surrender immediately. Send the boy out now. Then come out with your hands up. We will use force if necessary," he said. Then, less formally, "Waiting is only going to hurt you. Eventually you will run out of resources."

He may not have known that we had food and drinks with us, but what he said was true. If we tried to stall too long, we could starve to death. But that was assuming that the standoff went on for days. The three of us knew, as he probably did, that it would end sooner. We wouldn't be able to keep up the charade. Unfortunately, we hadn't gotten our hands on a megaphone of our own, and we couldn't exactly respond to his threats by running out and yelling back in person. If they guessed for even a second that I was not being held there against my will, it would be over. We were cornered like rats in our own trap, but I held on. I reminded myself that if they had brought the money at all, which I was certain they had, we'd already won.

"We have been given approval to open fire," he went on. "Don't make this harder than it has to be. Just give up the kid, and we won't have to draw this out longer than it has to. If you do not cooperate, I can promise you this won't end well."

"What do you see?" Sam asked me.

"He's just standing there, telling us to give up," I said. "But I think he'll fold before we do. Just stand by and stay ready."

For a while, that was all there was to be said. Minutes slipped through our fingers like grains of sand. Of all the waiting I'd done over the past months, this was the most excruciating. Over half an hour had lapsed since we'd first seen the police. I wiped sweat from my brow with the back of my free hand.

The officer, or whatever his title was, relaxed his megaphone arm and said something into his walkie-talkie. I was about to open my mouth to ask Sam and Jeff how much longer they wanted to wait before we moved on to Plan B, but before a word could escape my lips, the man turned around and started walking away.

"Hold on," I said. "It looks like he's leaving. Yes, he's heading back to the other police. He must be getting the money now. This is it. Get ready."

Sam flicked the flashlights on one by one, lighting the entrance from the sides like a runway. I turned to Jeff, who stood on the wall opposite from me. His flashlight was off and no daylight poured in from the blacked-out windows near him, but I approximated where he was.

"Hey Jeff," I called over. "I'll be sixteen next week. What're you getting me for my birthday?"

For a minute he said nothing. Then, from within the folds of darkness, he said, "It'll be a surprise."

I grinned and turned back to the eyehole I'd scratched out from the painted window. A swarm of officers surrounded a man in a suit. The whole party was working their way across the battlefield toward the entrance to the warehouse. Every officer in the pack was partially crouched and held an automatic weapon aimed at a different section of the face of the building. The man in the center of the group—the unarmed man in the suit—carried a briefcase.

"Jesus," I muttered. Then, loud enough for Jeff and Sam to hear, "Incoming. The money's on its way, but he's not alone. I count...thirteen or fourteen armed guards with him. I wouldn't be surprised if he had a vest on under his suit, too. If we're going to shoot, try for head shots."

"Shit, now what?" Sam asked.

My mind raced as they closed in on us. I had never fired a gun before. We had not set time aside for target practice. Shooting trapped cops sounded easy before, but my hands begun to shake as the men drew nearer.

This isn't going to end well.

We would have a hard time isolating the man in the suit, regardless of whether or not the whole lot of them came inside. But we couldn't open fire on them and then run out to snag the briefcase. Our best bet was to lure them all in, wait until they were inside, and then shoot them like fish in a barrel. Then we could shine our lights on the pile of dead bodies and root through their corpses to locate the briefcase. I preferred the scenario where we had a hostage—it gave us a better chance at gaining some distance before we shot the hostage and ran for our lives—but in our current position, we didn't have a whole lot of options. I tightened my grip on my handgun and licked the gap in my teeth where my tooth had been knocked out from the guy in the church.

"On the count of three, open the door. We're going to let them in and shoot them, then take the money and run for it through the back. There are a lot of them, and the others will hear the gunshots, so we have to act fast. Very fast. Ready?"

Sam swore and then reluctantly agreed. I took a deep breath and let it out slowly as I watched the officers and the man in the suit approach the warehouse. They were only about ten or fifteen yards away.

"One," I started.

The world stopped spinning. I felt every muscle in my body tense as I counted down to the moment of truth. Somehow, it had all come down to me. Our lives rested on my shoulders.

"Two..."

I raised my gun and aimed it at the entrance, prepared to destroy every living thing that crossed the threshold. I imagined my friends poised and ready, waiting for me to complete the countdown. The monster inside me growled. It craved death. Fresh victims were on the way.

"Three."

Three things happened at once at the second the word left my mouth. A long, deep horn sounded as if to signal an attack. I didn't know what it was, and I didn't have time to consider it, because at the same time, Sam swung the door open and began to turn and run back to the far end of the room.

Before he got there, the third thing happened. A loud *bang* resounded through the entrance, and Sam dropped to the ground on his back. He was splayed out in the high-intensity light, and I saw a large black splotch on his shirt. The splotch grew until it covered his entire chest. More bullets exploded from the entrance and struck the part of the wall that hid the exit to the building.

"Get down!" I yelled.

I ducked down just in time to avoid a hail of bullets ripping through the blacked-out windows. Glass shattered to millions of jagged shards which rained down around me. I covered one ear with my free hand and reached over the wall with my gun hand, firing away at random. I took only enough care to avoid shooting Sam, who was bleeding profusely from a large wound on the right side of his chest. It didn't really matter if I hit him or not. He was dead.

Sam was dead.

Gunfire filled every inch of air around me. For a minute, I didn't dare to move. Bullet holes tore through the walls. Dazzling sunlight filled the once pitch-black room through the broken windows. Dead cops collapsed in the entranceway, stepping and falling on Sam's body. The horn sounded again, followed by a low rumble. I couldn't stand up to look out the window without getting turned to Swiss cheese, but I pictured a stampede of cops and cars rushing straight at us. I thought I heard Jeff hollering on the other side of the building, but if I did, the rhythmic banging above and around me drowned out his voice. I had to get out before I wound up like Sam. And judging by the scene unfolding before me, I didn't have much time.

I had no idea how things had escalated the way they had. It made no sense for the police to suddenly open fire on us just as, for all they knew, we could have been about to surrender. Didn't they believe there was an innocent boy being held captive? I hadn't had time to fully process the fact that Jeff and I were the only ones left on our side. Unlike the courageous superheroes and suave secret agents in the movies, I didn't have a solution to my dilemma. There was no time to think. I found myself in the eye of the tornado. I fired my last bullet and dropped the gun.

My ears were ringing and my eyes were squeezed shut as I lay on the wall and prayed for the rain of bullets to cease. Our weapons were spent long before theirs, and the two of us didn't stand a chance against an entire police force who had trained for years to face outlaws who were stronger and deadlier than us. My plan had failed miserably, and now the blood on my hands belonged to a close friend. He never even got his glasses.

Loaded guns splattered in blood were strewn about the warehouse floor. They were useless to me, though, because as soon as they saw a gun in my hand, they'd mow me down. Bullets whizzed through the entrance and punched through the walls of the warehouse itself. The two of us were moments away from death, soon to join Sam in hell.

I realized my only escape was out of the frying pan and into the fire. Or, in other words, the front door. I would give up and hope they believed I'd been a prisoner all along. It was a terrible thing for me to do—abandon Jeff and hand him over to the cops—but that's nothing new to me. I'd been turning my back on the people I cared about all my life. Why stop now? If anything, I could learn to start taking responsibility for my actions and quit running from my problems. If one last lie was all it took to get out alive, so be it.

I rolled off the wall of junk and tried to slide down the side of it, but wound up tumbling down wildly and landed on a carpet of bodies. In my panic, I had no idea if I'd fallen on Sam. I hope not. One of them felt like they moved, and I quickly jumped to my feet and ran. I put my hands behind my head and ran through the tunnel-like doorway and into the warzone.

It was surreal, like running through a dream. A dream I would never wake up from.

"Don't shoot!" I screamed at the top of my lungs. "Don't shoot! It's me!"

I ducked my head low to avoid the oncoming bullets, but none hit me. Two big hands grabbed me by the arms and nearly swept me off my feet as they hurled me out of the range of the gunfire and off to safety. I looked up to see the man in the suit close-up as two armed officers pulled me away. The four of us ran behind a police cruiser, which was parked between the warehouse and the line of officers waiting behind the orange cones. The man in the suit said something to me and I nodded, but I didn't hear a single word. I was out in the middle of the commotion. The police had taken me. I'd betrayed and abandoned Jeff no more than five minutes after getting Sam killed. Sam's words echoed in my brain.

You might be the villain, but you're the one who's coming out on top.

Yes. I was the villain. There was no question about it. I was within reach of the briefcase that, I'd hoped contained a million dollars. I'd left my only friend for dead. I couldn't even bring myself to lie and tell them my captors were dead so they would cease fire. I was in total shock. Gone was the invincible Tom Rollins who survived on half a meal a day and showered in the cold rain. Gone was the kid who'd made it through fourteen agonizing days in utter darkness with influenza. I was just a scared, stupid boy with no friends or family. I was pathetic. But I was alive.

The man with the suit opened the back door of the cruiser and started to gently but firmly push me in, when I stopped him. The rumbling grew louder and the ground shook. The horn I'd heard earlier sounded again, and equally louder. I turned to my right and saw a train rolling down the tracks.

"What the hell?" The suited man shouted. "We didn't give them clearance yet! Those tracks were supposed to be blocked off! What the hell is going on? Thomas, listen to me, get in the—Thomas!"

He reached for me, but he was too late. I was already running for the train. I hadn't grabbed the briefcase, but it didn't matter. Nothing mattered except getting out of there. Bullets ripped by in both directions, reminding me that Jeff was still doing what he could to survive.

Whatever it takes.

Men shouted behind me. I didn't check to see whether it was in anger, pain or both. I was vaguely aware of the sound of an engine starting. I ran faster. Something exploded, and I thought of the remote-control helicopter. I ran harder. The tracks ahead of me were my finish line, and I was racing against death. The train, my last promise of safety, came rushing along.

My life depended on it, and I no longer wanted to die. I wasn't running to throw myself onto the tracks so that the tons of speeding locomotive could crush me and rip me limb from bloody limb. Sam had lost his life for me, and I was determined to ensure his death was not in vain. I pushed myself even harder, seeing him collapse again and again. In my head, I saw him standing over me the night we'd met. I saw him holding a woman's hands down as I bound them and searched her for a wallet. I saw him walking next to me in the rain and eating burgers in the gazebo. I saw him kill for the first time. And now he's gone.

I leapt into the air just as the police cruiser that was tailing me swerved and skidded to a screeching halt, shooting up a cloud of sand and dust behind me. My fingers locked around a handhold on the side of the train car, and my body slammed against it. I dangled there for a moment before gaining my footing and swinging myself into an open car. I hit my back hard and fell to the floor. I lay there for a second, but just before the train carried me out of sight of the warehouse, I took one last glance out the open side. The front of the warehouse had somehow become engulfed in flames. Red and blue lights flashed on the ground for a moment, and then they, along with the warehouse and hellish gunfight, were gone.

Like my old life, they were gone. Like Katie, and the missing girls and boy in Delaware, and my parents, and Rachel Owens, all gone. Everything I was working towards was up in flames. My present was quickly disappearing into the past. I sat slumped against the back wall of the car and closed my eyes. The better part of a year was gone in an instant. I let the train take me away from it all. My father's girlfriend didn't know his son had murdered him in a twisted act of revenge. Vinny and Leslie didn't know that the brief news of my resurrection would be followed by a bloody tale of an unsuccessful rescue and a high death toll. I didn't know if Jeff had died from a bullet wound or the sudden conflagration, or perhaps had somehow survived. My mother? She and I might never know what has become of each other. I felt small. A boy standing ankle-deep in the waters of crashing waves as a terrible, impending storm built up in the blackening clouds above. I braced myself for whatever the future held for me. I gave in to the unknown.

***

It's still a mystery, even now. What will become of me, and all of this? You may find the boy I killed in the church, and the girls we brutally murdered and left piled up in garbage bags in an old, run-down glass factory. You might even find Jeff and Sam in the wreckage of the warehouse. But there are two bodies you'll never find.

***

I came back to the only place I could think of to use as a hideout. I slipped in through the tight squeeze of the tiny window as Jeff had done on countless occasions, wriggling in the opening until I fell into the basement of the businessman's house. By memory more than from the little light the windows offered, I found the stairs leading up to the ground floor. I pulled the knife—his knife, the one Sam once gave me all those months ago—from my pocket as I crept up the stairs. Carefully and quietly, one slow step at a time. His wife's car was in the driveway, accompanied by a rental. They were both home. And maybe there were better places I could've hidden, but it was too late. It was the closest house I knew, and if nothing else, I'd find in its attic a place to hide and rest. My little secret escape.

I turned the knob slowly, cringing against the possible click or squeak of the door as I opened it.

"Hey," the man said, with a hint of humor in his voice. "What were you doing down there?"

I swung the basement door wide and slashed my knife-arm out as I jumped from behind the door. The blade tore a deep, thin gash in his throat, emitting an awful spray of blood from his jugular. The man staggered back, clutching at the wound, eyes wide. The hair on my arms and neck stood on end. More blood gushed from his mouth as he choked, possibly trying to form words to warn his wife. I ran at him and stabbed him again, hard, in his stomach and then bolted into the living room as he fell to the floor. She wasn't there. Upstairs, a hair dryer was running. I rushed back into the kitchen and finished stabbing him until I was certain he was dead. Then I tiptoed quickly up the steps. I'd take care of her husband's body later. First, I had to kill her.

A golden beam of light shone from beneath the closed bathroom door. The woman whose face I'd seen scattered around the house in several photos, frozen in time with a smile, was right there. Her husband had lied to and mistreated her. He held her chained to him by a loveless marriage, or at the very most, a broken marriage. She deserved so much more in her life. She should have been happy. She could have changed the world, if only she hadn't given in to the idea that this was how her life ought to be.

I knocked twice, lightly.

"I'll be done in a couple minutes," she said. "What do you want?"

I knocked again.

"Dammit, Tom, I'll be done in a minute," she said. I froze for a second, caught off-guard by her use of my name, before realizing it must have also been the name of the man

I'd just killed. I heard a single footstep, and then she opened the door.

I stared at her in terror. She stared back, mirroring me. Her mouth formed an O, but no sound came out. Our eyes locked for the longest moment of my life. The last moment of hers. My reaction had been so automatic, I couldn't even believe that I'd stabbed her until I looked down and saw my hand holding the knife. It had pierced her heart. I'd come to kill her, and I did, but I'd done it so reflexively that at first I couldn't comprehend it.

She was so beautiful, and so deathly afraid. Horrified by me and my unexpected intrusion into the safety and privacy of her home. She'd have been done in just a minute, and then gone on with her day. And then I came and killed her.

"It's okay," I whispered, taking her by the shoulder. I pulled her down, laying her gently on the tiled floor. Her eyes fluttered and her throat contracted. "Shhhh, it's okay. I've done this before, and it's all right. You're going to be fine. You won't hurt anymore."

Her blood flowed freely from the hole I'd torn in her and dripped onto the tile. So quiet. So serene. I turned her on her side and then took her hand and lay down next to her. I kept my eyes locked on hers, and we lay there together on the bathroom floor as she bled to death.

"Everything is okay now," I whispered. "I'm setting you free."

ACKNOWLEDGEMENTS

First and foremost, I must credit both my mother and my sister, Jessica, for being so supportive and encouraging while I wrote this book. Perhaps if Tom had such great ladies in his life, he would not have run off in the first place.

I would also like to thank my family and friends who refused to let me abandon the novel halfway through, when I was close to giving it up. This is no exaggeration: Without them, I never would have completed the novel, and you would not be reading this.

Special thanks, in no particular order, go to Brian Tudor Leeds, Bobby Gregg, Elaina Unger, Omarey Williams, June Bug and Christopher Gross. Mr. Leeds is the creative writing teacher responsible for the assignment which sparked the concept of *ASHES*, the initial starting off point of the Tom Rollins series. It was a vignette I wrote for him in high school that has grown into the sequel to this book, and it's an important reminder of the incredible impact we have on the people around us. Bobby, thanks for being one of my closest friends and supporting my creativity, be it prose or lyric. Our long talks and loud shenanigans inspired some parts of this series. Ms. Unger is the artistic genius whose fingers painted the beautiful cover art and whose eyes were the first to see a completed draft. It has changed a bit since then, but the important parts are still all there. Thanks to Omar for the hilarious conversations and loads of music recommendations; they helped get me into character and also to separate me from Tom's mind when things got too heavy. June, your love of horror is surprisingly matched to mine. I hope you'll enjoy this series as much as the Stephen King books and gory films we always discuss. Finally, thanks to my brother, Christopher. When we aren't trying to kill each other, we get along as the best of friends.

Whether you're a stranger or someone I know well, and you've read this cover to cover, I greatly appreciate it. I spent a lot of time working on it, and even more time wondering why I did. The answer is this: There is nothing else I would rather do. You all make it worthwhile.

ABOUT THE AUTHOR

Kevin Gross is a multi-genre writer from New Jersey. He graduated from Rowan University in 2012 with a Bachelor's degree in Journalism. He is most inspired by thriller novels, alternative/punk music, unusual films, and art of all kinds. Follow Kevin on Twitter: @Kevin_C_Gross

ABOUT THE COVER ARTIST

Elaina Unger is a freelance artist from New Jersey who has painted cover art for published books, including *A Prelude to Nothing*. She has shown in galleries and is a comic colorist for her clients. Elaina is also a licensed artist who owns her own brand "Puttiko," which is licensed and sold on various products internationally. When Elaina isn't making art, she's usually reading or watching horror movies. Elaina is also an avid metal fan and has a love for red velvet sweets. Follow Elaina on Twitter: @ElainaUnger